FINAL FEAR

PHILIP HARPER

SIMON & SCHUSTER

NEW YORK LONDON

TORONTO SYDNEY

TOKYO SINGAPORE

SIMON & SCHUSTER
Simon & Schuster Building
Rockefeller Center
1230 Avenue of the Americas
New York, New York 10020

SIMON & SCHUSTER and colophon are registered trademarks of Simon & Schuster Inc.
Designed by Pei Loi Koay
Manufactured in the United States of America

1 3 5 7 9 10 8 6 4 2

Library of Congress Cataloging-in-Publication Data
Harper, Philip.
Final fear/Philip Harper.
p.   cm.
I. Title.
PS3558.A62484F56   1993
813'.54—dc20   92-45660
                              CIP

ISBN 0-671-74532-8

For Lillian, Jesse and Anci.

With special thanks to Fred.

FINAL

C H A P T E R

1

The resident told Dr. Walker two things about the young woman in room 512. One was that she was pretty. The other was that she was having panic attacks—a sense of anxiety so severe she thought it was a heart attack.

Walker went to see her early in the evening. She was lying in bed when he entered the room. Her eyes were closed, and she had the sheet pulled up to her chin, clenched tightly with both hands. She was attractive, just as the resident had said: long reddish brown hair, a light complexion—pale with freckles—and smooth skin. Her breasts and hips were outlined by the sheet; she was well-curved and small-boned.

Panickers. They experienced fear as intensely as anyone could. He didn't get them as inpatients very often. Their typical course was outpatient, seeing several doctors, one after the other, pursuing useless remedies and tests, and for years. They searched for the cause of their disabling and intense experiences: the rapid onset of waves of anxiety and its accompanying physical changes, the tingling and numbness of fingers and toes, the drumbeat staccato of a racing heart, the dizziness, the frantic hurried breaths. They usually believed their sensations were warnings of death, or madness, or loss of control. And that was the core of it, the catastrophic way they misread the reality of their bodies. They had an instant and relentless certainty they were in great danger. The root of their problem was fear.

He drew up a chair and sat down next to her. She opened her eyes, which were blue-green, and then she opened her hands. As she did, the sheet dropped a few inches down her chest. The sudden exposure to the coolness of the room stirred her. She looked hesitant, then closed her eyes again. Every panicker he'd known had rituals. Perhaps she hoped that by taking a few moments, in the dark stillness of a world defined by closed eyes and a tightly held body, she could forestall the dread before reentering the other, frightening world. Hers was a life, Walker knew, made up of careful calculation and superstitious prevention. He only had one thought as he looked at her: She is of interest to me.

She opened her eyes again and sat up.

"Hello," she said. Her voice was shaky.

"Hello," he said. "I'm Dr. Walker. Just looking in to see how you're doing. How are you feeling?"

"I'm not sure," she answered. "Do you know what's wrong with me yet?"

"I know you were told you may have a problem with your heart; that was our working diagnosis. But you have no heart disease. You do have a serious problem that requires treatment, though, a condition called panic disorder. For reasons that are not well understood, some people— and you're one—experience anxiety very strongly, and in a very physical way. This is called a panic attack. Does what I'm describing make sense to you?"

She took a deep breath. She needs to brace herself, Walker thought, just to answer the question. That's the extent of her fear.

"I don't know," she said, upset. He could relax her, teach her some breathing exercises, give her medication. That's not what he had in mind.

"The way I can tell if that's what you have is to see if your particular symptoms can be reproduced, right here." He moved the chair closer to her. "Do as I do," he told her, not giving her a chance to think about what he had said. "You don't have to say anything. Just follow my movements. This will be good for you."

He moved his head slowly from one side to the other, the motion steady, the turns quick, all the way to the right, then all the way to the left, back and forth. She moved her head as he did, and when the two of them were in sync, he moved faster. He didn't feel dizzy, and knew he would not. But in someone susceptible, the dizziness would come. He watched her face. As she moved, her mouth opened, her jaw tightened, and her eyes grew wider. She was getting dizzy. Her whole body moved as she turned her head, her long red-brown hair swinging, covering her face from one side to the other. She did it with a sense of hope, he could tell, following his instructions carefully. But it brought on a sensation she dreaded.

Her chest heaved as she took shallow breaths in and let even shorter ones out. She held her arms stiffly at her sides, her hands pressed flat against the mattress as if the bed was a magic carpet, rolling a skyward course. She needed to brace herself to avoid falling. The sheet was now down to her thin, bare legs. She was shaking.

She got up on her knees on the bed, and looked around as if she wanted to leave the room. She glanced toward the window, and Walker wondered if she was thinking about jumping. It wasn't unlikely, he knew. Panickers, more than any other population, even the depressed, were most likely to kill themselves. Walker stared at her face. He wanted to see the expression of her fear.

"Dr. Walker?" Her voice was high, strained. Clearly a plea. He was supposed to help her. He got up and took her hand.

"Come with me," he said. He half-lifted her off the bed. He walked her into the bathroom, stopping in front of the sink.

"This will help," he said, already aware of what he wanted to do. He reached around her and turned on the water, running it cold into the basin. She held herself up with her hands on the edge of the sink, her shoulders slumped, her face turned down. She was sweating. A line of wetness appeared on the back of her hospital gown. It was half-open, and in the mirror over the sink, Walker could see the bare top of her breasts. He was close enough behind her to feel the warmth of her body against his. He held her by the outside of her arms, and it would have been easy to press her against him. He felt the beginning of an excited, aroused state, but it wasn't only sexual.

"This is what you have to do," he said. "Listen to the water as it runs." He put his hand gently under her chin and asked her to look into the mirror. The sharp light off the white tile walls shone in her fear-widened pupils, and made glaring spots of her eyes, as the two of them studied her reflection.

"Listen to the water," he repeated. "And try to relax." The words were hollow. Her relaxation was the last thing he wanted. But he did want her to stay exactly where she was, and in that state. He knew she couldn't relax, whatever she tried. She was unable to control herself. He could see it in her mirrored image. She was locked in fear.

Walker was forty-three and had been the assistant chief of critical care at Clarke Hospital in Philadelphia for six years. He was five foot nine, solidly built, with a full head of curly brown hair, dark blue eyes, and a mustache. He had the manner of a man who liked what he did, and he did it with confidence and ease. He enjoyed medicine. For him, the technical demands were easy and the routines of the medical day, the nuances now well known to him, were comforting. Clarke was a rundown city hospital, and Walker was by far the hospital's best doctor. He knew he was seen as a gem in a rough place. The medical staff admired him. Patients liked him or regarded him with awe. To the younger doctors, he was Clarke's fountain of medical technique, the master of bedside manner, the one it was never a mistake to call.

If only they knew.

Walker himself had been overwhelmed by fear throughout his child-hood. There was so much to be afraid of. Don't touch a hot stove. Don't put your hands in the dog's jaws. Don't touch the dead squirrel in the woods. Don't play too rough with your friends. And other more frightful things, which he discovered for himself.

He was afraid to be alone in the dark, to be in the attic with the double solid door closed; he was afraid to be out in the big cornfield by himself, even in daylight—in the middle where you couldn't see the house, and all around you were tall stalks, and you might not know how to get home.

He was afraid of his mother's old beat-up doll, the one with the bald head and missing nose. He always thought it was about to speak. He was afraid of his mother, too, afraid at night that she had crawled under his bed, transformed into some malevolent version of herself. Afraid that he might open his eyes and look over the side edge of his bed and see his mother's head, the sharp teeth grinning, the white face and blood red eyes.

He was afraid that his parents were not really sleeping, but dead. That the rhythmic movements of their bodies, up and down, up and down, were not the reassuring rhythms of sleep, but the convulsive persistent motions of death.

He was afraid of the back of people's heads. Afraid they might turn around and become someone else. Afraid. Afraid.

He was racked by one fear after another. It was as if, when he was born, he acquired a special sense and knowledge of fear. And from that time, until he finally decided he'd had enough, his life would be dominated by fear.

Then, when he was nine years old, and each one of his fears had plagued him over and over, something strange and even more terrifying happened. His father died of cancer. Right after that, Walker somehow found within him the strength to have no more fear.

It was mid-afternoon on a hot July day when he decided to go into the cornfield by himself, something he had never done before. He walked off the wooden porch hesitantly, but moved effortlessly across the grass to the field, as if a wind was guiding his steps. He reached the edge of the field and stopped. Then he went in, passing one stalk after another, moving slowly. He kept moving until he was surrounded by nothing but stalks as far as he could see. He looked up and saw the free, comforting open space of blue sky and soft pillow clouds—white, safe, familiar. He forced himself to kneel down so the plants seemed to close overhead, and the sky disappeared.

Enfolded in the field, the stalks were now linked parts of some unknown whole, a single form of continuous borders, but in an unknown threatening shape. The thought produced in him a familiar trembling state of fulsome, wrenching terror that controlled his very insides. His stomach heaved and pitched, and sent fire back into his throat. Something else controlled him. His instinct was an urgent command, his shrill thoughts were pleas to himself to run away, to leave there and never come back.

Daytime sounds of life outside the field were gone and he was surrounded by a dead, empty silence. The plants stretched high above him, closing off all light, and darkness pressed in against him. The stalks touched his skin like an enemy's flesh, all teeth and grabbing hands. As he stood there, he heard angry voices taunting him. He saw animals in the dark, and other ugly sights in the corners of his eyes, ghosts with twisted bodies.

He felt panic, and wanted to turn his head up for a moment for a reminder there was still a world outside this horrible place. But he stopped, because if he looked up he knew his fears would win. And he'd decided he wouldn't live with them, wouldn't live that way anymore, not even for another day. So he kept his head down, and his body still, and he didn't move, didn't look, didn't run, didn't tremble, didn't flee. And hours passed just that way in the field.

He was surprised, in the end, at how easily it happened. Merely by staying there, and doing nothing at all, thoughts that had scared him all his life now came and went like zephyrs of wind inside his head. They became harmless, then they left him, one by one. Fears left, and feelings left, and there was less and less inside him to be stirred and grasped and moved to fear. He felt empty, but also less afraid, and therefore more at peace. And when he was as empty as he could be, he finally allowed himself to move, casually taking big strides out from the center of the field. The previous dreaded place was no longer a source of terror, but only plain stalks and leaves. He had removed one source of his fear.

In the next few months he repeated the process—with his mother's doll, with the dark place under his bed, with the backs of strangers' heads, with everything he knew he feared. And in a short while he had overcome all of his many fears.

It was only later he discovered that the less he felt any trace of fear within himself, the more he was attracted to the terrors others experienced. And the greater their discomfort, the better it was for him.

"Relax," Walker said to her. His voice was hard, excited, the tone in contrast to what he said. Standing behind her, he pressed her to the sink, the steel gray metal of the rounded edge against her belly. He felt the strong, rapid beat of her heart, the raging pulse, the driven metered shaking of her arms. She was hard, muscled, tight, all of the softness of her flesh removed by the surging of tension and fear. He knew the thoughts within her, and bent his face close to hers, as if he were hearing them aloud.

"Afraid you'll go crazy," he said, and watched in the mirror her distorted expression. Her mouth was drawn tight, thinly open, the edge of her teeth against her lip a white razor line, sharp enough to draw blood.

"Afraid you'll lose control," he whispered, one hand on her shoulder to feel her try to move away, the other at the side of her face cupping her cheek, forcing her to stay symmetrical and forward. Walker kept the full picture of her in the mirror so he could see the fear.

The water filled the basin. The sounds of the running stream grew louder as the volume of fluid in the silver timpany rose up. Walker put his face next to hers, pressing cheek to cheek so that the image that loomed in the glass was no longer just hers, but theirs: the wide, frightened, pain-filled, shining depths of her eyes; the flat still glare of his, both numb and thrilled.

"Afraid you'll die," he said, and pressed her head down. Down to the full basin of the metal sink, past the visible line of water until the two planes of each object met: the thin film of the water's surface broken by the line of her flesh. He pushed her head under water, pressing hard against the straining with which she sought to live. The water filled the cavities of her eyes and mouth and nose. He held her until he felt the last jerking spasms of her dying.

He lifted her up now, one hand gently under her chin. With his other hand, he slowly, softly brushed back her long wet hair. He leaned slightly to let her rest on his body, her head against his chest. The two of them were visible in the mirror, now both faces emblem of one mind. No strain, no tension, no wide-eyed gaze. There was only composure, and in the placid, unlit stare, peace.

When she was found, they'd assume she'd had a heart attack.

He held her, and with a towel, dried her face and hair as best he could. Then he carried her back to the bed and laid her down, her face looking up, relaxed. It was the end of life. And therefore the end of fear.

C H A P T E R

2

I always came down to Florida for spring training. The heat felt good after a long Philadelphia winter. I'd played here myself for a couple of years, at the Phillies' Clearwater training camp: George Gray, number three, third base. But I'd torn up my shoulder sliding into home fourteen years ago and that was the end of my promising baseball career. It was a long time, but I hadn't forgotten a thing. I remembered how dry and rough the grass was on the B field, where I'd been watching all morning as a rookie third baseman worked out and took ground balls. He was smooth, though he took his share of bad hops.

The kids on the field looked younger and younger to me every year, and there was nothing like seeing them to make a guy feel old, though I was only thirty-eight. Most of the players weren't near their peak yet, but they had time to develop. And you usually get stronger with age. I had. In fact, so far at least, I still looked pretty much the same as I did in my playing days, successfully fighting off the usual post-athletic bodily slump. I had a few more creases under the eyes, and a few more scars, but I also had the kind of face that didn't show the years. I was still tall and still thin, but wide on top. Lots of wavy light brown hair and hazel eyes. My ex-wife said I was built like a tree, and she had a good eye for bodies, always did. Some players get their power from their legs, but I got all my strength to throw and hit from my shoulders and arms. As it turned out, my marriage lasted only a little longer than my minor league career. I wasn't the only body my wife had an eye for.

Everything about my life had changed in fourteen years, but I still followed baseball. I had an arrangement with the Phils that let me file scouting reports, and once in a while I still sent in a column to *Baseball America*. It gave me a good enough reason to visit a minor league ballpark now and then, and, best of all, to get to Florida for the spring rites, every single year.

The sun was hot for early March, even for Florida. The rookie at third had enough and headed for the water cooler, so I went back to the clubhouse. That's when I ran into Hank Merrill, a seventy-year-old coach who'd been around baseball three decades before my playing days even began.

"I hear that Joe Taft is in a hospital back in Philadelphia," Merrill said. "And he's in bad shape."

Taft was a guy I'd played with and gotten close to, in minor league ball. I'd kept in contact with him all these years, but only in one particular way. Every time I got back from Florida in the spring, I called him and we met for dinner. He was always the first person to get my informal Florida scouting report about the year's crop of rookies. As usual, I hadn't seen or spoken to him since last year. Still, it happened to be the time of year I'd be seeing him, so hearing he was in the hospital took me by surprise. I wondered what was wrong. He was basically a bull of a guy, and always looked strong, if not particularly flush.

"What is it?" I asked Merrill. "What's wrong?"

"Don't know, Gray. Just heard it by phone from a friend in Philly. Knowing Joe, though, if he's in a hospital, it's bad. He's not the type to go in for a cold."

I nodded. Taft was the kind who always played in pain.

Merrill didn't know much else about Taft, other than how he played the game. There was a reason for that. Taft didn't talk to people. Most players thought of him as a malcontent, a loner and complainer. That was how he was—with them—but he talked plenty to me. He always had, although mostly about baseball and not much else. He'd picked me out as someone he liked, for some reason, all those years ago, and that had been fine with me. Even back then I always made up my own mind about people. I'd learned to look past the negatives and see other sides of Joe. I'd ended up thinking of him as someone pretty special, a person unlike anyone else.

He was a catcher, far from great, but as solid a baseball player as I've known. He was in the majors for only parts of four seasons and always second-string. The rest of his years he was a journeyman in the minors. We both thought that had as much to do with his conflicts with managers as with whether he could play. I was with him in Double A at Reading for two years and he taught me a lot, maybe a little bit about life too, as baseball sometimes does. But I don't know if that was Taft's intention.

What most people did know about him was that his wife and newborn son had died in childbirth when he was twenty-six. Of course, everyone felt sorry for him, but most of the players thought he was a bitter guy before the tragedy and they didn't see a big change in him after. His life was the game—the sport and not the business—and he made that clear in everything he did. He practiced hard and played hard. And he hated the way the newer players cared more about their contracts than the game.

We both hated the money thing in major league baseball. I learned to hate it from him, in a way: the obsession players had with getting a bigger contract than the next guy. Taft cried like Cassandra about money tainting the game. He had a lot of complaints, and when you took them one by one, they all made sense, at least to me. That's why both Taft and I liked the high school kids who hadn't yet been signed, or the minor leaguers who hadn't made it up yet. Because they were eager and hungry, willing to do anything to get their shot, and they played the game that way.

What angered Taft most—even more than the giant salaries—was that no one ever thought about passing along some of the new-found billions from television revenue to the old-timers, the players of the forties and fifties and sixties, and the guys from the Negro Leagues. They made the game what it is and never made more than a few thousand dollars a year. There are hundreds of them out there still, having a hard time paying the rent. Taft knew plenty of those guys. He was clear and prescient about baseball and about how people did business. That was a quality I'd come to respect.

I'd hoped to finish out March in Florida, watching the players as they worked through their kinks, the teams as they winnowed down the rosters. But I knew as soon as I spoke to Merrill that I'd go see Taft instead. I couldn't help picturing him in the hospital, no fans in the stands, just gutting it out alone, as he had for most of his career. There was a three o'clock nonstop from Clearwater to Philadelphia. Merrill said Taft was in Clarke Hospital. I could be there by nightfall.

It was raining hard and cold in Philadelphia. After the hours it took to get in and land, they made me wait in a sixth-floor corridor at Clarke for half an hour before I could see Joe. The nurses said he couldn't have any visitors while they were putting in a line to give him something intravenously. The place was cold and damp, as if being indoors here was no respite from the rain. It wasn't the building I hated, but the fact that it was a hospital. As I stood there, I could hear occasional moaning coming from one room or another, and it sounded like someone was in a lot of pain. I hoped it wasn't Joe. I walked to the far end of the hallway, to a small lobby. There was a sofa and a chair, both pretty worn, and a low, dark wood table. On the table was a vase filled with flowers—red, yellow, and blue—plastic. The isolated attempt at cheer in a dreary place like this made me feel as if I were at a wake, in the home of a very poor family.

I didn't recognize Taft when they finally let me in. He looked generations older than the man I'd known, still the big body, but somehow empty, like a shell. He also only had one leg, and the last time I'd seen him he had two. On the right side was a large bandage where the leg used to be, and a tube connected to an IV. His hands and wrists looked bloated and his face was red. His eyes were open, but I wasn't sure he could see.

"I came as soon as I heard you were in the hospital," I said.

At first there was nothing in response.

"Gray the rookie," he finally said, speaking slowly, his eyes clearer now, and his voice a little stronger than I expected. "How's the shoulder?"

It was true my injury was the low point and peak event of my baseball career, but it was a long time ago, and that wasn't his usual greeting. I wondered if he knew where we were, or even what year it was. There wasn't that much suffering in his voice, it was all in the way he looked.

"I was down in Florida, watching the kids try out," I said.

"So give me the report," Taft said. "Did you see Glancey?"

It always surprised me how much he kept up with the game. Mark Glancey was a new pitching prospect for the Phils, and I had, in fact, seen him down in Florida. So I told him about Glancey and about all the others. While I did, I looked around. There were no greeting cards in the room, no flowers, no sign that anyone had visited. I'd imagined his loneliness right. The curtain next to Taft's bed was pulled shut, hiding a silent roommate. I kept talking about baseball, but it seemed more and more distant and strange. I had just finished telling him about another new pitcher who threw hard, but was very wild.

"Control comes last," Taft said, in a tight voice. I could see him clenching a fist, biting down hard on his lip.

"What happened here?" I asked him, putting the other stuff aside. I didn't see a chair, so I crouched down next to him by the bed. "What happened to you? Tell me."

"I don't really know," he said. "My foot was hurting so much I couldn't walk. I had a fever, too, burning up. I lost track of time. Now my leg is gone. I don't even know why. I don't remember anything, but it's gone."

There were long pauses while he talked, and the strength in his voice quickly faded. I was afraid to push him to talk about the leg. I'd known people who had teeth pulled and got depressed about it. I couldn't imagine what he was going through, but considering his situation, he wasn't showing that much. People could be like that, stoic about almost anything. Maybe stoicism helped you survive. If that was so, Taft would live forever.

The room had no furnishings other than a small dresser. No decorations, nothing pleasant. And cold. I stood up and went to lean against the wall. I didn't know what to say. After a few minutes, I walked out and found a folding chair in the hallway, and brought it into Taft's room. Once I'd sat down and looked at him again, it occurred to me for the first time that when I'd been with Taft in the past, he usually did most of the talking.

But a lot had changed over the years. In my case, after my injury, I tried to get a job as a sportswriter and got hired as a news reporter instead. I ended up liking the job, and even had what my editor considered a real talent for it. But it didn't work out. I got onto an investigative story about lawyers and doctors who set up a complicated swindle to strip some old people of everything they had. I knew that a newspaper article wouldn't get anyone their money back. So instead of writing an article, I went to the lawyer who ran the swindle, and I offered him a deal: they stop the rip-off and pay back the victims, and I don't write the story. It was my idea but I was still surprised when he immediately agreed to the deal.

First he offered me money if I'd simply lay off, but I insisted on the payback to the victims instead. I never did take a cut for myself that first time. But the next time I did a deal I pocketed my end of it, too. Like anything you get paid for and do more than once, it starts to feel like work. I'd stumbled onto a new career.

As it was, I needed a new career because the deal I'd made with the lawyer got me booted from the newspaper business forever. Burying a legitimate story is the highest crime in journalism, an open-and-shut violation of newspaper ethics and everything newspaper people hold dear. The way I looked at it, though, I was still a kind of reporter. I used the same investigative methods. But now I was free-lance. There were people like those doctors and lawyers everywhere. They always steal money, always have victims, and always believe no one can stop them—until someone does. They act like gods in their own little worlds. They make the rules and expect everyone to follow. But it doesn't have to be that way. I'd found that I could force them to stop their scams. And I could do it on my own, without a newspaper behind me. So instead of collecting a paycheck, I take a cut when I make a deal. That was how I made my living. Blackmail.

"I was thinking about Sandberg, and that play-off game against New Britain," Taft said. He started telling me a story, as if it were the first time, as if it had happened only days ago. It happened over a decade ago, and he'd told me the story numerous times. But I figured wherever his memory took him was better than where he was, so I let him go on.

As I listened, I thought about Ryne Sandberg, and why the story meant so much to Taft. Every once in a while, you get a player in the minors, on your team, who will turn out to be one of the great ones. At Reading, twice blessed, we'd already had Mike Schmidt, the sure Hall of Fame third baseman I was once supposed to replace. But a few years after I left, Sandberg, a second baseman, arrived. Sandberg has since gone on to make his tens of millions. But he also happens to be one of the modest players of our generation. A decent, hard-working, no-nonsense guy. The kind Taft admired and rarely found. When Taft first saw him, Sandberg was just another minor league unknown—but Taft saw the greatness very clearly.

Taft worried about Sandberg, like a nursemaid with her charge. He considered it a personal mission to move Sandberg along to the Hall of

Fame. What worried him was that some of the most dangerous plays in baseball take place at second base. Wind up on the wrong end of one of them, and a career—even a great one—could be ruined.

In the New Britain game he was telling me about, there had been one of those plays. The batter hits a ground ball with a runner on first. The second baseman has to cover the bag, take a throw, and dodge the baserunner coming in. No matter how great the second baseman is, a bad throw from the shortstop can leave him with his face in the dirt and a spike in his eye. Joe was always proud that as a catcher he never made a bad throw in any of Sandberg's games. He went beyond that, though, and did everything he could to protect him in other ways. That meant talking tough to jealous young shortstops who were tempted to make a bad throw because they wanted to see what the great second baseman could do. The shortstop in the play-off game was one of those kids. Taft could see that and he dressed the kid down before the game. When the time came, the shortstop didn't make a bad throw. Taft probably saved Sandberg's body that way more than a couple of times. He never told Sandberg about it, not once in those few years. Because Joe didn't do it for credit or notice, I was the only one who knew.

When he finished the story, Joe finally fell asleep.

Years had passed since Sandberg and Taft played together at Reading. I wondered whether the second baseman, now one of the best players in the game, ever knew how much of his future Joe Taft saw back in those early days. I wondered if Sandberg, when he gave his Hall of Fame speech some years down the road, would remember Taft. Or if anyone would.

I drove home in the chilling rain.

C H A P T E R

3

He pushed the gurney into the hospital elevator. In twenty minutes, Dr. Walker would have morning rounds on the critical care unit. The old woman on the gurney had been recovering well from the flu and was in decent shape, aside from being eighty-two. She was ready for discharge. But Walker was taking her down to the morgue. She would be dead by the time they got there.

Walker was moved by his patients: their imaginings, their frenetic and distorted assessments of their peculiar states, the knots into which their minds tied their bodies, and sometimes the other way around. He often stood at the back of the long high desk in the rear of the emergency room and watched as they came in, bringing with them their one lifelong howl of pain. In the end, their common denominator was that they all had their fears, and brought them transformed into bodily complaints to their doctors. And it was this indirectness that killed them: their tight chests and thin smiles, their unexpressed desires and sad, empty longings. It was their fear that made them sick and killed them. And it was the one thing nobody could ever heal.

Walker had decided to become a doctor when he was eighteen, when he worked on his hometown rescue squad. He was always fascinated by other people's sickness and crises and pain. In the same way, he felt drawn to the mobile emergency workers, and he took a volunteer job on the squad at the earliest age they would allow.

One day, Walker's team was the first to arrive at a fire. A burning building was lit up from within like a carved pumpkin, delicate licks of flame visible, gasps of fire trailing whorls of smoke from every opening. The three men with Walker didn't think it was worth the risk to go in to search for possible survivors. It would probably be five minutes before the fire trucks arrived, and they believed there was little they could do before then. So Walker went in by himself.

He wasn't sure what he wanted, or why. But if people were in there and desperately needed help, there was something Walker needed that they had. He approached the building calmer and more at ease then he'd ever been in his life. When he pushed open a door to enter, smoldering wood singed his hands, but he felt nothing at all. The rush of air from his entry fed the fire and stirred the smoke, and he bent down low so he could see. In the room nearest the door he found a man, crouched on all fours, charred like a piece of smoldering brush, his face and clothes all smoky gray. Walker squatted over him.

He felt the heat around him in the gathering flames, and knew the man did too. Walker could save his life simply by picking him up and getting him out of the smoke immediately. The man grabbed onto Walker's arm and said something Walker barely heard, one particular thing, repeating it over and over, trembling as he spoke. "I'm scared," the man said. "Scared."

The deep numbness Walker had felt since he was nine surged within him anew, and then began to ebb, leaving in its place a growing thrill. He was curious and excited. He wondered how he'd feel if the man died. He ripped the man's shirt open, and lay his head against the bare chest, the echoing sound of a pounding heart lost in the roar of the flames. And Walker felt, then, in a distant, measured way, the labored shuddering rhythm of the man as his life slipped away. When he was sure the man was dead, Walker got him up into a fireman's carry, and crawled with the weight of him through the burning building and out the front door. He could hear the whine of the fire engines now, and as he reached the sidewalk, the rest of the rescue squad came running toward him.

He heard everything they said. "Amazing," from one of them. "Great," from another. "Good job, Johnny," from Joe. Walker was entranced by death and thought for a moment that somehow they knew what he felt. But it was not death they were aware of, he realized, only that he'd rescued the man. They didn't even know the man was dead. They worked hard on the body as Walker stood back and watched, every one of them engaged in great urgent motions, trying to start once more what Walker had felt with his own hand disappear. The breath of life.

Life and death. In him the two were forever joined. And he'd found the perfect profession in medicine. He could do what people expected, and also meet his needs. It was in his first year as an intern that he learned he could kill and not be caught. He was treating a man, slight of size and in his thirties, who had a chronic problem with his blood—too much iron in the cells. The normal treatment was to occasionally remove some blood. Walker tried something else; he slowly bled the man to death. And it did for Walker again what the death in the fire had done. It left him aroused and aware in the presence of another's fear. No one had any problem accepting that the death was the result of the man's illness. For Walker, it was the proof he needed: He could live life as he wanted with little risk to himself.

Now Walker was a senior doctor, a specialist in critical situations. His job required him to be with people—and help them—when they were most afraid, often when death was near. In most cases he did what was required to save his patients, and he did the job well. He restrained his impulses because he feared being caught, and because there were virtues to hiding behind charitable works.

That morning, he had done an emergency room tracheotomy on a fourteen-year-old girl. The family was frantic and the nurses and other doctors, though they hid it well, were frightened too. Those were the situations Walker liked best. When everyone else was in a panic, Walker was always calm. And no one else could have gotten it done. Sometimes, when he saved a life, felt the gratitude and heard the praise, he had a fleeting vision of another way to be. Then, at other times, he killed.

He'd been thinking about the old woman on the gurney, he couldn't say for exactly how long. Perhaps only since that morning when he saved the girl. He became aware as the otherwise routine hospital day went on that the old woman and her anxiety about dying had become of interest to him. Old as she was, the way she fought to live stirred in him a vision like a palpable force, and an impulse he couldn't resist. His numbness was the dark in which he always lived, and all of her fears were flashes of light, inevitably drawing him near.

He had walked down the corridor toward her room, the image of her dying already in his mind. He took deep breaths, not to relax but to feel the thrill as fully as he could. He had removed her from the room, strapped her on a gurney, and wheeled it down the hall. She was his for the taking and no one would stop him, because he was a doctor. Now, as the elevator door closed, he looked down at the tag on the old woman's wrist. It had the name Martha Stenton in small purple letters on the pale white band. He touched the metal frame of the mobile bed. He felt through the frame a slight rumbling, the woman's trembling shaking the gray metal. He hadn't touched her yet, but she was fearful just the same. He heard what she had said to the nurses: "The doctors give me drugs, they keep me alive, but they don't care about me." But Walker did.

"You're afraid to die," he said. The woman stared at him. Her face was framed by a full circle of thin white hair. He spread his arms and filled his body with giant gulps of air, then he pressed his lips against hers, and sealed her mouth with his, and emptied his breath into her as completely as he could. He held her face hard between his hands, his palms tight over her ears, his fingers pressing her nose. Her body jerked and her thin arms tried feebly to push him away. Her eyes became bright for a moment, brighter than Walker expected they could be. He dulled her eyes with his two forefingers and pushed down steadily until the brightness faded and two clear lines of thin red blood appeared. When he took his mouth away he was surprised to find her still, though that had been his intention after all.

Clarke housed one of the city morgues. Walker was well familiar with the paperwork he needed to place her there anonymously. He had done everything in advance. Thin as the old woman was, the name tag remained tight around her wrist, the small white square of metal holding the plastic against the patient's skin. Walker reached down and snapped the narrow bones of her wrist. With old ones, it was easy. The band was now loose. He took off the tag and reached into the big pocket of his white coat. He pulled out another tag, one that was common at Clarke. It was marked "unk. wh. fem." He put it on her wrist and took her to the morgue. Another unknown white female.

C H A P T E R

4

I'd been in the city for a week. It was cold and rainy in Philadelphia and the warm green of Florida and spring training seemed far away. Over the years, I'd gotten to feel a bit like a chameleon; where I was had a good deal to do with how I felt. For instance, every time I completed a deal with a corrupt business, I recovered by getting myself down to the Caribbean. I had gone there the first time twelve years ago, on money that was part of a payback to some victims. The Caribbean trip was the personal payoff for me, blackmail's reward. Going to a distant, beautiful place, getting away for a while—I needed that to survive. Sometimes I even felt good just being home, staying days at a time in my two-hundred-year-old carriage house in rural northwest Philadelphia, a small place I'd renovated nicely with a combination of hard work and dirty money. I was eating and sleeping there in between my visits to Joe at Clarke, but I hadn't even called anybody to say I was back in town, so I was feeling like a stranger in someone else's place.

Every day when I visited Joe, his condition was worse. He usually lay absolutely still, a blanket wrapped around his ankle and up between his thighs, his big hands pulling it taut as if he was strangling an enemy. He barely seemed to notice I was there. The room was cool but he was always sweating, drops of it on his forehead as if he'd just played a few hard innings. I kept thinking that if he wasn't sick, we would have been talking baseball right now, the way we had every spring for the past fourteen years. I tried the subject two or three times without much response. I wasn't surprised. It seemed to have so little to do with what he was going through. That was one of the many things I hated about hospitals: the way being there made everything else about your life seem irrelevant.

He had stopped talking to me except when I said something to him, and after a week of visits I realized how little I knew him, in a way. I tried bringing him magazines but he didn't look at them. I ordered a TV for him but he didn't use it. I was sitting there this afternoon lost in thought when I noticed he was looking at me. He reached into the drawer of the table next to his bed and took out an envelope.

The envelope was the big manila kind. It was like the ones the police use to store the personal effects of the dead, an old envelope, purple ink stamps all over it. I took it from him automatically, but it surprised me to be handed it at all. He had suddenly gone from being blank and distant to being right there with me. I had the impression that we now both knew he was going to die, that this was it. I settled back in the chair, and left the envelope untouched in my lap.

"I wrote that for my boy," Joe said, the words coming out slow and dry.

I heard him clearly though his voice was low. I also heard some more of that keening moaning kind of sound, the background noise we'd had from other patients in nearby rooms all week long. This time the sounds were coming from Joe. He was punctuating his sentences with pain.

"Last words and all that," he said. "Not a will. Nothing to leave. But some things I should have told him. You'll give the letter to him, right?"

There was something pleading about the way he asked. He needed to know that letter was going to get to his son, whether Joe lived or died.

"Sure, Joe," I said. "I definitely will."

But I felt like a liar as I said it, because I knew he was no longer lucid, no matter how clear his voice. He had somehow gathered his last bit of energy and scribbled out a message to a son he no longer even had, last words to a child who was long since gone. His son had died at birth. Last words usually had something to do with unfinished business, things you felt guilty about, things you wished you'd been able to say. I had the weight of his final thoughts in a brown envelope on my lap. There were all kinds of pain.

I tried to think of soothing things to say or do for him but I kept coming up empty. What was the point of reminding him he didn't have a son? He wrote the letter because he needed to, and that was all that mattered. But he had given it to me. I wondered if perhaps he meant the letter for me. I was here with him at the end like a member of his family, after all. Maybe that's what I'd become.

It should have occurred to me he'd lose touch, especially considering how bad he looked today. The leg that was gone was sewed up like a package of flesh, the stitches so large it looked like a kindergarten sewing exercise, the ones they did with big colored wool. The other leg was larger than it should have been, the foot swollen grotesquely. His whole face was sweaty, not just his forehead, and the skin was as white as if he'd never been out in the sun in his life. If I found him on the street with just his face looking that way I'd have called an ambulance to get him to a hospital. But he was already in one, and he was fading fast.

I wanted to do something for him but I didn't know what. The other day I'd told a nurse how bad I thought Joe looked. She said they were doing everything they could but that he was very ill. Joe was quiet now, his eyes closed. He had the blanket wrapped tight around his arms. He'd had a week's worth of things going their ordained and ordinary way and it wasn't working out. I wasn't sure why I'd been inactive for so long, but the time had come to create some options. I decided to look at Joe's medical records.

I went to the nursing station down the hall. There was a set of patient files arranged by room number in gray metal bins on a carousel behind the desk. A woman in her late forties sat at the desk talking on the phone. No one else was around. The way she was sitting, she couldn't even see the charts. It seemed likely I could get away with it if I simply acted the part. So I went straight to the charts as if I knew what I was doing, did it all the time. I located Taft's file by his room number and pulled it out. Then I stood there and read it, the way any doctor would. And no one bothered me as I read.

There were some technical medical notations I couldn't follow, but most of the record was in ordinary words. Joe had been admitted March 8, two weeks ago. He had come to the emergency room with an infected foot and a fever of a hundred and one. His right foot was red and swollen, so blown up he couldn't wear a shoe. The notes said he asked for treatment as an outpatient but they insisted on admitting him instead, and he agreed. He was given an intravenous drug called Amigalycin. But his foot didn't get better and his fever rose. On March 17, five days ago, the notes said Dr. Wahdi decided to take off Joe's leg. The pre-op note said Joe had "severe cellulitis," "poor peripheral pulses," and "septicemia" coming from his leg. It concluded that amputation was "necessary." It also said: "Patient delirious, cannot sign consent, and no family available."

The day after the amputation, according to the charts, Joe's fever went up to a hundred and three. He had an infection in his leg above the amputation site. He was still on intravenous antibiotics—the notes said another one, Cedrahyphinal, had been added—but his fever didn't go down. The nurses' notes said he complained repeatedly about pain. They gave him morphine. They asked him several times a day to rate his pain on a scale of one to ten, and he always said six. It was obviously the kind of scale that varied from patient to patient, but I'd have bet anything that Joe's six was someone else's ten. In the dispassionate words they use in charts, it was clear the pain did not stop. "Patient cannot sleep because of pain," said one nurse's entry, written at four in the morning two days ago.

I couldn't understand every detail in the entries, but I got the overall point. What it all meant was that Joe had gotten worse since entering the hospital.

I returned Joe's file to its bin. I had read his chart but I wasn't satisfied. I knew his case had gone poorly. But was it just his case, or was this the kind of place where things went wrong with patients all the time? I wanted to know more. The lobby directory said medical records were on the second floor. I went up. It was after five already and the doors to all the offices were dark and locked. Some of the locks were deadbolts, but the doors had small panes of glass. I figured I'd break into a records room later that night. But the room that said Patient Records had the kind of lock you could open just by slipping a credit card through the crack. I looked around for security, saw no one, and let myself in.

The file cabinets were arranged chronologically, with the month and year written in a small white tab on the front of each drawer. I pulled a batch of charts from last month and sat at a wooden chair next to a small table. I opened the first chart and started reading. I took notes. A half hour and twenty charts later, I had a visitor. A woman opened the door, went to a cabinet, pulled out a drawer, located a chart, and walked out. She didn't say a word to me when she came or when she left. I wasn't surprised. I had been in situations like this many times over the years. It was human nature. When people arrive at a place, they assume anyone who is already there belongs. I'd actually had people ask me for help when they came upon me sitting in a place I'd broken into.

The charts were full of the jargon and the practices that made medicine so much its own world, closed to outsider understanding. After a while, I got the rhythm of it down, helped by the standard way the notes were organized in sections. I ran across Joe's doctor, Dr. Wahdi, six times in the first thirty charts. I couldn't see any pattern in his cases. Of the thirty patients, only two things stood out. Four patients had had their stomachs removed because of ulcers. That seemed odd to me because ulcers were usually treated with a drug these days, not with a "gastrectomy." I knew a bunch of people with ulcers and all of them still had their stomachs, as far as I knew. Six patients had other parts of their bodies removed—legs, arms, or internal organs—but I didn't know if that was a high number or not.

I read another thirty charts and two more things stood out. Many of the patients had infections of one kind or another, and thirty-five of them were given Amigalycin, the same antibiotic Joe had taken. Some did better than him, some didn't. No pattern. For the other patients, four or five different antibiotics were used in most of the cases, and I could see no clear similarity in the course of their illnesses. Most of the patients complained frequently about pain. Almost all of them were given morphine, sometimes as pills, sometimes as intravenous solutions. It was common for patients to complain of pain after they got the drug. Considering the kind of area Clarke was in, I wondered if those patients were addicts and just wanted more. I doubted that was true for Joe. I needed some help interpreting things, that much seemed clear. I wasn't sure whether Clarke was using the best antibiotics or whether pain medications were supposed to provide total relief.

I noticed one other common thread in the records. A number of patients had "discharge planning" notes in the social work section of their files. Those notes typically described the patient as living alone, with no family, often elderly, and in need of constant care. Twenty of the discharge planning notes recommended transfer of the patient to a nursing home. Half the notes referred the patient to a place called Brook Hall Convalescent Center. It occurred to me then—I'd skipped right over it when I'd read Joe's file—that Joe also had a discharge planning note recommending him as a possible transfer to Brook Hall. I didn't know what to make of that.

No one came along to kick me out of the records room, and by the time I got outside it was night. I knew I could find some doctors to tell me whether my impressions from reviewing charts were a cause for concern. But I was already concerned. I didn't like Clarke. Maybe it was that the place was rundown and too cold, or that so many people were suffering there, one of them my friend, and there was no reason to believe he was going to get any better.

I decided to have Joe transferred. I headed for a fancier part of town and a fancier hospital, William Penn. The only thing the admissions desk woman there wanted to talk about was money. Joe had Medicaid, but that wasn't good enough for them; they didn't take transfers of patients that poor. I ended up showing her my American Express. That solved the money problem. The next major step required was to have the doctor from Willian Penn talk to a doctor at Clarke.

I called Clarke and asked for Dr. Wahdi. It turned out he was on duty, and he answered his page after a minute or two. I told him I was a cousin of Joe's and wanted to talk about arranging for a transfer. He asked if I could come to the hospital.

I met him at a patients' lounge on the fourth floor. Dr. Wahdi was a few years younger than me, a few inches shorter, and had a lot more of an attitude. Maybe he'd had a rougher day. I'd only been with one dying man and maybe he had been with more. I thought about asking him to review Joe's case with me, but I didn't want to waste the time. The only thing I cared about was the transfer.

"I've been over to William Penn," I said. "They'll take him if you call and make the arrangements with a doctor there. Is that something you could do?"

He hesitated before responding. I wasn't sure why since it was probably a routine request. I thought for a minute that maybe there was something wrong with the case that I hadn't turned up in the records and Wahdi was reluctant to have Joe looked over in another place. That was the way my mind always worked. But this time I was wrong.

"I'm sorry to tell you this," he said, "but your cousin is dead."

The official cause of death was pulmonary embolism, post surgery. Whatever the cause, in the small amount of time I was away, looking for

reasons and making arrangements to save his life, his body had stopped
working and he was gone. At the age of forty-four. A more fundamental
transfer than the one I had in mind had taken place.

He was gone, removed from all his lifelong gripes and from the game.
I had memories. And his letter. And that was about it. I had spent a week
with him when he was sick and been with him when he would otherwise
have died alone, and that was certainly worthwhile. But it was also a fact
that I had run out of the time I needed to get reacquainted with a friend.
Of course that was a pretty commonplace story. You let things go because
you think you'll have time eventually. And then you don't.

We'd met and become friends at a point in my life I still looked back
at with longing. The big problems I had then were how to do the best I
could at one very narrow thing, and whether I'd ever be good enough at
it to satisfy me and my dad. Taft, even with his cynicism about the men
who played the game, had a taste for its innocence, and I appreciated that.

I didn't know all the details of what had happened to him from the time
we played ball at Reading until he became a patient fourteen years later
in one-half of a room at Clarke. I might have come up with a lot of
questions, but there wasn't much way to get them answered in between
the moans. Or maybe I just didn't find the words. One of those questions
I would have asked was answered every time I spent another hour by his
hospital bed and not a soul came by. It was only me, Joe, and the nurses.
No other visitors. No family. No friends. In a way it made sense he was
alone. He had always been different, and not an easy man to like or
understand. But he had, after all, gotten married once, and even almost
had a kid. It seemed like somebody should have come around.

Dying alone was a bad thing. Dying alone at a place like Clarke was
even worse. I had a sense that Joe's care—the quality of it, or lack of
it—had contributed to his death. It wasn't even anything particular I'd
seen in the records. It was more that Clarke was a place that served the
poor. Putting business people with access to big money together with
people who didn't have any clout to complain was a sure setup for
corruption. Hospitals in bad areas were an ideal breeding ground for
suffering of every kind. And greed. If corruption was, in fact, Clarke's
way, and Joe had gotten caught in the middle of it and hurt, then I was
determined to do something about his death. In baseball, he was always
trying to get me to see what went on beyond the plays on the field, the

realities that shaped the game. I eventually found myself doing that for a living, though not on a baseball field. I think Joe would have enjoyed my latest incarnation, but I had never told him about it.

If Clarke turned out to be a relatively honest place, and all that had happened was that somebody I cared about had died, then that was where I'd leave it. I'd make arrangements for his burial. I'd remember all the stories. And I'd get a stone made. But if Clarke was corrupt, I would fix things at the hospital in his memory. I'd do it as a parting shot for Joe. I'd find another way to make a memorial in his name.

5

Nancy Abbott had moved up fast at Clarke. In only four years, she'd become the hospital's top administrator. She was thirty-four, dark-haired, less attractive than she thought a woman needed to be to have real power, and, similarly, a bit shorter and thinner than she liked. She had tried to gain weight, to have a little bit of a lusher look. She often thought of her body and appearance as an asset to be restructured and used. She resented it when she couldn't make her physical self change to her dictates, as she had been able to do with the other parts of her life.

From her earliest days in administration, Abbott had worked hard to become familiar with the world of contracts—with pharmaceutical companies, medical equipment leasors, insurance companies, federal health agencies. It was where the money and the power were in health care. Everyone pushed for a piece of the action, everyone had a deal. The drug companies had their discounts to offer (they never called them kickbacks). The equipment leasors had their version: take this new machinery, and you can have it for six months with no payments. That is, the hospital books can show payments, but you can do what you want with the money.

Insurance money was always available, too, she had learned. Refer enough patients to a particular nursing home, and they were glad to split the insurance income. She eventually learned all the games the health care industry played, and now she played them well. She didn't view what she did as corrupt; it was just the way of the world, and certainly the way business had always been done at Clarke.

Her simple goal since she'd arrived was to find methods to run the corruption more smoothly, and to organize it all under her hand. Everyone benefited, no one complained. She saw her own profits as well-deserved bonuses for good administration. She enjoyed the power of the job, and the money it could bring. Most of all, she liked the creative twists involved in developing new schemes and profitable deals.

She looked across the desk at Brandon Gilbert, a pharmaceutical company rep. Abbott considered pharmaceutical reps guardian angels, vital to a poor hospital like Clarke. They provided extra money that no one else offered—for research, conferences, books, "special projects," lunches, parties, and the occasional outings. Even the hospitals in wealthy neighborhoods used them for such support. In fact, no institution in the entire world of medicine, she liked to remind herself—even the fanciest medical schools and academic medical centers—functioned without their largesse.

She worked most closely with Gilbert and his company, Rex Pharmaceutical Distributors. Every so often he had ideas that brought in more money—for him, for the hospital, and for Abbott. It was in this spirit he had approached her with an idea eleven months ago.

What he'd proposed was foolproof and, he said, time-tested. She had no doubt there was a well-established line of such schemes, perhaps for as long as there had been hospitals and drug companies. He had proposed that for every batch of morphine the hospital ordered from Rex, he would substitute, on his end, a diluted batch. Seventy-five percent of the drug was withheld, and a diluted, twenty-five percent version of the drug was delivered, packaged identically, down to the IV packets or individual capsules.

The scheme worked wonderfully, and had already provided vast sums for them both. Gilbert's company billed the hospital and its government reimbursement funds for the full, original price. The siphoned morphine was packaged and sold through associates on the street—at a price much higher than the pharmaceutical rate. Although morphine was a cheap drug, as medications go, it was expensive on the street. She and Gilbert split the profits. Her role was simply to take no notice that the drugs were diluted, and deflect any complaints that might arise.

She knew few complaints would arise, and when they did, it didn't matter. Patients in a place like Clarke were always complaining about pain, and wanting more drugs for relief. And most of her physicians were cynical about what patients told them.

Shortly after beginning that venture, Gilbert had suggested a similar though far more profitable scheme. He proposed that while the hospital was paying his company for the usual large orders of extremely expensive antibiotics, he would deliver instead cheaper substitute drugs. The scheme would work, he said, because much of the supposed crucial medical value of the newest and most expensive antibiotics actually amounted to no more than pharmaceutical company hype. The supposed value of the new drugs related mostly to convenience in dosing, or was a benefit for a minority of patients with rare strains of bacteria. In fact, most patients would do just as well on the cheaper drugs, he said, and the ones that failed to improve would hardly be noticed in a troubled place like Clarke. Abbott had liked this idea. They had put it into operation nine months ago.

Gilbert was tall and strongly built, handsome in a rough sort of way. Though he was in his late thirties he looked younger, and wore his blond hair long. He wore expensive suits, and looked, to Abbott, very out of place at Clarke. His voice was soft, and he pronounced every word carefully and clearly. She had seen him often at medical conferences he catered or sponsored. He always stood perfectly still as he spoke, his face impassive, hard to read. He had made her plenty of money, but she trusted him not at all.

His visits to her weren't scheduled. He stopped by several times a month, always unannounced. It was usually because something was bothering him, and he rarely said directly what it was.

"What's up, Brandon?" Abbott asked.

"A routine check of supplies," he answered, his tone so low she marveled that she understood his words.

"If you think something's wrong, just ask me," she said. "What's the problem? You can't be worried about the drugs. It's not like they're valuable or anything." She laughed.

He smiled warmly. "I just want to make sure nobody's disturbing the supply."

He had brought that concern up before. "Don't be that impressed by the neighborhood," Abbott said. "Or by the way the hospital looks. It doesn't matter to me much if things walk when they're not nailed down.

You're going to get a certain amount of that with this kind of population. But not in the pharmacy. You know my drug security is good."

"It's not the patients I'm concerned about," Gilbert said. "And it wouldn't be your fault. But there are always problems at hospitals." He appeared to try a weak smile. "So I check every once in a while." He had a way of making everything he said a matter of routine, of business. It was a talent she admired.

"It never hurts to check," he said. "Addicts are clever. Especially when they're doctors. Or nurses. You have addicts in hospitals, like everywhere else. They'll take their drugs either from the floor or from the central supply. It's a hard thing to control completely, no matter how good your security. We don't care about the theft, but if a doctor or nurse here uses some of our morphine, they'll notice it's been cut. I don't know what they'd do about it, but there's no reason to take a chance."

She knew he was right, but she found it hard to see any of Clarke's doctors, addicts or not, as a threat. Walker was the sole exception, in her opinion, and he was on her side. The hospital relied mainly on a mix of older private attendings and temporary hired doctors as staff. The private attending physicians had all been at Clarke for many years. Most of them were losers, unable to muster the skills or connections or luck to leave Clarke and hook up with a better place. They had little inclination to worry about patient care or notice hospital conditions.

The house staff doctors, for different reasons, were similarly irrelevant to Abbott's point of view. They were temporary hired help, most of them foreign medical graduates and unlicensed, seeking additional experience, credentials, and recommendations. Others had had problems in medical school or training programs elsewhere. Most of them only stayed one year. They didn't identify with the hospital or its patients. They made no waves. Gilbert knew all this.

She remained skeptical, but saw no reason to argue. "So let's go check the drugs," she said.

She escorted him up to central supply. When they got there, she sent the pharmacist on a break; he was more than glad to go. When he was gone, Gilbert moved into the room.

Abbott watched as he deftly opened boxes and ran bottles and packages of multicolored pills and capsules through his hands. She stood by the doorway and held open the spring-loaded weight of the metal mesh door, the cold feel of it on her calves. She had always believed, with an administrator's feel for the monied heart of all human affairs, that this place was the key, the essential core of a hospital's life, the storehouse of the magic that underlay the power of physicians. This was what made it all work. The powders that promised relief and cure, the crystals that gathered at the edge of the poundstone, the potions created by pestle and mortar. Drugs, which doctors and junkies used equally well, and to similar ends, after all, were what made the whole thing credible, what made it work. The drug companies owned the land. And this was their home.

Gilbert moved from box to box. Abbott was struck by how many boxes there were. The sheer color of the pills was striking. It was like sifting through a roomful of jewels. Though there was something childlike about them, as well. Not jewels, she thought, but crayons, or bits of colored glass. Everything was in primary colors. Yellows and red and blues. She wondered why that was. Everything they did was calculated, she thought. There was no business in the world so planned for its effects as the drug business. Color must be important, then. She voiced the thought aloud. Gilbert turned around, holding a collection of capsules in his hand.

"Oh yes," he said. "Very important. For one thing, the brighter the color—and the larger the pill—the better the patient thinks it works. And for doctors, making the pills easy to recognize has its advantages."

Abbott nodded. Very organized. Everything deliberate. Always sweating the details, lining it all up. It was the same when he checked the inventory; he knew exactly what to look for and what to disregard, and he did it as efficiently as it could be done. She appreciated the skill.

"You were right," he said, when he was done. "No tampering."

"Come on, then," she said, waving him out. "I've got work to do."

CHAPTER

6

I knew I'd be spending a lot of time at the hospital, and there are only a limited number of reasons you can give for doing that. So I decided to become a patient.

I was familiar with the symptoms of a heart attack. Very familiar. My father had a bad heart, and he was hospitalized when I was a child. My mother was always watching for the symptoms, and never said so, but always wondered whenever he had indigestion if he was weak, or sweaty, or nauseous. She had subtle ways to check if his pain had spread to his neck or his shoulders, or whether he felt heavy in his chest. Over the years, I had gotten to know these silent rituals and questions.

My father himself never showed any concern. He came up the old-fashioned way, raising hell, then settling down, then raising hell again. He was a ballplayer, a longtime minor leaguer who finally stopped playing while I was in grade school, but he never lost his taste for the game. He liked to talk for hours about baseball and its players, but never about himself or his feelings. When I was twenty-two, he died in his sleep of a massive heart attack.

The dying was sudden, and it was months before it really hit hard how much I missed him, and how much we had left undone. That was when I finally let go of baseball, and started going my own way instead of his. As a small token of that, I dropped my first and middle names. Nobody since then has called me anything but Gray. My father had named me George Herman, after the Babe. Dad was a big believer in finding destiny in a name. If he could have, he would have changed our last name to Ruth, but there my mother drew the line.

It was damp and chilly on the evening I went to Clarke. Florida was gone for the year. I left my car parked at a meter on Broad Street; I couldn't find a parking lot. The entrance to the emergency room was around back, a wide curved driveway with no sidewalk leading the way. There was a high fence on one side, the metal weathered and rusted brown and topped with ancient strips of barbed wire. As I approached the entrance I looked up at the hospital's chipped and faded cement walls, and wondered whether the fences kept intruders out or patients in.

The first thing I noticed when I stepped through the double doors was the smell. It was something like vinegar, something familiar like the rubbing alcohol in the trainer's room at the ballpark. But the odor was deeper, fuller, more cloying. More than the alcohol smell was the acrid odor of fear.

The place was crowded. People sick and old and in pain, the pain slow and deep and raw. Everyone in the room looked sad. Most of them sat quietly on green plastic chairs, waiting their turn, taking a place in line, one at a time standing to sign papers at a reception desk. Some made pleas to move quicker or to go first. The pleas were ignored. I got on line.

As I waited, I saw that everything in this place, even the machines and supplies, not only the patients, looked incomplete and battered. Each door of every cabinet hung open, reflecting some frantic hurried passage, or damaged hinge, and nothing inside them was straight up or arranged. Bottles lay on their sides, tops off as if long ago emptied, and rolls of bandages were everywhere, mostly used up, last strands barely clinging to their cardboard cores. Some of the machines looked damaged, tubes stopped short of their endpoint connections, small metal wheels at the top of cannisters broken or dangling at odd angles. The lights were too dim, the fixtures attached to a ceiling that was too low, unevenly plastered, and dark. The walls were a dull enamel green. The floor was made of huge tiles of gray and white.

I could see a big room through parted heavy curtains, our destination for the healing this group sought. The room was divided into small cubicles. The only barriers between them were heavy cloth curtains of pale orange, the color much darker or lighter in odd places because of wet stains and patches of dirt. The dirt had meanings of its own, traces of life and history, blood-smeared markers that had piled up over time. It looked as if the curtains themselves had been used for covering or wiping or bandaging the ill. They made the cubicles seem temporary despite the solid floors and walls, the semblance of a hospital created in a field, to take care of soldiers during a war.

In the midst of this faded and impaired display, there were a few new things here and there; wrapped unopened boxes of cotton, sealed and colorful packages of medicine, some machines that still had a metallic gleam marking their recent arrival. I had the impression of intermittent attempts to make repairs, erratic efforts to keep things going, efforts that perhaps gave way to despair.

The cubicles were arranged in a semi-circle facing the main desk and there were no curtains in front of them. You could look right in.

A very fat white man, tall and huge, was positioned carefully on one of the beds, trying to make room for his immense legs. They were swollen to the point that his long socks seemed full of nothing but fluid. He was smiling, I didn't know why, and people who walked by were careful not to look in.

In another cubicle a young black woman rocked herself on the flat thin pallet of the cot, her right side red and raw all the way from her hip to her foot. Her jerky movements sometimes rolled her partly over onto her bare fiery skin. When that happened she screamed, one loud fierce yell which quickly turned into a low sobbing.

In a cubicle across from that, a woman sat in a metal chair, and cradled a very small child in her lap. The baby was laid across the woman's arms, mouth open, small lips cracked and blistered. The child was quiet as if spent, not crying or moving at all. Not dead, I thought, because the woman wouldn't sit there like that if the baby was dead.

In the cubicle closest to me was an old man, extremely thin, with dark black skin. His chest rose and fell with a brittle, shivering quake, and each time it did a loud sharp sigh filled the air, then there was silence. A moment later, a new small shaking began, this time in the thin reedlike legs and delicate bony feet. The effect was like some injured bird trying to fly.

I found myself looking into every cubicle, compulsively holding my hand over a flame. But before I was able to see them all, the people in front of me had been processed, one way or another, and I was the one at the front of the line. I told the nurse at the desk my problem.

"I'm having chest pains," I said, my voice low and anxious. "The pain goes right up to my neck and shoulders. I feel weak, nauseous. It's hard to breathe and I'm sweating like crazy."

She hesitated, and seemed genuinely concerned. She asked for and took my Blue Cross card, and that seemed to relax her. Private insurance; a rare gift.

"Let's get you to a doctor right away," she said, and stood up.

"Come inside." She pointed me to a cubicle, guiding me into the small curtained space.

I sat on a metal chair, and she left. I put my hand on the dark green wall behind me. It felt cold. I was hot; I was sweating. It didn't take as much effort to feign illness as I thought. I was nervous. In this place, it was hard to feel good. This was a hospital that served the poor in a city that itself wasn't doing too well these days. It was nighttime, Center City, and this was one of the places people ended up when daytime expectations didn't pan out, or life got interrupted in unimagined ways. On one side a flood of desperate living and bad surprises; on the other a very small number of helpers. I was about to take up some care and time—I already had taken some—from a people and place who didn't have much of either.

In a few minutes, the nurse came back.

"The doctor'll be right with you. How are you feeling?"

"Not sure," I answered. "I've still got the pain."

"Hold on," she said, and left again.

Through the curtains, I saw a young woman in a white coat work her way toward my cubbyhole, and something happened as she went from patient to patient, a current of feeling in her wake that quieted people. Watching her, I could guess what it was. In one of the rooms, she smiled broadly at the man I'd looked away from, before she tended his wounds; in another, she sat and listened to a woman for a minute after she finished her work. She was nice and she was warm, and she took the time. Those were hard qualities to sustain in a place like this, and people probably noticed and appreciated it, sick as they were. Whatever effort it took for her, it was worth it. She bandaged a kid's burned arm, shoulders tensed as she leaned into the circular motions, and I wondered if the hardest part of her kind of work in a place like this was how it felt to hear the way some of their injuries occurred—that burden even harder than the skill it took to heal their wounds.

I was taken by the look of her—short light brown hair with slight curls above a face that was clearly Irish. She was about five-five, had an athletic body, and carried herself in an easy way.

The nurse came back. I gave my discomfort a nod. "I guess I have to wait," I said.

"No you don't," someone said. "It's your turn." The doctor I'd been watching was in my cubicle. "I'm Dr. Molly Hale."

"I've never heard a doctor do that before," I said.

She was already mid-motion, pulling the stethoscope off her shoulder and moving closer, but she stopped for a minute and smiled.

"Do what?" she said.

"Throw in a first name after the doctor."

She smiled. "How do you feel?"

"Not too good."

She put the stethoscope on my chest. "I'm just going to listen," she said, bending down. Then she put it on my back. For a moment, there was silence. All I did was breathe.

"So far, pretty good," she said. "I don't hear anything distressing in there. Tell me how it started. And when."

"About a half hour ago. I was driving, on my way home. At first I thought it was indigestion. A pain high in my chest." I put my hand on the area below my throat. "It got worse. I had to pull over and stop driving. But the pain spread up my shoulders and neck. I got dizzy, so I drove straight here, the closest place."

I volunteered my medical history, and, although it was true that my father had died of a heart attack, I added some to it. "My father and brother both died of heart attacks, my brother when he was thirty-nine."

She didn't need to hear any more. She kept me in the ER for some tests, but I knew they had no way to really rule out a heart attack, and my description of the pain and the history made it possible I'd had or was having one. She admitted me for observation and more tests and told me I'd probably be in for a few days if all went well.

I had my entry to Clarke.

CHAPTER

7

Despite my private insurance, they put me in a standard-issue room, just like Taft's. Maybe standard issue was all they had. My roommate was a thin old man who snored. It mattered, because he slept all the time. They stored my street clothes in two drawers of a dresser opposite my bed, and folded my jacket in there too, because there wasn't a closet in the room. I guess family members were supposed to take your things home, and if you didn't have family members, you probably had the kind of jackets you could fold and stuff.

I waited in bed until two in the morning, then got up and put on my clothes. I took a large towel, soaked it with water, squeezed out the excess, and folded it into a square. I peeked outside the room, saw no one in the corridor, and went right to the stairway. I walked down to the second floor.

The hallway in the administration section of the hospital was dark and empty. I went to the door of a contracts room I'd spotted two days earlier, a door with a deadbolt and a small window. I pressed the wet towel on the glass and covered it; the moisture almost held the towel in place. I spread my left hand flat and wide against the cloth and used my right to give one quick, hard poke. The glass popped out, most of it in one large piece, and shattered on the floor. The hole was covered so the noise was mainly on the other side. I still hoped no one heard. I reached through, unlocked the door and went in, clearing away the broken glass before going to the files.

I was interested in hospital contracts and purchase orders. There is a silent rhythm to any business that can be picked up by leafing through its contracts. Contracts are often overlooked because they're boilerplate and boring. But I'd learned as a reporter—and relearned many times since—that contracts are a key. When a place is corrupt, contracts are a good trail, a written record of deeds otherwise kept secret.

Pharmaceutical contracts and purchase orders seemed an obvious starting point, antibiotics in particular, since I'd already seen that most patients on antibiotics were getting the same five drugs. To my surprise, the files were meticulously arranged and the listings and cross-references remarkably complete. Administration had matters well organized and under control; it seemed inconsistent with the generally sloppy feel of the hospital.

I tried the files under "A" for Amigalycin, the antibiotic Joe had been given. There was a file under that name, but it contained only one index card with a cross-reference that said: "See Rex Distributors." The Rex file contained a half-dozen large orders for Amigalycin that month, as well as orders for several thousand doses of the four other antibiotics I'd seen most often cited in patient charts. It was clear from the records that Rex was a marketing and distribution operation and not a pharmaceutical manufacturer. The records also showed that three of the drugs were made by pharmaceutical companies nearby in New Jersey, which sold the drugs to Rex. I wondered why the hospital would use a middleman to deliver locally made drugs.

The earliest Rex contract went back only nine months. I searched through the period before that. In the nine months with Rex on the scene, almost all the antibiotic purchases were through Rex, but in the year before that, the purchases were split among a number of different distributors.

Next, I looked at purchases of morphine, and was again referred to Rex. They had been the exclusive morphine supplier to Clarke for the past eleven months. Before that, the hospital had purchased morphine from several other companies.

In another cabinet there were records of the hospital's contracts with the federal government. I wanted to go through them but it was getting late and I wasn't sure what kind of bed checks the nurses might be making, if any. I'd pick it up some other time.

I got back to my bed at five in the morning. It was still dark out and the old man was still snoring. Nobody seemed to miss me, so I went to sleep.

At ten that morning, a doctor walked in.

"I am Dr. Karanjme and I will be taking care of you," he said. He was thin and short. "We're going to do some tests on you," he said. "Nothing too much, but very important, to find out what's going on." His manner was cheerful and bright. He spoke quickly, and though his accent—India or Pakistan, I thought—was strong, the words were clear.

"What kind of tests?" I asked.

He looked toward the door as if anticipating leaving. He glanced a lot in the direction of the old man, and I wondered if he was his patient, too.

"We put a tube in, like an IV, you know. And then we do an X-ray so we can check on your heart. You don't feel it. Nothing, really. Simple. We give you a sedative, so you relax, and there's no pain. It's very quick."

"How long will it take?"

"Half an hour," he said. "We must do it to make sure you're all right. Okay?"

I didn't understand his description of the test. But I was there to be a patient. I wasn't too happy with the idea of having something done to me at Clarke. Even when I absolutely needed to have operations, I'd fought them. When my shoulder went to pieces and they wanted to go in, I spent a good while trying to heal it myself before I agreed. And of course, at the moment, there wasn't anything wrong with my heart. On the other hand, I needed access to the hospital. There was always a price. That's what it came down to in the end. And I had a certain talent for surviving. I found myself thinking about Joe, and everything he'd been through. Karanjme handed me a consent form. It was only three paragraphs but every single one of them was chock full of details about the dangers of the "simple" exam he proposed to do. The contrast between Karanjme's mild assurances and the dire language of the form was great. The truth, as always, was somewhere in between. I had to decide. I could refuse. But it was time to give a little blood, and get some in return. I scrawled my name on the form and handed it to the doctor.

"Okay," I said. He looked relieved. He nodded, and a minute later he was gone. In a short while, a nurse came in with a small paper cup. "This is for you," she said. I took the cup, and she poured some water into a glass. There were two pills in the cup. They were white, flat, and small. In my baseball days, the players always had pills. Greenies and reds. Uppers and downers. I swallowed the white sedatives and the nurse left the room.

Back in the fifties and sixties, the old-timers told me, they'd keep a big glass bottle on a table in the locker room. Greenies. Take what you needed. They'd raise your heart rate and made you feel like you could run and hit, when what you really needed to do was sleep. Occasionally, someone got into the pills more than the playing, or took the pills as well as their failures home. Everyone knew about the drugs, including the sportswriters, but the newspapers never wrote about them. I remembered how the old-timers laughed their heads off in the early eighties when Pete Rose took the stand during a drug trial and said he didn't know what a greenie was. Sure. Just like he didn't know what a curveball was.

I laughed at the memory, right there in the hospital bed. That's when I first noticed a tingling in my thighs. It felt good, relaxing. It spread across my body, a feeling of warmth, a great weight disappearing. Just keep your mind on the game. The phrase jumped out at me, a voice from within. Speed and power, kid. You've got all the tools. I'd pinch-hit and then they'd keep me in to play third base.

I let my eyes close. Good time for a nap. I opened my eyes when I felt hands on both my arms, lifting me. The nurses wanted to put me on a small cot with wheels. I braced myself to move over, but my arms and legs were leaden. I had no energy. No matter. They didn't speak to me anyway, just slid me down the few inches onto the cot. Then one of them said, "Time to go now." She had a very calm voice, and spoke slowly.

I remember rolling past a nursing station and getting on an elevator. I must have dozed through part of the rest of the trip. They left me in some kind of procedure room. Two men walked in, one of them Dr. Karanjme. He had a mask over his nose and mouth but I recognized him anyway.

Things registered but I didn't react. A pair of hands, which seemed disembodied and moved too quickly to follow, passed over my head, then attached a small bag to a metal pole that stretched above me. Someone pressed a hand on my side. I looked down. A tube was attached to my arm, the liquid flowing.

The fog deepened and I couldn't make out voices or sensations or anything. I was drifting along in a distant river, calm, quiet, peaceful. I was drifting alone now, relaxed. I swallowed something, a taste of liquid metal. I tried to spit it out but gagged and choked. I tried to get a breath. Couldn't. I felt a surge of pain in my throat, then my chest. My arm was on fire. I tried to move but didn't, the table shook instead, and I saw the metal pole and the bag swinging wildly. My vision turned shades of red, dark, then darker. I wanted to get some air but my throat was dry and raw. Then I was sick, nauseous and heaving. But nothing was in there. I opened my mouth. There was still pain. I kept moving, or trying to. Someone yelled and a nurse leaned over me.

"What's wrong?" I heard her say.

I tried to answer. "Dizzy." I thought it was my voice but I couldn't get out any more words.

She moved toward the others.

"Hold it," another voice said. He took his hand away from the IV bag.

"Shit." The same voice. "Doctor . . ." I couldn't hear her say anything else. She had a low voice, sweet.

"Pressure's a hundred in a sink." The same voice. "He's dizzy. He's diaphoretic." Their voices climbed a ladder of loudness, going up.

"Eighty," someone else said. I tried to reach up to grab the pole but couldn't. They didn't seem to notice me. They stopped moving.

"Going down," a woman said. "Going down . . . seventy, not palpable, systolic."

They pressed something metal against my chest.

"Can't hear it."

"Afib or what is it? Bolus him!"

I got feeling in my legs and kicked something, sending it into a wall. The crash of glass.

"Jesus Christ!" A man's voice. And then: "Hold him fucking down!"

"Maybe it's burst. Get a monitor."

"It doesn't work. Oh God!"

The door opened. New light flooded in.

"What's happening here?" A new man. Urgent voice, demanding.

"We need a monitor." The other man. "It's his heart."

"No." The new man. "It's anaphylactic. He needs epi."

Metal drawers were pulled out. A box ripped open.

"Come on. Come on!"

"Don't have it," the nurse with the low voice said, almost as loud as them now. "There's none in here."

"Go out and get it! Run!"

The door slammed against the wall. There was total silence for a moment and no movement. Then more pain. I needed air, but couldn't get it. Sounds faded and I drifted again. I couldn't catch my breath. I thought I was dying and I couldn't do a thing.

Someone grabbed my arm and I looked up. I saw him put the top of a bottle to a needle's point. I could see the rubber stopper split and a golden liquid spill upwards into glass. The man put the needle in my arm and pressed down.

In seconds, with one massive shift of sensation, like a tornado driving rain out in front of it, the whole world changed. Dark to light. My senses returned. I could see the room clearly. I could hear everything. I could move with no difficulty. I could breathe. I sat up, took in gulps of air quickly at first, then I slowed. I let out a deep sigh and moved my body around a bit, to see if it worked. One of them gave me some water and I drank it.

I felt okay again, just like that. I didn't recognize the doctor with the syringe still in his hand. He hadn't been there when they wheeled me in. A woman was at his side and I recognized her, the doctor I'd met in the Emergency Room. Molly Hale.

"Diazepam, too," the doctor with the syringe said to a nurse, still watching me. I got another shot. He saw whatever he wanted to see and turned away.

Dr. Hale came closer to me.

"You're fine?" she asked.

"Sure," I said. I was breathing as if there was nothing to it. My bedclothes were soaked with sweat.

A woman opened the door and gestured to Dr. Hale.

"They called you from CCU," the nurse said.

She said she'd see me later, and left. When she was gone I lay back down. I wanted to sleep. But I didn't.

CHAPTER

8

I was alone in the room. Light was coming in from the window, but it was a dim light, not the daytime sun. My head ached. I looked around. There was the dresser with my jacket folded in the drawer. And the curtain was partly drawn between me and the next bed. But the old man was missing. His bed was made. I stared at the empty bed. Some storm had swept by but I had survived. The doctor, Molly Hale, walked in. She looked in first to see if I was awake.

"Am I still in one piece?" I asked her.

"You tell me," she said.

I moved my arms and legs and hands, then settled back, satisfied to find everything in order.

"The old man," I said. "Where is he?"

She didn't hesitate. "He died." She sounded unhappy about it, not matter-of-fact. "He was eighty-six. There was nothing we could do for him. Died in his sleep, of old age. He was a nice guy. It was an easy death, for what that's worth."

"What happened to me this morning?" I asked.

"It wasn't this morning. It was yesterday. It's Thursday." She stopped talking and looked around the room as if she wanted something. She looked tired. "Mind if I sit?"

"I think I came close to dying in there," I said. "That's what it felt like, anyway. Tell me what happened."

"You came in complaining of heart problems and we thought you might have a dissecting thoracic aortic aneurysm."

"I need it in English."

"Sure, sorry. It's like a bubble on the surface of the main artery from the heart. It's dangerous because it can burst at any time, and the heart stops working when it does. That's one possible reason for chest pain, when the EKG—the test you had in the ER—doesn't show a heart attack. To find an aneurysm, you do a CAT scan of the chest, with contrast. That's a kind of X-ray where you first put dye into the heart through a thin tube. The dye highlights the aneurysm, if it's there, and then you can do surgery to fix it."

"What went wrong? I know something did."

She hesitated. I was curious why she'd come to see me. She'd admitted me to the hospital and I'd gotten into trouble. She might have felt responsible in some way. Perhaps she wanted to apologize, if not for herself then for others. In medicine, as in most other jobs, there was probably a thin line between helping outsiders understand the things that went wrong, and not blowing the whistle on coworkers. Most of us walked on tiptoe all the time, but sometimes you had to cross the line. I wondered if she would.

She took a deep breath. "You're right," she said. "A lot of things went wrong. Let's face it, you might have been better off in a better equipped hospital, like Penn."

"So what happened?"

"You were allergic to the dye. That doesn't occur too often, and you can't predict it in advance. When it does, the allergic reaction is pretty intense—it's called anaphylactic shock. It's like getting a dozen bee stings if you're allergic to bees. Your blood pressure falls to almost nothing. You have difficulty breathing. You get dizzy, sometimes pass out. Oxygen helps. They didn't give it to you because they didn't have an oxygen tank in the room. There should have been; standard procedure."

Her tone of voice when she described things at Clarke was similar to the way she sounded when she described the old man's death. Mournful.

"You don't sound surprised about that," I said.

"I'm not. It happens here a lot. Anyway, they thought the aneurysm had burst. The symptoms are the same as in shock, and they didn't consider that you might be allergic to the dye. What saved you was that Dr. Walker was around. He's the chief of critical care and really good. He suspected you were in shock and wanted to give you epinephrine to bring you out of it. But there was no epi in the room. Again, there should have been. There's a crash cart in procedure rooms, sort of an emergency kit, just for problems like yours. But the cart didn't have the supplies it was supposed to have, so we had to wait until a nurse brought the drug from another room."

"Could I have died?"

"I don't know. You look like you're in excellent shape. You might have survived it. Some people wouldn't have. Anyway, as soon as you got the medication, you were fine. Brought your pressure right back up. Your breathing returned to normal. Dr. Walker gave you a sedative just to put you to sleep. Your body needed the rest."

I got the picture. Lucky me. They did everything wrong but I came through with no scars. I was impressed she told me the truth. No excuses, no covering up. She was honest. Some people just were. I considered telling her the truth in return. That I'd faked my admission, that there was nothing wrong with my heart, that I was here to investigate the hospital because my friend had died. I thought she might help. But if she had a bout of loyalty or misguided conscience and turned me in, I'd lose my access. I didn't want to chance that happening yet.

She stood up. "I'm glad you're feeling better. I've got to go now."

"Wait," I said. "Just one or two more things." She looked puzzled, but she stayed.

"Was the test really necessary?"

I could see her hesitate, weighing things in her mind, then she plunged in—and did the right thing.

"I don't know," she said. "Perhaps they shouldn't have. We're all a little too quick to do tests, sometimes."

I was testing her ability to tell the truth, in effect. She was passing easily.

"But they didn't have to do it, right?"

"I probably wouldn't have," she admitted.

"Why do you think they did, then?" I persisted. "For the money?"

"It's more complicated than that." The question didn't seem to bother

her. On the other hand, she moved toward the door. "I really better go."

I didn't want her to leave yet. "I'm sorry if I'm making a nuisance of myself with these questions," I said. "But I think you can understand. I almost died here last night. I'm curious, that's all."

"I understand," she said. "And if you're angry about what happened, that's understandable, too. But it's hard to be exactly right or wrong about every decision we make. Should I say they probably shouldn't have done it? Given what happened, they'd probably tell you that themselves."

It was her first lie.

"No," I said. "I bet they wouldn't."

I thought she would defend the other doctors, if only because of professional loyalty. If she couldn't, she'd leave. Instead, she nodded her head. "You're right," she said. "They probably wouldn't."

I didn't want to ask her any more questions, at least not now. "It's been a really crazy week," I said. "Not only my experience last night. Other things. A friend of mine died."

"I'm sorry," she said.

"The worst thing about it was that he was in so much pain, he went crazy at the end. It was the saddest damn thing. He wrote a letter to his son and gave it to me to give to him. And his son died a long time ago, at birth."

She shook her head, emphatically. "People don't do that," she said.

"What do you mean?"

"People don't do that when they're dying," she said. "Unfortunately, I've seen enough people dying to know. When they're in a lot of pain, or delirious, people ramble, they say things that make no sense. But they don't write letters to loved ones who have died."

"My friend did."

"I don't think so. If I had to guess, I'd say there's a son out there somewhere. Or someone he thought of as one. And that's who he was writing the letter to."

It had not occurred to me, but the minute she said it, I thought she might be right. I didn't know if she'd ever met Joe, but she knew death. She had a set of experiences no one wanted. A small group of people—physicians—were there at deathbeds over and over, as part of their workaday routine. But it wasn't just experience with the dying that mattered. A lot of people become familiar with the dead, and it provides them no new wisdom at all. She told me something about Joe I almost had missed. Taft might have a living son. If he did, I would find him, and deliver his final words.

C H A P T E R

9

Walker's week had been routine. On Wednesday, the day after he killed the old woman, he helped a resident who'd botched a trach. On Thursday, he'd calmed and healed a teenager who came in with a knife wound; he also made a good friend of the boy's mother by assuring her that her son would recover quickly, and doing it in a nice way. On Friday, he supervised two codes. Both patients died, but that was expected; it was rare that cardiac life support kept a patient alive for long.

After a week of such routine, without having planned it, he stopped by Nancy Abbott's apartment on Saturday evening. He and the hospital administrator had been seeing each other for years. It didn't matter if she wasn't in. He had the key, and could wait. And if she was there, with someone else, he knew she would send the other man away. It didn't occur to Walker she had another choice. He had always gotten his way with her, right from the day they'd met. It was a sexual attraction. The prostitutes he called were available to anyone. Abbott was available only to him. To all others she was a figure of power, a woman who would not submit. Those were qualities whores were paid not to have. As Walker entered her apartment, he heard her in the bedroom.

She heard the door open and knew who it was. She wasn't dressed so she slipped on a gown. He'd come in whether she wanted him to or not, even if she wasn't ready. He came and went as he pleased. She tried not to let it affect how she lived, tried to be aware of whether she curtailed her social life or didn't have people over because of the possibility he'd arrive. As far as she could tell, she was living the way she otherwise would, but it was hard not to take him into account. Sometimes when she felt especially private, in the bath, or ill, or masturbating, she expected him to open the door at any moment. He had a knack for that.

She had a hard time reconciling the man who visited her in her apartment with the man she saw handling responsibilities at the hospital. She thought of him as moody, and he was. Sometimes they spent hours together and hardly spoke. Neither minded silence. The only important thing, she often reminded herself, was how much profit and power the relationship brought her. She had arrived at Clarke Hospital as a low-level administrator. That changed when she met Walker. They became lovers quickly, and after that Walker was happy to use his prestige at Clarke to convince board members that Abbott should move up the administrative ladder quickly. In most cases, the board did what Walker asked.

Being with him was both a gift and a constraint. He excited her, yet his assumption of power over her made her angry. She had a new ally in Gilbert. Perhaps she could continue to do well at Clarke without Walker's help. She had mentioned none of this to Walker, nor would she.

He came in and went right to her bed. He looked at her but didn't say anything. He lay down, crushing the thin bedclothes underneath him. He covered his face with his hands. His fingers were huge and she couldn't see anything of his features or expression, as if he had withdrawn behind a wall. He kept his hands there for minutes, pressing hard on his cheeks, digging into the bony structure of his forehead, using the center of his palms in a circular motion to rub his eyes. He sighed, and the sound, muffled and deep and low, was strange to hear. She stood by the doorway like a visitor outside the bear cage at the zoo, looking in at the big creature.

A bystander, passive and peripheral in her own room, she lost herself in thought. She thought about her favorite things, the projects she had under way at Clarke, each of them faultlessly moving along, generating money and power, seeing them in broad perspective, how each of these deeds had their place in the overall scheme she pursued, the inventing and structuring of the new life she had created for herself.

As a teenager and young adult, she went out with a succession of men who slept with her a few times, then left her. She reached a point at which she stopped seeing men as a solution or a goal, and instead put her energy into finishing college and beginning work as a high school teacher. She taught handicapped children for three years while continuing her own education at night. In graduate school, she met a man, a doctoral student studying chemistry, who seemed different, more interested in her than the others had been. When he finished his degree, she left school and went with him, her studies incomplete. They moved from New York to Philadelphia, where they married and he taught at the University of Pennsylvania.

The marriage lasted less than a year. He had an affair with one of his students. She kicked him out, and to his chagrin she stayed right there, refusing to leave the college or the house, refusing to return to New York. Instead, she decided to get a master's degree in hospital administration because it seemed to be an area where there was great need, and therefore the guarantee of a job. It also gave her a chance to live well on her own, without a man.

Her first job after she graduated was at Clarke. The place was poorly run, apparently corrupt, and after a few months she contemplated leaving. Then she met Walker. For the first time in her life, she saw accumulating money and power as a challenge she could enjoy. She never thought of herself as corrupt, but she refused to be a fool again. It was clear to her that the staff at Clarke who were honest or interested mainly in patient care made the least money and had the least power. She decided to stay, and take care of herself.

She succeeded because she saw that the corruption at Clarke Hospital had never been organized or controlled in any way. Every scam, and there were many, was handled separately by different people. A cancer doctor falsified information about his patients to get them admitted to drug studies, and benefited greatly from the grants. Another doctor fudged the results of studies to get more federal funding. An administrator in purchasing and several doctors bought unnecessary equipment to get kickbacks.

Abbott realized that as top administrator she could coordinate and centralize all of the schemes, increasing everyone's profits while giving her control. She found ways to help everyone else with their projects.

The scheme she liked the most was one she created entirely on her own. She had a private deal with a nursing home in Montgomery County. She arranged frequent referrals of patients from Clarke into the home. The nursing facility collected a hundred and fifty dollars a day from government insurance for each patient. It was common enough for a hospital administrator to get a kickback for a patient referral. What made the deal sweet—with the new twist she created—was that the patients she referred to the home were already dead. When certain patients died—usually patients who were very old and had no families—she kept their deaths from being recorded at the hospital. Instead, she had their bodies taken to the morgue and marked "unknown." Their files were then sent to the nursing home as if they were still alive. The nursing home collected insurance just as if the patients were there and being cared for, and every dollar of it was profit. Abbott split the money with the nursing home fifty-fifty. Walker helped her by selecting the patients for transfer, and making the necessary changes on the medical records. For this, he received a substantial share, though she sensed he didn't really care about the money. He seemed mostly to enjoy watching her wheel and deal.

For all of her business at the hospital, Walker was an invaluable and reliable helper. What she liked most was having a man assist her with her plans, for a change.

Walker liked the sex with Abbott much of the time. Aside from the way it felt, there was pleasure in the way she pushed herself to go along with his whims. He understood that she used him, trading sex for his favors at work, and, perhaps less clear to her, using him to test a new view of herself. Initially naive, though hungry for money, she'd been changing over the past few years and he knew it. More and more, control mattered to her. She didn't have to tell him that. He could see it in the way she constantly broadened her schemes at the hospital, and made them less and less dependent on him. As a lover, she remained available for whatever he wished, but no longer quite as openly.

She came to the bed and he pushed her gown off her upper body, exposing her breasts. He ran his hands down her back. He felt the warmth of her stomach and thighs against him. He pulled the gown down to her feet and off, looking at her, enjoying her shyness, the way she turned her face away. He took her thin, tightly muscled calves in his hands and raised them, spreading her thighs, sliding his hand between her legs. She didn't help him, or move in any way, though she never did at first. She always let him do it, but she was easily aroused. He stroked softly inside of her, his other hand at her ear, then her breasts. She took a deeper breath and he watched her begin to respond.

It was the reluctance he sensed in her that excited him. He was hard now and he let her feel him press against the soft flesh of her thighs and then her belly. He put his hands on her shoulders and moved her slowly down his body, feeling her warm breath against his nipples, wanting her below him, at his groin. He took his hands off her for a moment and she stopped moving and just lay against him. Whether she ever truly enjoyed this or not, he thought, she no longer does. He wondered if she had always tried to please him out of fear. He wanted to explore that more, at another time.

He felt his usual impulse to do something—be someone—different. He needed someone else but that was easy to obtain. He pushed her aside, gently. She let him and didn't try to reconnect. He picked up the phone and dialed a number he knew very well, a service where he had an account. He asked for someone new. Soon, she would come.

Walker often wished Abbott knew the full extent of him. For example, he provided her with dead patients for the nursing home scheme, but she didn't know he had killed some of them. She wasn't aware of the extremes he could reach. He wanted her to know he could be wild; that was a secret to everyone else. There was a knock at the door.

CHAPTER
10

Abbott went to the living room as Walker opened the door. The prostitute who entered was striking. They always were.

She was closer to thirty than twenty, which wasn't uncommon for the call girl services. She had light brown hair, combed up big, a short leather-look skirt, and a tight white blouse. She was thin but with large breasts, good legs, and a way of standing still at odd moments, as if suddenly struck by an impulse to pose. Walker's own movements were deliberate and slow.

From the moment the woman entered the room her eyes were riveted on Abbott. But Abbott only stayed a minute, then went back to the bedroom. Walker introduced himself and they sat across from each other on an L-shaped couch near a large picture window. Walker assumed the prostitute had found a category to put this arrangement into: a man and woman call a prostitute for some added excitement; that was well within the range of the routine, and safe.

"Well, this is nice," she said. "Why don't I just get comfortable, honey." She stood up and started taking off her clothes, moving slowly.

Walker interrupted. "Just sit there for a minute," he said. "Let's talk first. What's your name?"

"Roxanne."

"I want you to relax first," he said.

"Oh, I'm very relaxed, sugar. I'm always very relaxed. How relaxed do you want me to be? Relaxed like this?" She smiled and sprawled out in her seat, her legs spread. She dragged one hand across the bottom of her thighs, pulling the trailing edge of the skirt across her body, like a tide moving on the beach.

"Not like that, not yet," he said. "Let's talk first."

She was still smiling, but looked puzzled.

"I'm not sure what you want me to do, cutie, just tell me."

"Talk to me, Roxanne. Talk to me."

She sat there, smiling. When she remained silent, he grabbed her by the arms and shook her hard, just once. Then he put his face up against hers.

"Talk to me now, Roxanne." His voice was low, but harsh.

That fear they have as children never leaves, Walker thought. She'd initially felt secure because another woman was present. Now, she was scared. She began to speak.

"I have this girlfriend . . . Sometimes I go up to her place at night and we take our clothes off and get into the shower . . ."

Her voice was tight, the tone of it hushed the way it sometimes is when people are keeping some part of themselves hidden. She also seemed to have an accent that was either southern or entirely made up, and he knew this way of speaking was also a version of herself she used when she worked. Beneath that—and the actual reason for the way she chose to speak—was some image of herself she had held since childhood, an image she didn't like.

"I'm not interested in silly stories like that," Walker said. "I'm interested in you."

She looked hesitant.

"It makes it better for me," he said soothingly. "Tell me anything at all about yourself."

"Well, I'm from Minnesota. How about that?" She laughed a little. "A small town, but let's not say which one, okay?"

"One thing about a small town," he said. "Everything gets noticed."

"You got that right."

"So tell me. Were you a bad girl?"

She smiled. "Yeah," she said, her voice casual, teasing, contrite, as if she'd now figured out what he wanted. "I was a very bad girl."

"And did they ever catch you being bad?"

"They caught me doing everything."

"And did you get punished for what you did? Sent to your room?"

"Oh, more than that," she said. "Sent to my room." She pouted. "Spanked in front of the class."

He looked at her. He imagined her as a child, shrinking her stature, compressing it, looking under the made-up face, seeing it as a coloring-book picture of an adult, the kind of drawing kids made of grown-ups, the invented self, the "draw-a-person" kit we all carried inside. He saw in her the less varnished elements of great surprise, of initial hurt, of yowling joys and outraged innocent angers. She had told him her name was Roxanne and he knew that was part of her fantasy life. He wondered what her real name was. Her tone of voice, the particular memories she had chosen, her easy endorsement of being "bad," and, specifically, having been hit in front of the class—which he felt was true—announced her background to him clearly, as if she'd put it in words. A Catholic school girl.

It wouldn't hurt to confirm it. Wouldn't hurt him, that is.

"So the nuns were mad at you," he said, in a soft, flat voice.

"Very," she said. Then she looked startled; his comment about the nuns surprised her.

"Let's get you undressed now," he said.

"Um," she said, "and you too."

But he made no move to undress himself.

She reached behind her back and undid her bra, letting it fall. When she had nothing on at all, she stood up, moving closer to him.

He stood and put both hands on the sides of her head. He moved his fingertips lightly on her skin, then felt her temples with his palms. He lowered his hands to her shoulders, as if measuring her, and leaned back slightly so he could see her better.

"What are you looking for?" she asked.

"Sit down," he said gently, and she did.

"Put your legs up," he said.

"So you just want to look, huh?"

"That's right." But he didn't just look. He continued his examination. He moved forward so that he was leaning almost into her groin, then put his fingers at the entrance to her vagina, and spread the layered flesh apart a bit. He could see and feel the tightened, irregular tissue. There was looser skin as well, and significant width and loose muscle tone. Only one thing had those effects, and it wasn't sex, whatever the frequency or the roughness.

"Get up on the couch," he said.

"What are you doing?"

"Please. Up on the couch, and turn around."

She did as he asked. He slowly checked her whole body with his fingertips. As he did, he began to feel a growing sense of intimate connection, of finding out as only the body could reveal, what someone had experienced. The body was the record, a collection of secrets written in flesh. What were hers? She had a small scar, short but deep, on the ankle of her left leg just above the instep. Something had driven into her there, and penetrated enough so it bled deep. On her hands he saw small scars. He held her fingers together to check a hunch, and saw the way the scars matched up. She'd had a graft, many years ago. That meant a burn. He wondered how it happened. Many prostitutes had histories of abuse. Was the burn someone's lasting reminder? He reached down to her calves and felt one, then the other, and found there hard lengths of muscles, tendon threads, and saw, in her feet, blue veins close to the skin. She jogged or perhaps it was aerobics, he thought.

He saw her with practiced eyes and he knew her well, both the young girl and the grown woman, the way she presented herself and the way she actually was. He smiled at her.

"Is there anything that troubles you?" he asked.

"What are you talking about?"

"How did you get that burn?" he asked.

She looked puzzled. He touched her hand, drawing his finger over the scars. She tried to pull her hand away, then thought better of it and let him hold her.

"Oh, that?" she said. "When I was a kid."

"Did your parents do that to you?" He let go of her hand and looked at her. Her eyes widened a bit but she didn't flinch at his question. She was acknowledging he was right, he realized, but it didn't mean anything to her. Not any more. It was buried deep in the angry past, long handled and sealed over, too deep and too buried to fear.

"How about the wound to your ankle?" he asked. "Did you get it while you were running?"

"You ask very strange questions."

"Were you running away, and someone got to you?"

She stood up. "Maybe I should get dressed," she said.

He didn't do anything to stop her. She picked up her panties and her bra, and stooped again to gather up her skirt and blouse and shoes. She put them on. He could see she was angry.

"Well, at least you had a child," he said.

She stopped. She stared at him. He knew she had borne a child; he had seen it. It was only the huge passage of a child that could distend the canal that way.

"I'm leaving," she said.

She has something dear to her, he thought, something to protect. It's not something long gone, like her scars, and it's not something far away. It's real in her life, and she has it in her mind. She has a child, and though he'd never seen her child, and they'd never been together before today, she was suddenly afraid. He felt his skin tingle the way it sometimes did at the touch of a cold wind. Something was open to him now. He stood up. People loved most what was most like themselves.

"A little girl?" he said.

She gasped and turned away, moving toward the door. "I'll call someone else for you," she said, the words rapid and distracted.

He didn't have to see her face now. All he had to do was go on. A pretty little girl, Walker thought.

"And all those children you could have had," he said. "You do think about them, don't you?" She had the marks of abortion, more than one. Enough scarred tissue for a number of procedures.

She backed up a step, her legs meeting the wood barrier of the couch. She edged off to the side. He followed her motion.

"And when you had the abortions, you were young and you didn't think much about them." His voice was soothing; the healing doctor. "But now, you constantly imagine what the nuns would have said. And their horror at what you've done keeps you up late at night. Isn't that so?"

"Stop it," she said. "Why are you doing this?"

He said nothing.

"How do you know these things?"

Her expression captured him, full of displeasure and still the fear, and now the anger. He reached out for her. She was trembling.

"All I'm trying to do is get to know you," he said. "You're another person. I'm lonely too sometimes, and I can't ignore that."

He saw in the wells of her eyes the thin, barely visible surface of tears.

"Damn you! What do you want?"

"You. I just want you."

He reached for her. She jumped back, holding up a hand to ward him off.

"I'm leaving!" She was visibly trembling. She turned to open the door. He lunged past her and leaned against it, holding it closed.

"Let me go or there'll be trouble."

"No. There'll be no trouble," he said. "I paid for you."

She tried to open her bag, as if she had a weapon inside. He ripped it from her. She slashed at him with her fingernails. He laughed and took her in his arms, pressing their bodies together. He kissed her, opening her mouth with his lips and letting her feel him hard. She tried to scream and he covered her mouth with his hands. He held her still for a while. He liked what he saw in her face: many feelings, more than he needed, tears glistening in her eyes; through them he saw the fear.

Once he knew she was properly silenced, he stripped off her clothes. He slid his hands over her, her face, her breasts, her thighs. He forced her onto the couch, picking her legs up from under her, undoing his pants and exposing himself to her, moving down her body, from her mouth to her groin. When he entered her, she just let him, made uncertain by her fears. He enjoyed the sensations, all of them.

He saw the bedroom door was slightly open, Abbott's face peering out, eyes fixed wide on the prostitute and him from behind the wooden shield. These days, she watched him carefully from her safe little territories, though she no longer joined in. She held herself back from what she needed and liked and could do. It was increasingly the difference between them.

CHAPTER

11

The official address for the *Reading Eagle and Times* was 475 Penn Street, but newsmen used the back entrance on Fourth and Court. I couldn't have gone in the front anyway. It was Sunday, and they locked it. In the back the big double doors were open, leading to a square entry, a big freight elevator, and a low glass booth with a security guard doing his time. In front of him, outside the booth, were waist-high stacks of Sunday papers, and, as I sat outside in the car and watched for a while, a regular pulse of people walked, or biked, or drove by to pick up a copy.

The security guard took their money and made change, but they picked up the papers themselves from the stack. The guard was old, maybe late sixties, with a crew-cut row of thick white hair, and a square face that seemed most natural with no expression at all. He didn't skip a beat when I didn't want a paper, and accepted my statement about being up from the *Philadelphia Inquirer* with a slow nod. I told him I was there to visit the newsroom. I waited while he called upstairs. A photographer walked right by him while he was calling. "Nobody's around to let you in," he said. He acted as if the photographer was a nobody. Every organization has its outsiders, I thought.

I told the guard I'd wait and traded him the buck twenty-five for a copy of the paper, then took it out to my car. He didn't have to explain that someone would be in soon. I knew that for a fact. It was only noon. By one or two at the latest, at least a couple of the early staff would come in. I wondered if I'd recognize anyone. I knew just about everyone on the paper when I played here fourteen years ago. I drove to get a sandwich and came back at one-fifteen. Even before I reached him, the guard pointed me toward the elevator.

"Up there now," he said. "Third floor."

The glass door entrance to the city room was locked, and it gave me a minute to watch Ted Coleman come down the corridor toward me, his image appearing through the slightly hazy glass like a reflection of myself suddenly showing up and enlarging. He hadn't changed much, at least at this distance. He was still thin, still tall, hadn't put on a beard, weight, or the diminished stature that came from carrying sad burdens. Maybe not enough time had passed. Only fourteen years.

He was a sportswriter then. He'd had two years of coming to me for quotes. I'd liked him enough to go to him after my shoulder muscles and my career had torn apart, and asked him about the possibility of my covering some baseball. As it turned out, the same Reading I'd always thought of as a very small place was too big a city for a rookie sportswriter to break in, and eventually I'd gone someplace much smaller, the tiny town of North Hampton, in Delaware County, where I met Mike Shannon, my first and only editor.

I wondered if Ted had ever heard about my having been drummed out of the reporting business. If he had, there were only two possibilities. He'd either be the kind of newspaperman who shared Shannon's views, and didn't like what I'd done. Or he'd be the kind of newspaperman who didn't care. The hard part for me was that all the people I respected hated what I'd supposedly done.

As soon as Ted opened the door, my concerns were eased.

"Hey, Mike Schmidt," he said, grabbing my hand and shaking it, while patting my shoulder with his other hand. It was a bittersweet thing to say, a teasing reminder of lost possibilities, but also a profound compliment. The truth is, I played third base at Reading only two years after the great Schmidt had left this town and made it to the majors.

We spent the first few minutes catching up. Ted wasn't a sportswriter anymore. He'd made his way to management, as he explained to me in detail. It turned out he'd started out at the paper as a mail clerk, ten years before I showed up in Reading. Sportswriter had been one of the stops along the way. He was now an assistant managing editor. He lived in West Reading, the upscale section of town.

When I asked if he remembered Joe Taft, he immediately said yes.

"He was one of those guys who didn't talk much after games," Ted said. "At least not on the record. He really didn't mind talking baseball, if you knew the game, but he was lousy for quotes. If he said anything strong and clear, like a knock on somebody, he didn't want you using it in the paper. He took his complaints straight to the ballplayer or coach he had his beef with. Face-to-face. Didn't like using the paper as a go-between. He thought that was cowardly. I guess I respected him for that."

"He's dead. Died a few days ago, in Philadelphia."

Ted took in the news without much reaction. It was true he didn't consider Joe Taft a friend, but it was also something reporters excelled at: hearing and handling bad news. They were even better at it than doctors.

"Was he doing something with the Phils?" Ted asked.

"No," I said. "Far as I can tell, he was doing nothing. Nothing with baseball, nothing at all. Living by himself on little money in a lousy neighborhood." I didn't like the way I'd put it, and I hadn't even finished. "Died the same way. In bad circumstances."

Ted was looking at me, showing some concern. I realized I'd gone on too long.

"What do you need?" Ted asked. "It's why you're in Reading, right?"

"Yes," I said. "I'm looking for his son."

"You and he were pretty close when you were here. I remember that now." Ted shook his head. "But one other thing I remember pretty clearly, too. Joe Taft was always alone. His wife and kid died in childbirth. Everyone knew that. He didn't have another son, did he?"

"Not that I know of." I didn't tell him about the letter. I wasn't sure why. Maybe it's because it wasn't so long ago I'd thought of it as a letter to no one. "I'd like to check the library. Maybe something's there."

"No problem," Ted said.

Asking for a favor after talking about dying was always good timing. In the moments after you invoked the image of the grave, people were always glad to do something. Anything. It beat standing around and feeling sad. We went to the library.

Even in the age of computers, newspaper libraries were big. One huge room for the newsroom, one equally large for the library. It was as if newspapers had the two major functions: to note the present, and to keep track of the past. Dividing up the space that way paid even-handed tribute.

"We're talking back two decades," Ted said. "Can't use the computers. Have to go to clip files. The old-fashioned method."

True to his word, he ignored a set of terminals near the front desk and we approached instead a wall of file cabinets, at least twenty, which lined three walls of the room. He went to the one marked "T," opened two or three wrong drawers before he got to the right one, then quickly extracted a fairly thick, large-size dirty yellow folder. "Taft," he said, and maybe it was right to sum it up that way, I thought. At least in one particular place, they'd kept track.

We walked over to a dark wood desk and sat down. Ted started looking through the pile, then picked up a handful of clips and put them in front of me.

"We can both read," he said. "What are we looking for?"

"Anything interesting," I said. "Anything that tells us about Taft the person, not just the ballplayer."

I spread the contents out as if we were about to do a jigsaw puzzle together. He reached past me and started a new pile, grabbing different stories, adding to it. The papers rubbed against each other with a dry, crinkly sound. Most of them were yellowed and stiff with age.

"These are just the game stories," Ted said, as the pile grew.

I let him separate those out, but, as he did, I took a look at them. They were the games where Taft had played a key role. There were a lot of them. Looking through the faded stories, I remembered how he had played. More seriously than most. The headlines and copy were a record of work hard done, of one narrow thing done very, very well. In all my thinking about how he'd died, and whom he'd left behind, I'd forgotten, for a while, what he himself considered most central to his life. It wasn't a thing most people counted for all that much, and arguably trivial compared to the general struggle to survive in the world, but baseball meant something to people who understood. I was one of them. Ted was apparently thinking similar things. He was reading one of the stories. "Haven't looked at these for a long time," he said. "Taft was some player, huh?" I nodded. "He caught Smalley and Taggart and Johnson, too," he went on. "Three good ones. Taggart, with that knuckler. He was hard to handle." He stopped, and looked at me, as if he'd just remembered I'd been there too. "You played with Trillo, didn't you?" I nodded again. "Hey," Ted exclaimed, holding up one of the stories he'd just seen. "Here you are."

He handed me the clip. I didn't remember the story in the paper, but I instantly remembered the game. "Gray hits two solo HRs to beat Vermont," the headline read. I remembered it very well. One homer came off a breaking ball, a hanger, a two-and-one count. The other was on a sinker that didn't sink, and I cleared the right field fence by thirty feet. Taft had also homered in that game, and afterward it had felt good sharing the feelings. I remembered that, too.

I finished the rest of the clip pile, and at the end of it had nothing at all on Taft's personal life.

There were two feature stories with Taft as the focus. They were both about his participation in off-season baseball clinics for kids. They had two clinics a year, in September and October, according to the articles. I'd never been there for them. Most of the guys, including me, were eager to go somewhere other than Reading as soon as the season was over. That's why it stood out when I read in the stories that Taft always stayed in Reading for two months after the season, and coached in both clinics. That seemed unusual. I wondered how many years he had done that. It was possible to find out. I asked Ted where they kept the bound copies of the actual papers, and he took me to another part of the room which had a wall filled with vinyl-bound holders of every paper, month by month, year by year. I pulled the ones for September and October for all the 1970s. Sure enough, they had clinics every year. And only two or three other players ever stayed to coach in any one year. But Taft was there every year, ten years in a row. I wondered why.

I did remember that during the regular season, when we were playing at home, Joe had a habit of going out to the stadium gate to watch the kids on line before the game. He always did that, and he usually looked sad when he did. All the players saw him do it, but we never asked why. We assumed it had something to do with his dead son, that he liked seeing the kids coming to the game, and he was imagining what it would be like if his son had lived. No one, including me, ever spoke to him directly about it. Maybe he coached the kids for the same reason; he was grieving the loss of his son. I went back to the clips.

When we finished reading, I realized there was something missing.

"What about Joe's wife and kid?" I asked Ted.

"What about them?"

"There's nothing on them in the files," I said. "Shouldn't there be an obit?"

"Yeah, you're probably right. But it wouldn't be in the Taft file. It would be over there." He pointed to my left, to a short steel gray cabinet. "In the obituaries."

I followed him over to that cabinet, and he pulled it open.

"Okay," he said, bending over to adjust his six-foot height a bit better to the three-foot cabinet. "What year was it?"

"I don't know. I think it was seventy-one or 'two."

"Which one?" Ted said. "It'd be a lot faster if we knew."

"I really don't know."

"Okay, we can do both." He pulled out a stack of yellowed folders, and handed them to me, then squatted down to look at a similar pile himself.

"You've got seventy-two," he said.

I started looking through my stack.

"They're supposed to be listed alphabetically," he said, "but usually they're out of order. So it's easy to miss the one you want." He turned back to the cabinet, and it took us both a few minutes to finish. Nothing. He stood up and looked at me.

"I know it's not seventy-three," I said, answering his unspoken question, "because I was here by then."

He started to stand up.

"Let's just try seventy," I asked, sensing his impatience, but willing to push it.

He stayed down, opened a new drawer below the first one, and started over. This time he didn't hand me a pile. He went through the clips by himself. It took five minutes. Then he stood up and held out one small clip. I took it from him. It was a single box, black-bordered in the curlicued fashion small-town newspapers tend to use. It was only an inch, perhaps five lines, and datelined October 16, 1970, a couple of months after the season. In bold-face, under the border, were the words, "Carolyn Taft, 23." The copy said: "Carolyn Taft, 23, died of complications of giving birth at Reading Memorial Hospital yesterday. She left her husband, Joseph, 26, and her one-day-old son, Peter."

That was all.

No mention of a son dying in childbirth.

It was crazy to think I really knew him, I thought. It was always guesswork, anyway, what people were like, who they cared about, and most of all, why they stopped caring. He had actually had a son, Peter, and he had not died in childbirth. Yet that's what he had told us, told us all, even me, and we were close for years. It was part of him, part of how we explained to ourselves the way he was. Embittered, sad, angry. Partly, we told ourselves, because of his loss. But the loss wasn't as great as we thought. Of course, he had lost his wife, but it was always our belief that he had also lost his son that gave his sadness its depth. There was something special about losing children. Even adults who faced death themselves were capable of cringing at the death of a child.

Yet it still seemed strange to me that I'd missed this one, not just the years I knew him, but even in the past week. I had sat with him in the midst of his suffering, watched the strong impassive face soften and tears come. I had seen him grow confused. And in the midst of losing himself, and losing his hold on the world, he had reached out and plucked one last story from the void, put a part of himself on a folded piece of paper and put it in the hands of a messenger sitting bedside. I had taken possession of a prayer and almost put it aside. Molly had somehow recognized a truth. And that was strange, too, that there should even be such a category of knowledge in the world, a way of understanding seemingly delusional notes to missing children, of knowing that a man might write a deathbed letter to a son, and that it was never a ghost they wrote to, but a living object of their love.

"Why?" I heard Ted say. "Why would a man tell friends his son had died when he had not?"

And as soon as he asked it, I knew.

Joe Taft had looked ahead, with that unsparing honesty piercing and hounding him as always, as critical of himself as those he railed against, and he decided he would fail as a father. There were so many ways. Fathers did it all the time. Ignored their sons. Made them be someone else. Walked away. Let themselves grow towering rages because the boy didn't look good, or act right, or ease enough the aching anger and the pain, the way they thought a son should. They didn't get to know them well enough from the day they were born, hidden from the start inside the circle of mother's love and women's ways. And it never got better, did it?

Maybe Taft, with his great thoughtful despair—his lifelong curse and flaw—had simply looked ahead, and seen the everpresent void between fathers and sons looming for him and his newborn boy. Maybe, at that moment, he felt too much the loss of his wife, his one soft hope for conveying love to a child, when he felt hopelessly incapable of conveying any, now gone. And like the great dissatisfied, complaining curmudgeon that he was and had been all his life, decided in that one fool's moment not to be a part of the sorrow he was convinced his attempt at being a father would inevitably create. And so he walked away.

"I don't know." I answered Ted's question with the simplest words that came to mind.

And I might have been telling the truth. Maybe it was a question no one could ever answer. Not even Taft himself.

The next morning, I went to the county courthouse to check birth and death certificates. The birth certificate was there: Peter Edward Taft, born on October 15, 1970. So was a death certificate: Carolyn Taft, his mother, who died the same day. But there was no death certificate for Peter. So Peter did not die in birth. I wondered where he was.

The place to pick up the trail was at Reading Memorial, where he was born. There are few things people care less about than eighteen-year-old hospital records. Most hospitals keep them in basement rooms that are the equivalent of unused warehouses. I was always surprised even to find the door locked in one of those rooms. At Reading Memorial Hospital, the records were indeed in a basement room, whose door was not only unlocked, but open.

The old charts were in cardboard boxes, and each box had a year marked on the outside. I spent an hour and a half going through the 1970 charts before I found the one marked Taft. According to the records, the baby stayed in the hospital for several weeks after the mother died. He had some minor medical problems, but the main reason he stayed was to await adoption. Times had changed since the early seventies. Privacy laws have tightened up everywhere, especially in medical matters. These days, when I wanted to know something like this, I either had to spend weeks cultivating contacts on the inside or get someone with subpoena power to help me out. But in 1970, in a small hospital in Reading, a nurse had actually written on the chart the name of the couple that adopted Peter Taft.

Craig and Renee Miller. But the Millers' address was not in the records. Unfortunately, it wasn't in the phone book, either. They could live out of the area, or they could have an unlisted number. I called information and asked for Craig Miller's phone number. The operator told me it was unlisted, as if that was bad news. But that was good news indeed. You can ask the telephone company to unlist your number, but you can't ask the Post Office to unlist your address.

When you call the Post Office, there's no receptionist, no secretary, no public relations spokesman, and therefore no one experienced in fending off callers. I got a mail carrier on the phone, and told him who I was: a former third baseman on the Reading Phils. I said I was trying to track down an old friend I knew in Reading fourteen years ago, but I couldn't find him in the phone book. I wondered aloud if he could help out. He said he could, and he did. It took him only a couple of minutes. He gave me the Millers' address in Reading. I thanked him and called Coleman at the newspaper. I told him that Taft's son was alive, and had been adopted by the Millers. The news that Peter was alive surprised him. I imagined it moved him, too. I asked him to check the crisscross directory, a book that lists every street address in the city, with phone numbers next to each address. Unlisted numbers are usually not in the book, so I asked Coleman to give me the numbers of a couple of the Miller's neighbors. He came back on in a minute, and gave me more than I'd asked for. The Miller phone number was in the book; apparently it had been unlisted only recently.

I called, and a woman answered the phone. I asked for Peter. And Mrs. Miller told me that Peter wasn't living with them anymore. He was in an apartment on his own, and she gave me the address. Simple as that. I left Reading Memorial in a hurry. I had something to deliver to Peter Miller. Something from a previous life, and a previous father, of whom he might know very little. Or perhaps nothing at all.

CHAPTER

12

Millway Avenue was a string of shabby two-story row houses. The neighborhood was in a small industrial town, the factories long shut down. The buildings had wide, high steps, and there were people camped out on them all up and down the block. Mid-afternoon, Monday, not a holiday. Must be a lot of people out of work. There were two overweight women outside number 367, and I said hi as I walked up the steps and into the vestibule. There were no buzzers or name markers on the walls, but there were mailboxes, decent ones, the federal government's ever-present gift to poor buildings. Peter was in 2-A. I went up one flight of dark wooden steps and knocked at the first door off the stairway.

In a half minute, the door opened. The kid inside was a teenager. I looked behind him into the apartment. It was one big room without much decoration, or color, or furniture for that matter. There was a double bed, which looked like it was doing extra service as a dresser, bookcase, and dinner table. The space that wasn't covered by clothes and junk looked like you could sleep in it, if you curled up tight. The kid himself was a mess.

He was the right color and the right age, but what didn't match was the body. There was no sign of the short, thick, powerful father in this boy. His body was more like mine. But his face was Joe's, no doubt about it. More than that was the feeling I had standing there. When I'd walked into

Taft's room at Clarke Hospital, it was like arriving in a place where there'd been a war, but there were no bombs or bullets or explosions anymore, just small lingering flames, the wind knocking over remnants of partly crumpled buildings. His son seemed similarly battered.

"What do you want?" he said.

"My name is Gray. I have something for you from your father."

"Really," the kid said. "Must be desperate for help at the store." He sounded as if the idea amused him, but he wasn't smiling.

"I don't know what you mean," I said. He seemed surprised, and made a big show out of looking me over. When he was finished, he announced the results. "You play ball, right?"

"Used to," I said. "With your dad."

"Oh," he said. "That dad. The one who played ball. I thought you meant the other one." He nodded to himself. "So you were friends with my dad. And you've brought me something from him, right?" He kept summing things up, and saying everything playfully as if he were teasing me or making a private joke. But his face was empty and dark, a good fit with the downcast, uncared-for way he looked.

"What's your name?" I asked him.

"What's the difference? Didn't my father tell you my name? Why don't you go ask him."

"How about letting me in?" I said.

That was enough to get him to start closing the door. I held it open with one hand. He didn't even try me. He just turned his back and walked to the window and looked out.

"Close it when you leave," he said.

He was standing at the windows, but looking at him was like watching someone walk into a tunnel, slowly fading out of the light.

"What's the matter with you?" I said. "I've got something—"

He cut me off, without turning around. "Yeah, I know. You've got something for me from my father. Well, listen, baseball man, I'm not interested in anything from him. Tell him that, okay. Tell him I'm not interested, and then give him back whatever he gave you. Is that clear enough?"

"If you're Joe Taft's kid, you ought to know," I said. "Your father's dead."

He still didn't turn around and he didn't do anything else. I considered dropping the letter by the door and leaving him to deal with it his own way, but the more he kept standing there, doing nothing at all, the less I felt like I could leave. After a minute I walked all the way in, shutting the door behind me. He turned around and I realized he'd assumed I'd left. But when he saw me still there he sat down on the bed.

"I was with him when he died," I said. "I'll tell you how it happened—if you want me to."

He looked up. "You still don't get it, do you? I don't want to know anything about him. I already know everything I need to know about good old Joe." It was anger aged bitter. It didn't build to rages and it didn't go away. "He had me. He abandoned me. It was a long time ago. And now he's dead. What do you think?" His voice was strained. "Do I have the whole story?"

There was one other piece of furniture in the room, a wooden chair. I grabbed it from the corner and pulled it over to the bed. I sat down next to the kid, and he didn't get up and move away.

"No," I said. "I don't think you have the whole story. I don't think I do, either. And I'd like to. I can tell you how your father died, and how I was close with him for two years on the Reading Phils, just after you were born, and I've stayed in touch with him since then. That's the piece of it I've got. I was with him a week before he died, and all of that by a hospital bed with him out of it most of the time. I don't know what happened to him, or you, or anything. But when I knew him well, I liked him, and nothing since then changed that. The only thing I ever knew about you until now was that according to your father, you were dead. I don't particularly like the idea that someone I like hurt somebody, but maybe that's exactly what he did. I promised your father I'd deliver a letter he wrote on his deathbed to his son. If there's anything I can do to help you, I will."

I waited for a response, got none, and said, "That's it. That's all I've got. Now what do you want to do?"

He put both hands to his head, maybe trying to keep his head from aching. His eyes were red, but it wasn't from anything I'd said; they'd been that way when I first saw him, along with the pouches under his eyes from not sleeping. He wasn't shaved, or combed, or anything else that showed he gave a damn. He brushed back his hair with his hands, as if he were thinking the same thing. The possibility that he was doing drugs came to me, but I let it go. He stood up slowly, walked over to a corner of the room where there was a small sink, small stove, small fridge. He grabbed a pot and ran some water into it. "I've got some coffee," he said.

While he was making it, I told him about his father. First I told him how he died. I left out a lot of the suffering, but none of the stories and nothing at all about how it felt to be there. I told him why I'd gone to the hospital in the first place. I told him as clearly as I could what his father looked like and acted like and talked like during the last week of his life and, most of all, what he'd thought about. The picture I painted was not ideal, but it was Taft as far as I knew him. I told how his father had given me the letter, and what I'd believed of it when he did. I told him how a young woman doctor thought he might still be alive and how that had led to my finding him. I took the letter from the inside pocket of my coat, and held it out.

"A lot of what you might want to know could be in here," I said.

He shook his head. "I can't deal with that. Talking about him is one thing. Maybe I can do that. But reading that thing—" he pointed to it but didn't touch it. "It'd be like—I don't know." He waved the letter away and I put it down on the bed. "I went looking for him once. When I was fourteen."

The way he said it made it sound like it was a long time ago, but it was only four years. There were stretches in everyone's life though, when years, even four of them, raced by. The days were lived one by one, but looking back they seemed instant, of a single piece. It is usually routines, like life on the job, that order days and force similarity on them, and the more they are the same the less we notice them. But when they are hard, the days become distinct. For this boy, four years ago had been a lousy time.

"I wanted to see him just once," he continued. "I knew who he was, but I never found him." He handed me the coffee. It was black and I drank it that way. "Guess that was my one chance. If it occurred to him to write me a letter when he was dying, why didn't he look for me when he was alive?"

"I don't know," I said. "You'd have to tell me some more."

"I'm adopted," he said. "Simple as that. Grew up around here and my parents always told me I was adopted, that my mother had died in childbirth and that my father gave me up. They didn't know why. My adopted parents were okay. They only had me, no other kids. Sometimes I used to wonder. You know when you're adopted people always say that it's a good thing because it means your parents really wanted you. So whenever they acted like it was a hassle to have me around, like parents do, you know, I'd be thinking to myself, What's so special anyway about how they wanted me?

"I just got screwed up somewhere along the line. Maybe the adoption thing. Who knows?" He looked around the apartment a moment. "My father manages one of those local outlets. Cardon Coats. I got out of high school, he got me a job. I just screwed it up. Partied a lot. Drank a lot. Lost the job. What I've got left is a motorcycle I still like to ride. Not much else. I let the friends go. I still haven't fixed things up with my father. Got this nifty place though." He almost smiled.

"You say you looked for Joe once?" I asked.

"My parents gave me some basics, like Joe's name and that he had been with the Reading Phillies—a baseball player, of all things. But nothing else. So I actually went to the baseball stadium and asked around." He shook his head. "My parents took me to the stadium once when I was five. I'd never been back there since then. Can't believe I did that. Going around talking to everybody about my father. I used some jerky explanation, which no one ever questioned. Told them I was doing a school project about career minor league players for the Phils. I don't even like baseball. Coincidence, huh? Couldn't even talk about the game with them, and they still believed me. Or didn't care."

I pictured him at fourteen on his own, with enough energy and ability to conduct a decent search. Just talking about it he seemed brighter and clearer than he had before, more out of place in the mess and scattered junk. He never told the Phils he was Taft's son. Maybe there was too much feeling to the simple act of calling Taft his father aloud.

For some reason Taft had made this boy and their relationship a secret, but in no other way had I ever known him to hold back anything, about himself or who he was or how he felt. What the boy had learned was that his father was a loner, a character, angry and outspoken and hard to get along with, with few friends. And then some of the players had mentioned that his wife and son had died in childbirth.

"I almost stopped right then," he said. "Can you imagine? People saying that I died in childbirth. Me! What a trip. I almost told one of them, 'Look at me. I'm a ghost.' But I didn't. I kept looking. None of the players or people at the ballpark knew where he was. I went to the directories, I tried Philadelphia and all of the 215 area code. I wrote to players' associations, the minor and major leagues. I got nowhere."

He'd kept going for a while. He'd taken it a lot farther than most people would have. Then he'd given up. And maybe in more ways than one. I'd known other people who were adopted. They also wanted to know their natural parents, or at least about them. And even when what they learned was bad, I'd observed, they still seemed to value the search. It wasn't just their parents they were looking for, I realized, but themselves. Taft's withdrawal from the kid, whatever his reasons or intentions, had left an emptiness, on both their parts, of which the kid seemed well aware. Perhaps that had driven him wild for a while, and he'd come through it, but hadn't arrived anyplace else. He was only eighteen, I reminded myself, and there was still a lot of time for him to straighten out. Maybe I could help.

"I don't know why he did it," I said. "Not really. And I was pretty close to him for those two years, and he didn't have many friends. I might have been the only one he would have told the truth, but he even told me the same fake story. I can't explain it. But now that I know he lied I've tried to imagine what he could have been thinking to abandon you. I don't know if it's true or not but this is how I explained it to myself."

So I told him what I thought I knew about his father, and how he could have abandoned his son, and I knew as I spoke that saying it didn't make anything better, not for me, not for the boy, and certainly no longer for Taft. All the time I was talking, and he at least listened, the envelope with Taft's true voice lay between us untouched, temporarily sealed from us both, by the boy's fear and by the simple fact that I had delivered it as Taft had asked and I had vowed, and it was no longer mine to open.

I gave him my number at home and told him I'd be back whether or not he called. I left, taking Joe's letter with me. I owed it to Joe not to just toss the thing down and walk away. When Peter learned what he needed to about his father, maybe he'd share it with me. And then I'd be able to share the letter with him.

CHAPTER 13

The staff had little luck with the five-year-old boy. Walker saw with pleasure that his favorite resident, Molly Hale, was there. He was more attracted to her than anyone he'd ever known, and he believed she was attracted to him. He was accustomed to having the admiration of the better residents at Clarke. But Walker felt she not only admired him professionally, but also had a personal interest in him. His life was too private, of necessity, for him to include anyone like her in it, he realized, but he sometimes found himself thinking, when he was around her, of another, easier way to live.

He was a little surprised they'd called him, considering she was there. She herself was excellent with kids. At the moment, though, she wasn't succeeding in calming the boy down. He was on the bed, lying down, and shivering so much the rails beside the mattress made a small vibrato hum. He was holding himself tight, drawing his breath in gulps, eyes wide. The boy was in the short pediatric version of patient whites and, as usual, the set of cotton strips tied into bows failed to hold the cloth fully together. Lying flat as he was, the sides of his body were exposed, his ribs pressing out against the thin skin from the pressure of his nervous breath-holding.

The room was cold. One of the nurses had taken a seat next to the boy on the bed, tucking up a blanket around him, and pushing back the hair from his eyes. She was talking to him in a low voice, but the boy hadn't

relaxed at all. Walker nodded hello to Molly, then approached the bed.
His voice was naturally deep, and he lightened the tone of it as he spoke.

"Hi there, your name is Jack, right? I'm Dr. Walker."

The nurse got up as he reached the bedside, clearing a space for him.
Walker had interrupted her explaining to the boy what a bronchoscope
was, because he knew that wasn't necessary. Most adults tolerated things
better with information, Walker had learned over the years. But with very
young kids, it was comfort and attention that was needed, more than
forewarning. A game would sometimes do. And to children, hypnosis was
a game.

He took over with his own left hand the nurse's occasional stroking of
the boy's brow. The boy's mother was there, but Walker was especially
aware of Molly looking on as well. He kept his concentration on the boy.

"I know there're a lot of people here, Jack, but you just talk to me, just
look at me." He took his stethoscope and said: "Did you ever see one of
these? Did the nurses show you? Would you like to try mine?" He
removed it from his neck and offered it to the boy, holding the plastic
ends to his ears.

"Listen, listen." Walker put the cold metal against his own chest.
"What do you hear, Jack?" Walker let the ear piece end of it drop, and
the boy uncurled himself just enough to pick it up.

The boy listened, and said: "Thump. Thump."

"That's right," Walker said. "That's my heart. Thump. Thump. Your
heart makes the same sound. That's how we all sound in the stethoscope."

Walker put the metal on the boy's chest, placing the small tubes in his
own ears. He listened for a moment, and nodded his head.

"Thump, thump. Sounds just fine," Walker said.

He knew what he wanted to do, and was certain the boy would respond.
Five-year-olds were often easy to hypnotize. He took the metal end of the
stethoscope and turned it over in his hands, rhythmically catching the
light from the bright overhead lamp on its shiny silver surface, making
it glint. "See this? You can listen to my heart, and see how this shines at
the same time."

The boy watched him and Walker noticed the exact moment when he
settled back a bit, his slight movement against the pillows barely pushing
them in. The boy held the tubes of the stethoscope to his ears, as Walker
had asked him to, and watched the twirling circle of the scope shine in
the light, moving slowly in Walker's fingers, bright then shadowed then

bright. Walker said aloud the sound of his heartbeat, thump thump, thump thump, speaking quietly while leaning over the boy, creating in the curve of his larger form a small private place for the two of them.

"You'll hear it even better if you close your eyes now, Jack," Walker said, and the boy did. When the boy was more relaxed and ready, Walker motioned Molly over to the bed. He wanted her to watch him remove the stitches from the boy's hand. He did it very gently.

That afternoon, Walker was alone, on call in the Emergency Room. He watched the patients as they drifted in, wondering about their lives. They almost all tried to avoid pain and suffering and dying at any cost, yet legions of them moved headlong into the fire, straight to the heart of the sun. The frequent alcohol and drug users, the overweight, the smokers. They were never deterred. And here they all ended up.

He was in the back getting coffee when he saw the techs bring a man through the ambulance entrance doors. He was young, with blond hair, dressed cleanly in new jeans and a blue cotton shirt. In good neighborhoods, people rarely dressed themselves up to be sick, but here, he saw that often. Perhaps it was a token of respect for the hospital or a way of holding off the spectre of death. The patient's neat, clean, casual clothes made such contrast to his slack, toneless stillness, it looked as if someone had dressed up a doll. Walker had a sudden desire to see him stripped and bare, for curiosity's sake. He could do so soon enough, he realized. He stepped forward.

The patient was unconscious, but breathing.

"OD," said one of the techs, a short woman with thick dark hair. "Librium and Tofranil, at least that's the two bottles we found next to him. The bottles were empty. Twenty five-milligram Librium, ten fifty-milligram Tofranil. How much he took? Who knows." The tech shrugged. "Rest of it's on the report. He was conscious when we got there, not talking though. Faded on the way."

Sounded like enough dosage to kill the man, Walker thought.

"Any sign of drinking?" he asked.

"Didn't smell like it," the tech said.

A simple job. The treatment for overdose was straight forward. He'd be out for a while, then gradually recover. At his age, complications were unlikely, unless he was sick some other way.

The nurses took hold of the ER bed the techs had transferred him onto, and wheeled it past the curtained cubicles, through a door, and into a small square room. It was a psych observation room; the door closed securely, no doorknobs on the inside, and a couple of straitjackets piled in a corner. The room had a window at the top of the door so staff could look in to watch suicidal or assaultive patients. The hospital was always short-staffed and no one ever bothered to check on such patients, but that's what the window was for.

The man's symptoms were the usual: pupils dilated, skin red and flushed, sinus membranes dry, fever of a hundred and two, heart beating too fast—tachycardia. The nurse, Miss Brown, a fat white woman with a big horsey face and stringy brown hair, moved automatically through the OD protocol, and Walker helped her. Each step was a simple mechanical response to a problem drugs caused in the man's body.

People were basically machines, Walker thought, and most of their problems were hydraulic, fluid piling up here or there, unable to get through tubes and valves. The treatments were often a matter of applying simple force.

"Ninety over seventy," the nurse said. She had an angry tone.

Walker had known her for years. She was always angry, and all it took was a patient, any patient, to get her going. She hated dealing with patients who weren't conscious, or with very young kids, or with the ones who didn't speak English. Those were the worst, because she liked to insult them and to have them understand. Patients who came to the ER over and over were a particular burden. Her favorite lament was: "Why do they have to come in here and smell the place up? Why not just die in the street?"

The man's blood pressure was too low. Walker pierced his skin with a needle and put in an IV while the nurse hung up a bottle of saline and let it pour into his blood. His pressure would come up just because there was more fluid to push. Walker popped an empty tube onto a syringe and drew some blood from the man's arm. Brown held out her hand, and he dropped the tube onto her open palm. He didn't have to tell her to send it out for toxicology.

It was likely he still had residues of the drugs in his stomach, slowly seeping through the wall into his bloodstream and producing their poisonous effects. Walker took a thin, clear flexible tube and threaded it down through the man's nose and into his stomach. It was easy to follow the hidden canal on down, to feel the tube dropping through the empty spaces and linked routes inside the body. He poured some saline through the tube, letting it slosh around in the man's belly with the remaining drugs, then used a small hand-squeezed pump to draw the drug-filled liquid out. When he saw that the fluid was clear, he poured a mixture of activated charcoal and castor oil back into the man's stomach. That would absorb the rest of the drugs and start some bowel movements so Walker could clear him out.

Brown came back in with the portable electrocardiograph, and Walker pulled the patient's shirt out of his pants so they could do an EKG. The drugs could cause changes in the electrical rhythm of the man's heart, leading to a heart attack. He watched Brown spread the thin lotion on several spots on his chest then attach the rubber cups, the strong suction dimpling his skin. Walker started the machine and watched the paper tracing of the reading ease out from the side. He scanned it quickly, his experience letting him make a quick assessment. No problem. He could rouse the man a bit right there in the ER, then send him upstairs to a patient room.

Brown detached the electrodes and dropped a gown on the bed. She bent over the patient to get him undressed.

"It's all right," Walker said, "just take the machine back. I'll do it."

Brown nodded, obviously pleased to be able to leave. "Bring some amyl or salts," Walker said to her before she left.

He leaned over and unbuttoned the man's shirt, opening it wide. He stared for a moment, and while he did Brown came back into the room with the smelling salts.

"Look at that," Brown exclaimed, and whistled.

Walker could see a pattern of old scars all over the man's skin. Clean, straight scars running the length of his arms. A self-mutilator, he thought. He wondered briefly exactly what the man's history was. First the cutting, now the drugs. The nurse shook her head with disgust and left again. Walker raised the man's upper body slightly with one hand and took off his shirt. He undid the jeans and slipped them off as well.

He immediately saw a crowded collection of crossed scars and long trailing calcified rivulets dividing up the man's otherwise tanned and smooth skin into a small patchwork of squares from the base of his chest to the top of his groin. His thighs were covered with long continuous horizontal cuts. They were thin enough for the skin to have scarred and grown over, but the parallel lines of the cutting were clearly visible, the slices so close together it looked as if his skin was some oddly textured piece of clothing. He had similar lines, sometimes vertical and smaller, but equally numerous, across the flat surface at the top of his chest and on the inside skin of his forearms. White dry patches of glue from recently removed bandages adhered to the skin all around his arms. He'd obviously been treated for a cutting episode recently.

Life sought its own ending, Walker thought. People gave up, over and over, and yet somehow they kept living. The thing that always struck him when it came to suicide attempts was not the fragility of life but its hardiness. It was only because people weren't built with the easy means to turn themselves off that they went on living. When they had the killing tool or easy access to it, they made their real choice. To die. Didn't need a war, didn't even need an enemy. People did it to themselves.

He knew self-mutilators basically controlled their tensions with their cutting, and that even suicidal people were only trying to get away from what hurt. But their closeness to death interested Walker, excited him. This man's willingness to part his own skin and expose the life inside him to dissipation, this ultimate waste, the spewing of life's energy into the air, this was exhilarating to Walker.

He uncapped the amyl nitrite and held it under the man's nose. The acrid odor flooded the air near his face for a moment, most of it going up into him, some of it into the air where Walker caught the harsh smell and turned away. The man stirred, his muscles clonic for a second, his head rising slightly off the bed and dropping back. Walker brought the vial to the man's face again, though not much of the gasses were left. His eyes opened, unfocused at first and with a fluttering rapid blink. He groaned, the sound low and weakly formed, more a simple expiration of air than a matter of complaint. His hands lay flat at his sides, palms up, perfectly symmetrical, arranged against the white sheet as if posed. Walker took one of the man's hands between his own and leaned over so the patient could see him.

He squeezed the patient's hand. He responded by curling his fingers over Walker's, holding onto the fingers as a child would. Walker sustained the feeling by wiping sweat from the man's face with a towel, soothing and parental. The patient made another sound, still wordless. His lips were dry. Though the man's eyes were open, his face was flat and neutral in expression. Walker noticed for the first time the rest of the man's body, unclothed, his skin in places bare and soft, in marked contrast to the old and new rivulets of cuts, both recently raw and darkly scarred.

But it was his absolute stillness that most intrigued Walker, the lock-step closure of the spaces at his ankles and knees, the bunched taut muscles of his calves and thighs, the armored rigidity of his neck and shoulders. The facial expression that appeared a bored mask of neutrality and disinterest was in reality frozen, he observed, as he looked even closer. He shook his hand loose from the tightening grip. He can't even let go enough to tremble, Walker realized. The notion seized him. The patient was frozen with fear. Walker felt energy and an anticipatory thrill take hold of him. He sent the patient off to a room.

Later that night, Walker decided to kill him. An hour after his shift was over, he went to the man's bed. He was partly covered by a sheet. Walker pulled it aside and looked again at all the scars. He tried to rouse him. He shook his arm. No response. He shook him again, patted his cheeks, listened at his chest for breathing. No response.

Walker took the scissor he'd brought from the nursing closet and held it up to the man's face. He ran the tip of it along the dry swell of his lips. He stirred a little. The feel of the metal seemed to rouse him. He opened his eyes. His pupils were unfocused. Finally he spoke. Walker put his ear next to the patient's lips. "No," the man said.

The confusion never stops, Walker thought. The endless shift between wanting to live and wanting to die, willing to do neither fully. They walk the line, lean too far in that direction and they get scared, lean the other way and feel empty. Never any balance. Never able to decide. There's a better medicine for you, he thought.

He pulled on gloves, then traced the point of the scissor gently along the short vertical lines on the man's chest. The wounds were old. He pressed harder, tracing one line over and over. Redder and redder. Then it was wet. He pushed the scissor in. Still sedated, he had little reaction. It was like puncturing someone on an anesthetic, a surgeon's cut. The man barely moved. The point of the scissor was still in him, new blood flowing. The scissor barely needed Walker's hand, falling easily into tracks the patient himself had once made. The process of dying had a life of its own. He cut another line. Soft. Another.

A thin but growing rectangle of blood fell slowly from the lines on his chest, some of it dripping down his sides. Walker only cut where the man had cut himself. Do it carefully, ease the tension out, just as the patient did in seeking his relief. He did the same at his thighs, each of the lines there longer. The patient was coming out of it now, jerking and moving at each new cutting of the skin.

Walker noted with curiosity and satisfaction evidence of arousal, the slow hardening of the man's penis. He hesitated, easing the pressure of the metal on his flesh. He had already lost a good deal of blood, and would be very weak, yet he was aroused. With his free hand, Walker touched the man's groin, letting the weight of the scrotum rest on his palm, then running one finger up the man's hard shaft. He did it gently, with a lover's lingering touch. He felt for a moment his own arousal begin. He had never felt that before, not when they were dying.

He moved his hand and pressed hard on the scissor again. Dying would remove all pain. Death was, after all, what the man sought. He moaned and struggled now. Walker put his hand over the man's mouth. Along with the effects of the drugs and the loss of blood, it was enough to keep him quiet. In the peace of his silence and the slowing convulsive movement of what was, after all, only life's reflexive holding on, Walker finished the cutting. He held him tight that way until he was finally still, at last relieved. So was Walker. He put the scissors in the man's hand. It was the patient's own desire, fulfilled. Let him get credit for the act.

CHAPTER

14

I parked at a broken meter a block away from Clarke. I wanted to meet the hospital's administrator, Nancy Abbott. If you only saw the patient rooms at Clarke, you'd expect the administration offices to have an old-fashioned feel, to see green blotters on wood tables, and hear the air moved by fans and not condensers. People would scratch pencils across paper, move files around by hand, and store things in old wooden cabinets.

What was there instead was the thoroughly modern working center of a successful, high-stakes business. The administration offices were large and airy, plant-filled, ergonomically designed, appealing and comfortable. The furniture was new, sleek chrome and deep leather.

There was new equipment everywhere, each desk wearing a gleaming modern metal helmet, a crown of sorts, with a matching keyboard underneath: computer monitors, laser printers, fax machines, and a big high-volume copier in the corner by a window, the kind that collates, sorts, and staples by itself. On the patient floors, people couldn't get an outside line to call home, and I'd heard doctors say it wasn't any better in the medical staff offices. But here in administration the phones were the multiple Merlin models, AT&T, top of the line.

A thin young woman with braided brown hair, green eyes, and an aloof expression greeted me at the reception desk. I told her I was the reporter from the *Inquirer* who had called for an interview with Abbott. I wasn't working for the *Inquirer,* I wasn't even a reporter anymore, but there was no way at all they could check on that. One of the quirks of the trade, little known and therefore useful, was that many newspaper stories are done by free-lance reporters. Free-lancers don't register anywhere, they carry no credentials, and there's no central record at any newspaper that lists who may or may not be working free-lance on a story. Reporter was a title to which society paid some respect and sometimes even feared, yet it was totally available to anyone for the claiming.

The receptionist asked me to take a seat, which I did, on a plush brown couch. She said I'd have to wait a while but I was used to that.

Two hours later she ushered me into Abbott's office. Her furnishings were less opulent than the outer decor. She wore a blue suit, and was attractive in a serious, subdued, undecorated kind of way. It was as if she was playing herself down. I wondered if she was as low-key as she looked or if it was her way of gaining an advantage, making others think they had nothing to fear. People have told me I carry myself that way. She sat behind a thin rectangular table that looked like an antique. There was absolutely nothing on it. On the large wall to her right were wood shelves that held lots of thick, black-vinyl looseleaf folders. Strictly business. She looked me over impatiently.

"Usually I see reporters when we have a patient here who's newsworthy or controversial," she said. "Like a crime victim or an injured police officer. Do we have anyone like that at the moment?"

"I wouldn't know," I said. "That's not what brings me here."

"Well, then. What can I do for you?"

I had nothing specific in mind. All I really needed was to see her, get a sense of her, a feel for how she handled questions. A test of the waters, before I jumped in further.

"We're doing a routine story about Clarke," I said. "We know there have been some changes in administration in recent years, and some questions raised by people in the area about services. I just wanted to check in with you, let you know I'll be interviewing people at the hospital. I don't know what we'll end up writing. It might be something general, like the portrait of an inner-city hospital, including vignettes of specific doctors and nurses or patients. Or it might be a story that identifies some problems."

"Why now?" she asked. "Is there anything in particular that spurred this? There's a lot going on with health care, of course, state-wide and locally, that affects us. Are you covering a number of hospitals or just Clarke?"

She was getting right to the heart of it. She was in a small room with a man flailing around; she needed to know if the punches were aimed at no one in particular or intended for her.

"We've heard complaints about Clarke," I said. "We may go on to other places, too, but for now, Clarke is the only place we're looking at."

"I'd like to know who's making these complaints," she said. "If you tell me exactly, I'm sure I can give you some insight into these people and what their motives really are. Give you an accurate picture."

Over the years I'd developed a list, guideposts for identifying people I thought of as "little gods." One of my signs was that they always have the names of enemies at hand, and any criticism they get always comes from enemies.

"One complaint is that the hospital is too aggressive in doing procedures," I answered. "Doctors doing too much surgery to increase hospital revenues and their own, for instance."

"Who said that?"

"A lot of people, not just one particular person."

"Well, it isn't true," she said. "The doctors here are very responsible. We have a lot of foreign graduates, so the training people bring to the job may not be quite as good as the Ivy League schools. But we're more caring and sensitive about patients than the bigger and fancier places. Closer to the community, for one thing. It sounds like you're coming into this with your mind already made up. Perhaps you think that because we serve poor people that automatically means we're taking advantage of them. Frankly, I find that offensive. Medicine is a complicated business. Do you have any medical expertise?"

I'd only been with her five minutes and she'd already challenged my credibility and accused me of bias. I checked off two more items on my "little gods" list.

"Okay," I said. "Let's say I've got it all wrong. Straighten me out."

She waited a while, thinking about it, sitting perfectly still.

"You won't find another hospital in the city that faces the challenges we do," she finally said. "Operating with as thin a cushion as we have, doing as well as we have. We've turned the place around in just the few years I've been in charge. To tell you the truth, the hospital was in a shambles when I got here four years ago. There was no one really running things and we were in serious debt. We've turned things around. In case you don't know, that's hard to do in the hospital field."

I scribbled a few notes on my pad. She waited for me to look up.

"A hospital—and it might not look like it to most people—is a business. Other hospitals, even community groups, are often no more than our competitors, and many have a bone to pick with us because we don't use their services or we take business away. We have to be tough because we don't have as much money as places like Jefferson or Hahnemann or Penn. Then there's the politics. The local politicians have a say in where the health-care dollars go, city, state or federal, and they have their favorites, too. You might want to look into that. We're at the bottom of a big totem pole in this city, and that's an interesting thing to investigate as well, the ways in which others could help us and don't, or actually hinder us in serving our poor population. There's a story there."

She was offering me a choice of targets, anyone but her. It was a game people often played with reporters—"I'll help you screw someone else (if you go light on me)."

"I've spoken to some people already, including employees," I said. "I asked about you. And they all say that you're great at bringing in money to Clarke. But the money doesn't get to the patients, and staffing and salaries are low. I'd have to add, just from the little I've seen already, your administrative area is a lot better fixed up than the patient floors."

She shook her head. Then she laughed and got up.

"Four years of improvements here and I still have to hear stuff like that. This job is too much," she said, and paced behind her thin table. "Sometimes there's nothing else you can do but laugh. What's next?" She smiled and sat down, more relaxed.

I had the sense of her I needed and I got up to leave. She motioned me to stop and picked up the phone.

"If you're going to be around the hospital and talking to people, you should at least be known to security. I'll take care of that."

She dialed an extension and asked for someone named Mike. While we waited she talked a little more about newspaper ethics and whether it was right to "pick on" a place like Clarke, and whether we ought instead to be going after the bigger guys. We debated the topic for a few minutes until a man walked in. I knew right away he was an ex-cop. It's not fair to judge people by their appearance, of course. There must be accountants and physicists and artists built thick, with pale skin, close-cropped hair, square-block bodies, white indoor skin, mustaches, and expressionless faces. But all the ones I knew were cops. Maybe appearance was destiny. We shook hands, overly polite the way you had to be with strangers you instinctively didn't like, and then we just looked at each other while Abbott spoke.

She introduced him as Mike Carter, head of security. She told him my name and said I was a reporter for the *Inquirer*. She used the word "reporter" like a curse, and that was clearly the way Carter took it. He pulled out a cigarette from a pack in his jacket pocket, and lit up. Maybe my presence made him nervous. Or maybe he wanted to blow smoke in my face. I wondered if the hospital had a no-smoking policy but maybe that rule didn't apply here. Maybe no rules did.

"So you're still a reporter after all these years?" Carter said to me.

"You know each other?" Abbott asked, surprised.

"No," I answered.

"We never met," Carter said, "but I know the name. He did some stories a long time ago about the police. A real hatchet job. Tar and feathers, no facts. A couple of my friends lost their jobs as a result. And they were good cops."

Abbott looked at me. "A hatchet job?"

"A few cops were indicted and then convicted of beating innocent people who were handcuffed at the time," I said. I turned to Carter. "Were those cops your friends?"

He took in a large volume of smoke then turned to Abbott. He kept an eye on me as if I might do something violent, like write an exposé.

"You want me to escort him someplace particular in the hospital?" he asked Abbott.

The invitation sounded like a threat. He didn't actually offer to put me into a hospital bed but it was close, at least in tone. He didn't seem too intimidated by my size though I was taller than him, and broader, at least up top. Either he knew more ways to win or it was the confidence that comes from having the higher moral ground.

"No," she said. "I just wanted you to meet him. He's going to be looking around."

I wasn't sure what legitimate functions security guys had in a hospital. Protecting the staff, that had to be top on the list. Maybe protecting what little cash there was, perhaps pursuing internal crimes, like watching out for addicts around the narcotics, or employees taking home stationery and pencils and paperclips. Whatever his normal functions, he certainly had no problem with this assignment—intimidating a reporter, which was obviously what Abbott wanted him to do. There must be some built-in, hard-wired, in-the-blood protection of turf thing that governed the way organizations dealt with reporters. And they always got it wrong.

Because the thing to do when confronted by a reporter, if your operation is clean, is to prepare a warm welcome, provide free access to your place, offer typewriter ribbons and paper and a nice desktop for work. Just stand back and let them go. For one thing, newspaper stories usually have no effect at all. At best, when they are absolutely first-rate in every way, and catch the public's fancy, they only have a temporary impact.

Another reason to leave reporters alone and let them do their work is that there isn't any way to scare a reporter off a story. Reporters are contrary by nature. Have to be. Comes from the inherent craziness of spending your professional life running toward the events from which other people run. Wars, earthquakes, volcanos, people with guns, riots. It doesn't matter what it is. Reporters go and cover it. Wars were the best example. Three kinds of people disappear and die in them. There are always soldiers. There are always innocent villagers. And there are reporters. So if bursting bombshells and crackling automatic rifles can't turn reporters away, what good were intimidating glances from big ex-cops?

"Nice meeting you, Mike," I said. "If I run into any problems, I'll be sure to call." Then I left.

CHAPTER 15

I'd been planning to see Molly again since I'd met Taft's son up in Reading. I wasn't sure exactly what I'd tell her, but I was thinking of asking for her help. In recent years I was more and more in the habit of acquiring allies. When I started out as a reporter, I always worked alone, felt I had to, couldn't imagine bringing anyone else along. Time changed that. It was hard to function totally alone in the middle of corrupt organizations. Finding good people out there was one of the small pleasures, and I valued it. Molly was a potential ally. Maybe more.

The last woman I was with went off to make her own way after six months, having decided she needed a new challenge in her life, and needed to be alone to find it. She'd spent a half year plotting revenge for her father's death, and then another half year recovering after she'd gotten it. I helped with both the vengeance and the healing, and in the process we grew close. But my feelings about her in no way stopped her from leaving. I even understood why she left. Understanding why they leave has long been one of my problems. It occurred to me that not understanding why they leave and therefore rendering vigorous protest stood me a better chance of eventually getting one of them to stay. I'd have to try it sometime.

The lobby entrance at Clarke was as rundown as the ER. There was a waiting room with the usual green plastic chairs. Beyond the chairs were a couple of bank-teller–type windows with bars in front. Another Clarke specialty was taking money at a fast clip from people in waiting rooms. There was no reception desk, no greeters, no guards. No one seemed too interested in why I was there, or that I had a name or place in life or some other destination. I could have sat if I wanted to. Or paid money at the window. Instead, I walked around a corner and found a working staff phone on one of the walls. I had Molly paged.

I hung on the line for a few minutes and then she picked up. I got a friendly hello and she asked why I was back in the hospital. I said I wanted to talk with her and suggested she come downstairs for a cup of coffee. She said she would, but I'd have to wait a few minutes. I found a small snack shop off the first-floor lobby and waited for her there. Everything they sold, other than coffee, was prepackaged. Probably for the best, I thought. I bought two coffees and sat at a small table. It was mid-afternoon and the place was doing no business at all.

I kept an eye on the elevators for her arrival but after ten minutes she came out of the stairway. She was wearing tops and bottoms in some color unique to hospitals, a greenish blue, the kind of clothes that tied with drawstrings. On her, they looked good. As she stepped past the door, she looked upset and it occurred to me that whatever she was coming from had been hard. But by the time she was across the corridor she had relaxed. She had the ability to put things behind her quickly and move on. I liked that. She smiled when she saw me. I liked that even more.

She sat down at the table. "I could use the break," she said. "How've you been? How're you feeling?" She reached for the coffee and thanked me for it. She took off the plastic top, put sugar in, and sipped.

"You were right. My friend did have a son. I saw him. I'm not so sure I was happy to find him. I still haven't delivered the letter." I told her about my trip to Reading and my visit with Peter. I realized as I spoke that I hadn't ended up doing much but taking a long drive.

"It's sad," she said. "Your friend, the letter, that boy. The whole thing." She paused. "It's good you found him though. Maybe at some point he'll accept the letter from you. And appreciate having it. Maybe much later on it'll help him."

"I hope you're right again. Anyway, I did want you to know what happened because it was your guess about it that sent me to Reading."

I knew that if I left it at this we were essentially finished. It wasn't clear that together we had anywhere else to go. I was interested in her; there wasn't any way I could deny that. I found her attractive. And I admired her as well. It was a potent combination. She drank her coffee slowly. She had an unusual manner. Little things. For instance, we had stopped talking for a minute. She just sat there sipping coffee, not making small talk, not uncomfortable either. She was different. She didn't try to fill in silences. Usually when one person doesn't make small talk, it makes the other person uncomfortable. She was nice to be around.

"There's something else," I said. She looked at me casually. I had this impulse to simply spit it out, the way it actually was, and I considered for a moment doing just that. But I heard the words echo in my ears without having spoken them aloud. "I'm a blackmailer." Or maybe I wouldn't use those words. "I'm an investigator. I find out things organizations would rather keep private, and then I threaten them, and they stop their scams and they pay me to leave them alone." I toyed with another way or two to put it, and none sounded like anything anyone with a good sense of right and wrong would find acceptable. Whatever the strength of my instinct to unveil myself, there was no way to be honest. Not yet. Fortunately, I had a well-rehearsed option for presenting myself to the world. Once it had even been true.

"Yes?" she asked.

"I'm a reporter."

"I'm not surprised," she said. "You had a lot of questions the other day."

"The friend I told you about, Peter's father. He died at Clarke. I don't think he had to die. Something that happened at Clarke killed him or at least contributed to his death. I didn't come to the Emergency Room because I was having heart problems. I came because I wanted to find out what was going on at Clarke. I needed to spend some time here, and being a patient seemed like the best way to do it. The questions I asked were based on more than curiosity, or my own close call. I'd already looked at some of the hospital records, medical and administrative, and there do seem to be problems at Clarke."

"How did you look at records? Who let you do that?"

"No one. I did it on my own."

She nodded her head but I wasn't sure if she approved of what I did or was shocked by it. Whichever it was, she moved on to the point. "What kind of problems did you find?"

"With antibiotics and morphine. Not just with one or two patients but across the board. There's something screwy about the hospital's purchasing practices. They're only buying from a few distributors to begin with, and most of the antibiotics and all the morphine comes from the same company. I don't know yet exactly who's profiting or how much, but I think patients are suffering as a result. And I think there's more. Procedures done unnecessarily. The kinds of mistakes we were talking about the other day but on a much larger scale. Not just individual mistakes by single physicians or inadvertent problems occurring on occasion, but something more systematic. I could use help from a doctor to understand it all better. Especially a doctor who's familiar with this place." I still wasn't sure how she'd react. "Would you be willing to help me out?"

"I'm worried about what you're saying," she said after a minute. "And you're right to check it out if you have concerns about how your friend died. And it's your job, too. I understand that. But I don't know if a newspaper story will help. This place, troubled or not, is the only way the people who live in this neighborhood get any health care at all. Clarke's an easy target but that doesn't mean it's right to go after it. And you're already sure that it's not just a doctor who did something wrong with your friend, but that the whole hospital is at fault. If that's true, and it's exposed, then people in this community could end up losing the hospital. They may not end up better off that way."

There was nothing fundamentally wrong with her reasoning. In fact, I had already considered that point of view. If I really were a reporter, my stirrings could indeed cause problems, not solve them. Because a reporter just tells the story. What happens after the story is up to everyone else. Often, when a story comes out, problems go under cover for a while. But problems have a way of resurfacing, smoother, and harder to catch the second time around. Change is uncertain and the rich usually find a way to at least stay rich, if not get richer.

It is less of a gamble the way I do things. The end result with blackmail is more predictable. You get to keep a hand on the bad guy's pulse, a grip on the organization's accounts. But Molly didn't know anything about my way of dealing with problems and therefore I couldn't reassure her. So I kept those thoughts to myself and only told her what I used to tell people when I was a reporter.

"If Clarke has a problem, there are only two alternatives. We can go after it and hope the story leads to improving things. Or we can leave it alone and assume it won't get better."

She nodded, this time it seemed in agreement. "I'll help you," she said. "If you do something first. I'm working here the rest of today and then I'm on call tonight. You spend that time on call with me. That's how you really get to see and understand the place—the patients and how we try to help. Maybe there's some other explanation for what you think is wrong here. That could be the way to find out."

I wasn't sure what spending the night on call here would help me understand, especially since I'd already experienced Clarke as a patient, but it was clear that this was her end of the deal, that she was asking me to prove myself in some way. It was also an invitation to share an intimate part of her life. I didn't want to turn that down.

"It's a deal," I said. "Tell me what I have to do."

She smiled. "Just follow me. Keep your eyes and ears open. Use common sense. And do what I tell you to do. That's the standard advice medical students and first-year residents get. It ought to work for you."

The hours passed quickly. For a while, the halls were busy with visitors and staff. A lot of the rooms we were called to, where patients were having the worst problems, had no visitors at all. Sometimes I waited outside while Molly was in with a patient because I felt like an intruder, uncomfortable. Standing there, I was very conscious of the physical state of the building. The corridors, the nursing stations, the elevators and stairwells—everywhere I looked there was dirt and disrepair. But when I went into the rooms with her, impressions of the patients brushed my other concerns away.

Most patients we visited talked about pain. Usually it was the first thing they asked about. They were all hooked up to pain drugs in one way or another, either with a pump that let them press a button and dose themselves with morphine a set number of times, or with pills the nurses brought. Often, regardless of the particular solution, it didn't seem enough. As Molly checked the patients, I checked their charts. The worst complaints about pain were from patients taking morphine. A few of them were also on one of the five antibiotics I had identified in my records search. Molly reassured them the drugs would eventually work. It was what they all needed to hear, but I had serious doubts about whether she was right.

It was the kids that got to me the most. We were called to Pediatrics to see a six-year-old girl with cancer. Her parents were angry about treatments because there was no sign of improvement, and she was always dizzy and in pain. The nurses had beeped Molly because an IV kept coming loose at the girl's wrist. The mother was in the room, and every time Molly tried to do something, the mother tried to stop her. It was hard for all of them.

At three in the morning, we went to Pediatrics again. Kevin was eight years old, stocky, with long black hair and a cute face. He was crying.

"What's the matter, honey?" Molly asked him, sitting on the bed, her hand on his cheek taking some of the flow of the tears.

From the waist up, the boy looked fine. For one thing, he had no tubes of any kind going into him. His left leg, on the other hand, was wrapped in a cast that fully enveloped him from the top of his thigh to his toes. It was hung up on a sling. He kept trying to grab his leg, but he couldn't do it.

"What are you doing?" Molly asked.

"My leg hurts," the boy said. "It hurts a lot." He said it with some anger and bitterness. "They told me it wouldn't hurt. But it does."

She tried to comfort him but it didn't do any good. She asked him if the nurses had given him medication for the pain, a question I had gotten used to through the night. I checked his chart. He had gotten codeine until a few days ago. It was now ten milligrams of morphine every four hours.

"Your leg is healing all the time," she said, "inside the cast. But it has a lot of healing to do, that's why it still hurts." She called me over.

I said hello and told him my name.

"I want to show you something," Molly said to the boy. She took a thick pen out of her pocket and when she touched the stem a bright beam of light appeared. "Watch this, Kevin," she said, and turned to me.

Molly put her hand on my shoulder and eased me down until I was at eye level with her. She shined the light in my eyes.

"Look," she said to Kevin. "Look at Gray's eyes."

The boy stared at me with curiosity. I stood still and let him look, tolerating the glare from Molly's light.

"Tell me what you see," she said. "In the black part of his eye."

"It's getting small," the boy said.

She gave the boy the light. "Take it. Now do it to me."

She leaned forward until her face was right in front of his. The boy held up the light and lit it in front of her eye. Without her prompting him, he leaned close to her and looked into her face, eye to eye.

"When there's so much light the eye shrinks down. Does it all by itself," Molly said. "That's just the way your body's working inside the cast, healing your leg, putting the bones together, all by itself." She got up from the bed. "You keep the light. I'll come back for it another time."

He wasn't happy, but the distraction had at least taken care of the tears.

At four-thirty there was what she called a "code." It meant someone was dying. A message came over Molly's beeper: "Dr. Pacemaker, room three-ten." It was repeated over and over. We ran through the hall and hurdled down the stairs. She reached the room before I did. Other staff soon appeared. The woman on the bed was very small and very old. She was unconscious and looked dead already. Two residents began massaging her chest and forcing air into her lungs with a bag they rhythmically squeezed. The flurry of effort, well coordinated, continued for ten minutes. As far as I could tell, the woman's condition never changed. After it was over, at what seemed like an arbitrarily chosen moment, one of the doctors announced the time—4:56—and a nurse wrote it down. No one used the word dead. They all left the room together and for a minute the woman lay alone on the bed. The oxygen bag was on the bed next to her, the floor was littered with a few empty packets of whatever they'd been injecting into her. Molly told me the nurses would come back in a minute to clean up. That was the last patient for us.

I wondered if I'd seen what Molly wanted me to see. I knew I'd seen enough.

CHAPTER 16

Molly and I sat alone in a small living room/dining room where residents rested during breaks. It was five-thirty in the morning and still dark out. Neither of us spoke for a while. I realized that she had been right. An overnight shift at the hospital added to my understanding of Clarke. But not in the way she intended. I admired her well-intentioned effort to help patients, but she seemed blind to an obvious truth: A lot of the drugs at the hospital didn't work. Someone was supplying the hospital with worthless medication. And making large profits, I was sure. The people who paid for it were the patients we saw in unrelieved pain.

"Is it unusual," I asked her, "for so many patients to complain about their pain medications not working?"

"No," she said. "It's real common. One reason is we tend to give too little medication for pain. I always have to remind myself to give them enough. It's because we worry people will get addicted to the pain meds but in fact that rarely happens. Another reason is patients in bad shape generally, and patients who have been in the hospital a while, like most of the ones here, tend to have more pain than we think they ought to have, given their particular disease and how much medication they're on. It's because they're just more fragile physically, and they're lonely and bored, or depressed, and less able to ignore it or handle it when they hurt."

"What about the people who run the place?" I asked, changing the subject. "What do you think of them? I met with the director, Nancy Abbott. What do you think?"

Molly said she had gone to Abbott a few times in the past to complain about shortages of supplies or bad conditions on a particular floor, but she'd never gotten a satisfactory response.

Nor would she ever. Good intentions and a few helpers weren't going to do the job. Clarke was a devastated place. Many of the beds in the hospital were taken up with patients who might be better off if they'd never gained admission. The ones who died here would probably have suffered less by dying in their homes, I thought. Instead, they spent their last hours and energies as patients. And so much of what was done to them was empty rite, things done to no effect other than to increase their suffering. Whatever the intention, whatever words doctors used to explain what was done, suffering was what occurred. Like the way that old woman died. What good did it do? Treated her final minutes as an exercise for healers.

In one way, though, the doctors and nurses were victims, too. They probably got into their professions out of a desire to help people, among other things. There had to be some price they paid, emotionally at least, for participating in events that caused suffering. Yet they had to be responsible at some point for standing up and saying no, I won't do that anymore.

In fact, the routine acceptance of conditions here by all the doctors and nurses convinced me that the problem wasn't just Clarke. It was the whole system, the medical profession itself, the business of hospitals. Clarke was worse than most, that was clear, but in whatever ways it was bad its worst excesses were nothing more than exaggerations of the things other hospitals did every day. Angelic, she might be, I thought, looking at Molly. But she was plying her trade in hell.

The fact that she didn't see the corruption around her meant nothing either. I'd seen that before too, many times—the inability of good people to see the wrongdoing being conducted in front of them. It's just that everyone has a vested interest in what they do, and so can ignore or blind themselves to unpleasantness. I could easily haul out examples from my own experience. And that's exactly what I decided to do.

"I started out as a reporter fourteen years ago," I said. "And one of the things I remember most clearly was how I sometimes didn't notice things—big stories, every one—that should have been easy to spot. But I didn't see them—and neither did any other reporters."

"I don't understand," she began.

I nodded. "You will. My beat was to cover the city courts. Every week, as I sat in on murder trials, the defendants would get up and testify that they had been beaten up by police during interrogations. The testimony was vivid and always similar: They all said they were handcuffed to a metal chair inside a small interrogation room and then questioned for hours. When they refused to admit they were guilty, a detective threatened them and then beat them on their ankles and backs with a wooden stick. Sometimes, they said, detectives put phone-books on their heads and hammered down on the books, which is a pretty effective way to torture someone without leaving marks. There was a lot of testimony like that, very specific and detailed. The beatings usually went on for hours, the defendants said, until they agreed to sign statements, give incriminating evidence, even write confessions—just to stop the beatings."

"Gray, why are you telling me this?" she asked, frowning.

"Just bear with me, Molly," I said.

"Okay, but—"

"I heard this kind of testimony every week and I didn't believe it. Any of it. All the lawyers, and other reporters, and the judges, and everyone else who'd been coming to the courtrooms for years, longer than me, assured me that the suspects made up the stuff. When defendants first got to the lockup, I was told, after their arrest, other prisoners in the cell coached them about what to say, how to testify so that the judge might throw out the case. That's what the lawyers thought—even the defense lawyers who represented these guys—so that's what I believed.

"It came to me slowly, and only after covering the courts for several months and mentioning the testimony to friends who'd never been in a courtroom before, that maybe the defendants were telling the truth. And if they were, that meant the cops and prosecutors—knowingly or not— were lying. So I checked it out, did a lot of research, and it turned out the cops *had* been lying. It was at that moment—and I'll never forget it—that I first understood how someone can stand right in the middle of a corrupt world and not see it. The people who surround you every day, people you work with, people you like, want things to go on ticking as they always have, for a lot of different reasons. Even when other people are getting hurt."

I stopped for a moment, unsure yet whether to turn the conversation to Clarke Hospital and Molly herself.

"How did you know the defendants were telling the truth?" Molly asked.

"Once I realized it might be true, I knew what I had to do. Get the facts. There are always facts, if something's true, and if you look for them. Nothing in this world is ever hidden completely. It was a matter of collecting evidence. Looking through a huge number of public records of homicide trials, one by one. But mostly interviewing people—defendants, lawyers, doctors, and the detectives themselves. This may seem incredible but when I talked to the detectives, not one of them denied using coercive interrogation techniques; instead, they explained themselves. Excuses, rationalizations really. All the evidence—pictures, medical records, the statements by defendants and police—showed that the detectives had in fact been beating suspects. Just as suspects had testified in court all those years. Nothing contradicted it. Nothing."

"What happened?"

"I wrote the story. It made a big splash. The cops stopped beating people, at least for a while. The hard part for me is that once I read my own words in the newspaper, I saw how obvious the corruption had been. But before that, for years, everyone believed the lies because that's what they all wanted to believe. Including me, at least for a while."

It seemed like the right time so I went ahead and bridged the gap.

"Maybe just like you believe," I said. "Like you told Kevin and all the other patients, that the pain drugs work, that it's only a matter of time before the medication takes effect. It makes sense. It's what anyone would think. But it may not be true. I don't have exact evidence yet, but I think a lot of the drugs in this hospital are fake. That someone may be replacing real drugs with phony ones, to make money. And there'd be a lot of money at stake. Millions."

"No one would do that," Molly said. "That's impossible."

If she really believed it was impossible, then she was naive. Finding people who would do things like that for money was not difficult at all.

"I don't know what to say," she continued. "If that's happening, we have to find out, get it to stop." She wasn't looking at me and some of what she said sounded like she was talking to herself, as if thinking about it hard enough would solve things. That might have worked for her before. Not this time. In a minute, she stopped trying and turned back to me.

"You should talk to John Walker about this. He's the doctor who brought you out of the anaphylactic shock last week. He's definitely the best doctor at Clarke, and he's been here a long time. He'll know what to do."

I knew what to do also but I wasn't quite ready yet. "I can't bring up the issue of fake drugs with him, though. I need to have more documentation. But we can talk about the general conditions at this place."

"Okay," Molly said. "We're having a staff meeting Friday, at noon. It usually runs an hour. Come by at one."

"I'll do that," I said. I knew she was upset. So was I. It was the only way to be. She went to one of the resident rooms to get some sleep. I went home.

CHAPTER 17

Walker stood outside the room and watched Chaney, a resident, draw
blood from an old woman's thin wrist. He fumbled, stabbing the skin
three or four times with the needle. The patient was old and sick and
demented. In that sense, nothing Chaney did mattered much. But he had
bothered Walker for months.

Chaney, a foreign-born resident, had a diffident, hesitant quality with
patients. He always took an inordinate amount of time introducing himself, and explaining what he was about to do. He did procedures slowly
because he was unsure of his knowledge and ability. And he was afraid.
Walker had seen the fear in him many times over the past several months.
A few weeks ago, Chaney and Walker had done a spinal tap together. In
that procedure there was always some risk of accidentally injuring the
cord and causing a partial paralysis. It often took several tries to get the
syringe properly inserted. Chaney had missed the first tap completely and
got blood on the second try, which meant he was getting close. But then
he froze, afraid to go on. Walker finished the job himself.

The old woman Chaney was with now was already nearly dead. There
was little at stake even if he killed her. But the resident was still afraid.
Walker could see it. What is he afraid of? Walker wondered. Blood, open
flesh, distortions in human symmetry? Afraid of the mere possibility of

death? He's caught up in her dying as if it were him, Walker decided. He sees the fading breath and in that moment he breathes deeper himself, reassurance that he is young and alive. He sees her thin skin, whitened hair, pallor, the brittleness of bone, and he senses the fragility of his own body.

Walker saw how Chaney's lips drew tight and his eyes turned away whenever the needle entered the woman's skin. He is bothered by the aesthetics of the sick, Walker mused, by the way flesh distorts itself and accommodates instruments of metal and glass. He gives in to the stirrings of distress. He lets the details of suffering and dying overwhelm him. He has failed to accomplish the main thing required of a doctor. He has not become numb.

The monitor patched to her breathing, silent until now, began making a regular sound, the simulated pealing of a bell. The sounds were slow at first, then quicker, closer together. The resident looked up at the line for the woman's track. At least he knows the sound means the woman's not getting enough air, Walker thought.

Walker noticed for the first time that the way the track was sitting in her neck was wrong. The flap wasn't slightly opened the way it was supposed to be. Chaney suddenly noticed it too. He grabbed the flap and held it open with his hand. The bell kept ringing. He shook the tube and pushed at the skin behind it but the sound didn't stop. His movements became quicker and more frenzied. He was doing two things at once, using one hand to maneuver the tube and his other to reach behind the patient, propping her up, trying to get her to breathe. Walker wondered why Chaney didn't call for help, then realized the answer: He's afraid he caused the problem, and he's willing to let her die, rather than call in a code and be found out.

Chaney reached up to turn off the monitor, probably to prevent any nurses on the floor from noticing the bell, which then stopped. He bent over the woman, putting his ear to her mouth. Sometimes, you could barely see if they were dead, but you could usually feel the slight remaining breath on the hairs in your ear. It was a decent way to tell, reminiscent of the days before monitors and bells. At least he knows enough to search for signs of life, even if he can't keep them alive, Walker thought.

The resident cursed aloud and straightened up. He grabbed the woman's shoulders and began shaking her, pushing her body down into the bed, the thin flesh and slight bones pliant beneath his hands. He pressed down on her chest as if he could squeeze air into her. "No," he said aloud. He brought a hand up to his head as if in wonderment, then struck himself with the hand. He thinks he killed her, Walker thought, looking at him with contempt. Her death was nothing. Why was there so much fear?

For months, Walker had felt more impulses to kill. Now he knew why. A few days ago he'd been walking behind a man on Walnut Street when he suddenly had a sense of sharp familiarity. He felt he knew the man, recognized his stride, the narrowness of his waist, the particular lay of the jacket on his shoulders. The man slowed at the corner and Walker paused behind him, making sure not to catch up. It was when Walker hesitated in that strange position, avoiding even standing next to the man, that he recognized within himself a feeling he had not experienced for many years: fear. Walker was sure the man would turn around, and that he would recognize the face. He was afraid it was his father, who had died of cancer thirty-four years ago. What struck Walker more than the notion that he might see the face of a dead man was that he felt the strong sensation of fear. He hadn't experienced that in himself since the year his father died. Understanding that now, he decided to return to his parents' farmhouse in Lancaster County.

He drove the hour and a half into the country early in the morning, before sunrise. He'd kept the house, locked and vacant, for the eight years since his mother had died. He hadn't been there in over a year.

Fear was something to overcome. That was the major truth of Walker's life. When he confronted and removed his own fears at the age of nine, he had become immune, powerful, and distanced from ordinary concerns. As a doctor, he could help people or hurt them, assist their recoveries or kill them. He had acquired that power not in medical school, but on that one day in the cornfield. He did not know the full meaning then of the gift he had given himself, nor anything of his eventual calling. Only that something special had occurred in the field across the way. And then in the house. Now something had changed and he knew he had to come home to see what it was.

He went in through the kitchen door. He flicked the switch for the light, then remembered all the bulbs were out and he'd never replaced them. He found one of the several boxes of wooden matches he'd left out on the counter his last visit and lit one. Then he saw the dark edges of the familiar room appear. The doors of the cabinets above the sink and stove were open, displaying the emptiness within. The white-topped kitchen table was in the middle of the room, surrounded by three matched wooden chairs, low and plain, and a fourth, with a tall back and thick black cushion. His father always used the one with the cushion. When his father was away—which was often, because he was a pilot—no one ever sat in the cushioned chair. Seeing it empty now, Walker recalled that it almost always was. For both he and his mother, things changed for brief intervals when his father came home between flights, but most of the time they existed more truly during his absence. Until he came home to die.

Walker went on into the other rooms. He lit another match though he really didn't have to; he knew the house so well. There was a small living room, and a sitting room beyond that. The rooms were almost empty, most of the furniture in storage. At the far end of the sitting room was a set of curved bay windows facing the back yard. To the right was the short flight of dark oak–bannistered stairs that led to the bedrooms and attic. Walker sat down for a minute on the top of an old schoolboy attached chair and desk his mother had picked up at a garage sale. He sat there, head in hands. What is happening to me? He turned the question over in his mind, again and again. But it remained a question with no answer. He stretched and tightened his hands into fists, forcing himself into movement. But the stretching did not do what it should have—make him relax. He stood up.

He climbed the stairs to a small landing around which were three small bedrooms. The one across from the stairway had been his, small, neat, a perfect square, with one big window above the bed and a small closet opposite. He and his father had built the bed, down in the basement, using wood from a tree on their land. He'd had a storybook in which two bears, a father and son, did that, and every time he read the book he felt strange, that something so similar had occurred, in the fantasy and in his life.

The second bedroom had been used as a den and his father kept maps in there of his flying routes. Walker remembered tracing the paths he imagined his father was flying, during the long intervals when he was away. The shelves were still up but books and maps were no longer there. Everything was in storage. He went to the largest of the three bedrooms.

He always thought of it as his mother's room because his father was gone so often. As he walked through the door, it was as if he'd stepped into—for a moment—another house. This room still had all of its furniture, including framed pictures on the walls. He had done that, Walker reminded himself. He had simply left the room alone. And he knew why.

It was this room he had always been reluctant to enter, and the reason he had been hesitant to come upstairs. He walked in, turned on a table lamp and sat down on the bed. Across from him on the dresser was an old doll, the body battered a bit, the nose and eyes askew, but in an elaborate dress. His mother had not been a collector of anything, though everything in the house was old. Everyone has objects they hold on to and like for some unfathomable reason. As far back as he could remember, she always had that doll. Sometimes, in the mornings, she stood there at the mirror, and while she combed her own hair or did other things, she absently fixed the doll's white dress with one hand, or patted the doll's matted curls back in place. They were gestures of rare affection. She had never showed Walker affection like that. As he now looked at the doll, he felt a tingling stirring at the back of his neck.

He stretched out on the bed and remembered how he had sometimes slept there as a child when his father was away. But he had also been afraid of the bedroom. It was the place his father stayed when he was dying, the cancer raging. His mother cared for him alone, with no nurses and no outside help.

Walker was suddenly struck by a sense of the reemergence of old fears, something long closed to him, clamped and locked tight, now wrenched open, taking their place as narrow streams that were part of some larger source, tributaries to a forgotten ocean. What he remembered now, clearly, was that he had opened the bedroom door and there was his father, dead, his face still and ashen white, and his mother standing above him. She wasn't crying. Walker saw her lips parted wide in a grin.

He only glimpsed the smile; it was too painful to look at for long. What did it mean? In the silence and shadows of the bedroom, Walker now felt a growing sense of dread. He got up from the bed and stood, frozen, in the doorway. Now, at forty-three, he was every bit as shaken as when his father's death had happened thirty-four years ago. He again felt small and still, without the brave airs that sent him into the cornfield, left with the sense of being little, only a boy. He tried to shake himself into motion, to seize within himself the implacable strength of empty curiosity so long his resource and retreat. He succeeded in moving, in taking quick steps backward as if shoved by some force radiating out from the room. He stood, his back stiff and wet, not allowing himself to tremble, but feeling something. The door was barely open, he couldn't see clearly beyond it, and he was suddenly gripped by the sense that his mother was coming, the grinning face moving toward him, skeletonlike.

He gathered himself again, rejecting not just the image but the very surge of emotion it augered, and yet, despite these efforts, he found himself measuring the distance to the stairs. Unable to control the urge, he ran down the stairs and in a moment he was out in the light, the just-risen sun throwing shadows off the wood steps. He straightened up, reminding himself of his size, needing to see himself adultlike again. He took a deep breath, shook his head, then, startled, grabbed at his chest, experiencing a pain so sharp and sudden it was as if he'd been struck. It's nothing, he thought, nothing, and he trembled, helpless to stop it, and, when he finished his trembling, he cried.

He knew what the grinning face meant, knew it as he'd always known it, but avoided facing it all these yearning years. The relief his mother felt was not just at the death of his father but the death of family as well. She had rid herself of her husband and could just as easily now rid herself of her son. Because she didn't care and never had. At that moment, this truth was clearer to him than it had ever been before, though there had been terrible clues, he knew—knew at nine as he knew now—and it was a truth he could never again deny. He was alone in the world and always had been. If he let himself feel anything at all he would be engulfed: the anger, the emptiness, the fear. He could not surrender. He wiped away the tears.

It stunned him in its precision, in the way a single idea could cut through confusion and suffering. Everything he had protected himself from all these years was too little, too narrow, too small. It wasn't fear of battered dolls, of the dark, of faces, of the body's transformations, of anything like that that mattered. Those were small things. He had done a good job all these years, made himself into someone powerful, who couldn't feel fear and sometimes couldn't feel anything at all. But it wasn't enough.

I can still die, Walker thought. He realized that he was breathing fast, his heart was racing, his fingers tingled from the rush of blood, that after all he had done, he had not protected himself enough. He could still die.

And he knew it was a fear he could never overcome. All of the fears people had—of pain, of failure, of being alone, of being discovered for who they really were—were only a mask for what they, like him, had to fear the most. Once, to conquer those smaller fears in himself, he had deliberately exposed himself to them, over and over. Staying up all night because there were terrors there. Turning off the lights, making himself still in the dark, until every shadow had a chance to take its fearful shape, and, in the end, declare itself an empty, harmless threat. Whatever he feared, he approached and stood near, for as long as it took him to feel calm and unafraid. He'd done it as a child. Now, as an adult, he had to face death, and the fear of it. By experiencing the death of others, over and over, perhaps he could conquer that final fear as well. It was important, and necessary. Because he needed to be ready for his own.

Chaney was weeping. Walker could see that his fear had been transformed by the old woman's death, fueled by the guilt of his inaction, made more intense by the shame of his incapacity to help her. He identifies with her death, Walker understood, when what he needs is to be immune.

He walked into the room, and Chaney, startled, turned to greet him. "Dr. Walker—" he began.

Walker picked up the needle Chaney had used minutes before. He pushed the plunger completely down, making sure it contained nothing but air, then pulled it back up to the top. He smiled, and Chaney relaxed a bit. Walker suddenly grabbed him by the throat. Bending Chaney back with one hand, Walker slipped the needle into the carotid and pressed down hard with his thumb, injecting the syringeful of air. The resident tried to push him away but the deed was done. Walker held him with his greater strength as the embolus of air sought his heart, kept him still until he felt the sudden jerk of a heart seized. And then Walker saw the empty rolling up of eyes, the absence of vision brought on by death.

He released the body. The resident lay over the flat thin form of his patient, the two of them in virtual embrace. Walker was lost for a moment in the sight, his senses full of not what was present but what was not. The room was empty, and that was good. No noise or motion, no cries of sorrow. No fear. No life.

Walker brought Chaney's body down to the morgue, then marked him as an unidentified corpse. This time, because he wasn't an indigent patient but a doctor who might be noticed in the morgue, Walker made sure the body was picked up and buried in a pauper's grave that same day.

C H A P T E R
18

I've never liked Philadelphia's City Hall. It smells like a subway station in a bad neighborhood. The rooms and passageways are scattered in a maze of dim light; I get lost every time I go there. The elevator buttons tell you there are seven floors in the building, but if you walk up you find nine. Actually ten if you count the little rooms attached to the file storage areas a few steps above the ninth floor. Over the years, inside some of these rooms, city councilmen and judges have become local legends by cutting deals, taking bribes, and taking falls. As time has passed the faces have changed but the games have more or less remained the same. So has the look of the Hall. Paint chips from walls everywhere. When you get to the seventh floor, some of the corridor ceilings are stripped open, thin metal pipes exposed and sagging. Many of the rooms have high walls displaying enormous paintings, the frames long tattered, the intricate woodwork surrounding them fine and elegant but intended for another age, a more civilized world.

The Hall also houses millions of files, documents, printed pages, and photos that have one thing in common: they are public records. These records, in City Hall and other public buildings nearby, contain the ignored but available pieces of stories of millions of people: anyone who lives or does business or commits crimes in Philadelphia. The records cover all the ground—from birth certificates to death certificates; marriage to divorce; business incorporation to bankruptcy; home purchases to tax liens; voter registration to campaign contributions; civil suits, malpractice suits, libel suits, and criminal proceedings of all kinds, shoplifting to murder.

Most of the details in the files are insignificant, and never reviewed by anyone. But some of the information, examined and pieced together properly with other facts, can be used to track dealings people would prefer to be kept secret, paper trails of corrupt deals. That was not the intended purpose of public record keeping, but that was the way investigators used them. They were a resource I'd relied on as a reporter, and I still did.

Nancy Abbott was not born in Philadelphia, the records told me, but she'd been married and divorced here. The divorce file was thin in pages but thick with rage. She'd sued him, charging adultery and physical abuse. She demanded and won the right to keep all their major possessions and property, such as it was: a BMW valued at $18,000; a twelve-foot sailboat, valued at $16,000 and stored at the Jersey shore; total liquid assets, aside from the car and boat, of $24,000 in savings and stock. She kept all of it.

Those possessions were extremely modest compared to what she'd managed to accumulate since then.

In Philadelphia, you can look up real estate records both by computer and by the actual paper filings. I preferred paper. Computer is faster— you key in the name, push a button, and in seconds you get a listing of every property purchased or sold under that name. But I liked the feel of paper better; it gives a more complete picture of the transactions. It bores you with the boilerplate language of the contracts but it also offers little details you don't find on a computer listing, such as the signatures of attorneys who represented both sides. You never knew when you might need those names.

The room with the real estate deeds was warehouse-sized, but other than two clerks up front it was empty; most people prefer the computers. I found my way to the old wooden file cabinet with small drawers holding index cards. They directed me to large binders which hold the deed to every property in Philadelphia. Locating each deed is mostly a matter of patience. If you have no time, then you need luck. Fortunately, I was in no rush.

The files told me that Abbott owned five residential properties in

Philadelphia, all in the city's most expensive neighborhood, Society Hill. The properties were worth a total of three and a half million dollars. The most expensive was a six-room penthouse overlooking the Delaware River and costing one point two million dollars. For a quick and easy check, I wandered down the hallway for a minute to the most available of all public records, the telephone book. Sure enough, Abbott was listed at the penthouse address. She was not listed at the other four properties she owned. Investments and rental income for her, I assumed.

Abbott also owned two commercial buildings in South Philadelphia. One housed a company called Hosp-Care, Inc. The other was a warehouse for a company called Medi-Systems Supply. The two properties were worth one and a half million dollars.

Incorporation papers were in another building. The clerk was a thin, pale, middle-aged man named Bob. He'd been there for years but I'd never gotten to know him. He just wasn't interested. I always wondered how he managed to stay thin with such a sedentary job. I told him I wanted to find the names of owners of the two companies in the commercial buildings owned by Abbott. He said he'd do it for me and told me to wait ten minutes. Then, as if realizing he was a fool to volunteer for the chore, he changed his mind and suggested I do it myself. He pointed to a row of metal file cabinets. The drawers were arranged alphabetically according to company names. I pulled the single sheets of paper that were filed to incorporate Medi-Systems Supply and Hosp-Care, Inc. Both companies had been created in the past three years. They were both solely owned by Nancy Abbott.

Back in City Hall I went to the office where they kept city Health Department contracts. The files were thick under both Medi-Systems and Hosp-Care. According to the contracts, the city awarded a total of eight million dollars to Medi-Systems and Hosp-Care to provide medical supplies and equipment for a half dozen hospitals in poor areas in Philadelphia. A lot of the supplies were for Clarke.

Most reporters who covered big-city governments learned over time that the concept of an honest bidding system for public contracts was something for college textbooks, not real life. Bidding was sometimes rigged, but more often there was no actual bidding at all. Contract proposals were written by city officials and contractors privately, before any public notice was given. They were written in such a way that only one company could meet the specifications—the company that helped write the proposal. And then the contract was awarded with no effort ever made to seek bids. The key question wasn't whether there was competitive bidding, it was what connection did the contractor have with the city official. There were lots of possibilities. Some of them could be found in public records. I went to the elections commission to look up records of campaign contributions.

I didn't know which politician to start with but, as it turned out, it didn't matter. I looked at the mayor's contributions first. He'd received five thousand dollars from Abbott in the last election. He'd also gotten twenty thousand dollars from employees of Clarke Hospital and fifteen thousand each from employees of Medi-Systems and Hosp-Care. All the contributions came in on the same date. No doubt all the money was actually laid out by Abbott. She paid employees to make the contributions, because federal law prohibits businesses from making donations; people do that routinely to get around the law. I checked the campaign contributions for the mayor's opponent in the election. Abbott and her companies had contributed the same amounts to the opponent. I started checking city council members alphabetically but once I got to the fifth one and found that all of them had received contributions from Abbott and her companies, I decided there was no point in continuing on that trail. Abbott made friends in City Hall. And her generosity paid off.

Facts don't always tell the whole truth but they usually don't mislead. The facts said that before Abbott had taken the job at Clarke Hospital she was worth a little under sixty thousand dollars. Today, in real estate alone, she was worth five million. And she owned two companies doing millions of dollars in business with the city. Whatever else she had in bank accounts or investments I wouldn't be able to determine from public records. My guess was she'd been putting away a good deal of cash. Either way, it was not likely she'd earned anywhere close to enough in salary to fund five million plus in real estate and corporate assets. There were two other reasonable possibilities for her newfound wealth: She inherited the money or she stole it.

I went to probate court the next morning and found nothing listed under Abbott's name. According to the divorce file, her parents lived in Manhattan. The Amtrak Metroliner got me to New York in an hour and fifteen minutes. It took me twice that time to find the right clerks and records at probate court downtown. What I learned was that Abbott's parents were still alive, and Abbott had received no inheritance from any other relatives and had never paid any estate taxes in New York. I was satisfied she had not become rich by the death of a family member. That left only one reasonable conclusion. She was a thief.

C H A P T E R
19

I took West River Drive into the city Friday morning. The college crew teams were out doing laps on the Schuylkill, and I pulled off to a grassy spot where I could park. I walked to river's edge and watched the slim wooden boats in quiet motion, the young arms moving in lockstep, the dark mass of water holding them all with a steady, uncomplaining hand. For the first time since I'd come back from Florida, the sky was clear and the sun was warm. The last place I wanted to go was Clarke Hospital.

By the time I got to the conference room at one, the presentation had evidently ended and the medical staff was standing in small groups, carrying on separate conversations. I spotted Molly right away, standing by the lectern, talking with three men and two women. When I was halfway across the room she saw me, and waved and smiled. She left the group and came over to me. The man she'd last been talking to looked disappointed. I empathized.

As Molly approached, I glanced over the rest of the room. Everyone was young—late twenties, early thirties—too young to be Walker. When Molly reached me, she gestured to someone behind me. I turned and saw a man in his mid-forties, average height, but broad shouldered and solid. He had dark hair, a mustache, and was good-looking. Now that I saw him, I could place him as the doctor who had taken over when I had my close call that night. He came over. Molly did the introductions and I stuck my hand out. Before I spoke up, he did.

"You're the man we looked in on last week in four-A," he said. "How are you? Good as new?"

He put it in such an understated way, as if he had breezed in last week to say hello, instead of finding me dying in a room full of frenzied doctors and nurses who didn't know what to do. It was as if we were talking about somebody else. "I never got a chance to thank you, Doctor," I said to Walker as we finished the handshake. "Molly explained it all to me afterward. I appreciate what you did."

"If she explained it to you," Walker said, "then you know everything I did was pretty basic. You never should have been in that mess in the first place."

Molly then spoke up. "Gray's a reporter." She was probably going to say more, but Walker took over.

"It makes sense you'd want to write about it," he said. "About everything that could go wrong in your case did. Except that you came out okay."

"He's actually doing a story about conditions at Clarke," Molly said. "He's already talked with me and I thought he ought to talk with you."

"With me?"

"Yes," Molly said. "Because you're one of the people at Clarke I respect. If there are problems at the hospital, I thought he might discuss them with you."

Walker grinned shyly. He seemed uncomfortable with her praise, which struck me as nice for a doctor in his position.

"I'm flattered," Walker said. "Really." He smiled at Molly. Then he turned to me. "I'd be more than glad to talk to you about your case and how it went that night. I have no problem with that. But as a physician, I just wouldn't feel comfortable having a conversation about conditions at Clarke. Especially about patients."

His stand sounded a lot like conscience speaking, and I respected that. On the other hand, his particular reason for not talking was the same one doctors always gave when reporters asked questions. Patient confidentiality. It was the invisible shield for doctors. One thing I'd noticed over the years, though, was that it usually wasn't the patients the doctors were trying to protect.

"You really ought to talk to administration," Walker said. "There isn't anything that happens at Clarke they don't know about. I know there are problems, but we try to do the best we can." He held out his hand. "Nice meeting you."

"It's terrific that she admires your work," I said to Walker, as we made our good-byes. It got him to stop.

"I know." He had that humble look again, almost a blush. "She once left me a note—a 'mash note.' " Molly didn't seem embarrassed at all.

"That's right," she said. "It was after you took care of the Wiley boy, with the clot." She turned to me. "He did a difficult procedure to start with, but the way he talked to the boy and his parents was what really impressed me. It was right after I'd arrived, and I actually wrote him a note, to tell him that. It was great to see, especially in a specialist. Rare."

Walker gave her a smile. "It was a very nice gesture. Most residents don't give you that kind of response." He paused. "Got to get going, though. If you have any questions about your case, call me," he said to me. "Good luck."

He seemed likable, and Molly's endorsement was high praise. But it was possible, if not likely, that as a senior man, he knew all about Clarke's problems, including the scams. Molly trusted her feelings about him, and he was good at his work. But that didn't mean he wasn't part of the problem at Clarke.

"Seems decent," I said to Molly. "Not too helpful, though."

"Maybe when you can tell him about the drug problem, he will be," she said.

"Not to change the subject," I said, "but do you have a day coming up when you're not working, or on call?"

"Sunday," she said right away.

"I'd like to pay one more visit to Peter Taft, and I thought you might like to come along. There's some beautiful country on the ride."

"I'd like that," she said.

Where was it? I thought, looking at her. Where was the numbness, the sense of distance, the concern with power, even in its everyday, routine forms, the arrogant confidence supposedly inherent in the job of doctoring? I'd now spent hours watching her work. She had none of that. Nor were there any of the usual games with men. Just now, for instance, when I asked her out. She would either go to Reading, or she wouldn't, and it wasn't dependent on what I said or how smoothly I said it. Her responses come from something more basic, something she was able to tap within herself. It was the way she had known about Taft and his living son. She's all of a piece, I thought, one weave, and I felt a tremendous surge of feeling for her. She was looking at me.

"What?" she asked, smiling.

"Remember I told you Joe was a baseball player?"

She nodded.

"Well, Reading isn't only where his son lives. It's where Joe played." I almost told her that I played there too, years ago. But it somehow felt strange to say that, when I was keeping so much else from her, at least for now. "There's a baseball park up there, small and open and pretty. As long as we're up there, I'd like you to see it. There's a plaque on one of the walls that has Joe's name, alongside all the other players who made it up to the major leagues."

"So let's go," she said.

Walker carefully watched Gray and Molly from a distance. He couldn't hear their words but he could tell from their expressions and by the way they moved that they weren't discussing medicine or newspaper stories. There was something personal between them. He felt it, knew it would grow. She's so good, he thought. If only she knew how good she was. For me.

Later that night, having spent the rest of the day thinking about her, he knew he had to be with her again. He waited out the hours until she finally finished rounds and went off to sleep in one of the resident overnight rooms. He had observed her carefully over the last few months. She was a person of strong habits, extremely well organized, in her life, he assumed, as well as in her work. She always finished her shifts on time, barring emergencies. And, when she had to stay at the hospital after call, she always went to the overnight rooms and caught up on sleep.

He waited a while longer, then entered the room quietly, using a master key, as he had done a half dozen times in the past month. If she woke up, he'd simply say he needed to talk to her about a patient. But not surprisingly, she did not wake up. He made sure to turn off her beeper. Then he reached into his pocket and took out a narrow brown bottle of thick glass, holding five ounces of clear liquid ether. Simple, old-fashioned, effective. Used properly, enough of it inhaled puts you to sleep and keeps you there, calm and relaxed, for about two hours. He poured drops of the liquid onto a handkerchief and held it in front of Molly's mouth and nose for a moment and she inhaled it while she slept. When she woke up later that morning she'd be totally unaware that anything had happened while she slept.

He sat on the bed by her side and counted her breaths, in and out. They had an effect on him, almost as if he was meditating. Similarly, the sheer akimbo spread of her, her legs laying lightly atop one another, the way her arms careened out from either side—it relaxed him, made him feel as if his own body was at rest, tensions gone, mind empty. He lifted the blanket from her body. She still wore her hospital scrubs. She had removed her sneakers and arranged them neatly on the floor by the bed. Order, always order, Walker thought. It was the doctor's lot. Her skin was pale, smooth, kept out of the sun. She was very attractive but it was a handsome face more than a pretty one. He reached up to undo the drawstring waist. The pants came loose quickly; it was easy for him to pull them off. He tossed them aside and they settled on the floor lightly, like a tiny parachute. Then he took off her shirt.

There is something especially exquisite, it occurred to him, about the sleeping form of an attractive woman. He had not experienced this particular pleasure enough. He looked at Molly with great concentration. She had long legs. He ran his hands over her calves. The muscles were hard. He pressed his palm against her skin. She was warm and he could feel the capillaries on both sides. He pushed a fingertip into the flesh just below the knee on the front and watched as the white indent made by his finger was filled back in by the reflow of blood, the flesh regaining its pale pinkness. He slipped his hand over her leg again and this time felt the slight stubble where growth was starting after her last shave. He sniffed the skin. Sweat. No body perfumes or powders like the prostitutes. He hooked two fingers under the elastic band at her waist and pulled her underwear down. The band caught for a minute and the material was held by her crossed legs. He gently slid a finger down the front of her thigh and then uncrossed her legs and pulled the panties off. The hair on her pubis was thick, brown and curly.

He rested his head on the inside of her right thigh, and heard, as he focused, the rush of the blood torrent making its way unimpeded back to her heart. He felt the warmth of the firm flesh against his cheek. He sighed. It was a peaceful place. He moved a lazy hand up the inside of her other thigh, walking his fingers forward like a spider until he lightly touched the soft wisp ends of her hair. The sensation should draw a response, but she was deeply asleep from the drug. He brought his other hand up to her vulva and used two fingers to part the outer lips.

He felt the heat of her on his fingers. He let his fingers rest inside of her, the moisture and slight warmth comforting. He lay like that, perfectly still, for a long while. Then he eased his fingers out and moved his hand back down her thigh. On an impulse he found irresistible he suddenly stood up and looked down at her, at her body spread out before him on the bed, the beauty and muscularity of her legs, the perfectly matched bones of her hips and pelvis, the soft slight roundness of her belly and then the swelling incline of her breasts. He moved automatically, thoughtlessly, slipping off his clothes, never taking his gaze from her form, not stopping until he was naked, noticing the feel of the cool air now, the breeze stirring his skin, raising slight goosebump welts. But it was not coldness he felt.

He crept onto the bed and straddled her, one knee on either side of her waist, bracing himself on his palms so that his face was directly over hers but up high and away from her. When he let himself down his penis lay gently on her groin just above the thin brown border of her curls. Oddly, it seemed to him, he was not hard and the feelings that raced through him he recognized as excitement but strangely absent of arousal. He looked down at her. The position itself, this dominant pose, felt wrong, not what he'd been seeking when he made himself bare. He let his weight be taken by her form. He felt the shift and warmth and firmness of her as she accepted his pounds and edges and aches. He had a sudden sense of himself uncontained, as if he'd been made over, reduced to some essence of himself. Like some formulary base for human, a fine white powder sifted smooth over her, filling and fitting the lines and spaces of her. Her. Not him. And then he no longer knew who he was; he wasn't Walker. No longer yearning or hurting or craving anything, or lost. No longer the doctor, no longer in fear of death. He felt what it was like to be her: at peace, unafraid. Now so was he. He stayed with the feeling, let it drift through his skin, his marrow, his veins, all of him. He was her.

And then, for no reason he could explain, he lost it. He felt again separate and apart—aware of her breathing, her rhythm, her life. He slipped off of her, mourning the loss of their identity, the feeling of her nipples pressed against his own as if her insides were a part of him. He lay by her side and kissed all the parts of her he could reach, wetting her breasts and chest and belly with his tongue. He rolled her over with one easy push and held her in that way, her back to him, the two pressed together hard. He buried his face in her hair, barely breathing. He held her as close as he could, but the feeling—the joining of feelings, his and hers—was gone. He tried to bring it back but he couldn't. He was alone and afraid. He dressed her, then, as he looked down at her, he felt a tear on his cheek.

He went to the door and looked back at Molly, still asleep. I love you, he thought, closing and locking the door as he left.

CHAPTER

20

There was a big black dog in the front yard of Molly's house. It had a look about it I recognized as starved for affection, which was impressive considering that at that very moment, a small boy had two arms wrapped around it in a lover's grip. I heard him call the dog Katy before I got to the gate. The dog had an old tennis ball in its mouth, and the boy took his arms off the dog's back, and tried to wrestle the ball out. He was having little success, but he didn't seem to mind. Neither did the dog.

Molly's neighborhood, the East Falls section of the city, was one of the many in Philadelphia that I liked. The Schuylkill River was at the bottom of the hill, and the houses all the way up and down were wonderful. Philadelphia has more good houses than any city in America. In East Falls, the houses were mostly turn-of-the-century, big, brick and stone. Small patches of the original cobblestone streets, a hundred years old, were visible here and there. It was only ten minutes out of Center City but there were still intact barns from the old days of farming, usually standing detached and simple and beautiful in the backs of some of the yards.

Molly opened the screen door at the top of the porch, and came down the small flight of stone stairs. She patted the dog, then put a hand on the boy's head. He was nine or ten years old, with straight dark hair, and a wary eye, except when he looked at the dog. He had on a T-shirt with the name Jesse printed on it.

"I used to take Katy with me everywhere, when all I was doing was social work," Molly said. "One of the main things I had to change when I decided on medicine as a career was my time with Katy. Dogs and hospitals don't mix."

I let myself in through the gate and gave the dog a pat myself. I left the kid alone. He glared at me. "Does that mean you actually tried it once, bringing the dog to the hospital?"

"Well, not to a hospital. But during medical school, my first clinical year, I did a month at an old-age home, and the recreational therapist and I decided that Katy would be a nice boost for some of the patients. So I took her with me. The director had a fit."

"I can imagine."

"It probably didn't help that she peed on the floor," Molly said. She looked down at Katy and shook her head. "And she never did that before, either."

"New environment. Probably shook her up."

"Imagine how the old people felt."

There she went again, I thought, being effortlessly empathic. It was something I fancied myself good at, but compared to her, I was someone who knew how to swim, hanging out with a dolphin.

I leaned over and gave my best effort to taking the ball out of Katy's mouth. I got it to budge not an inch. The boy looked up at me and grinned. Katy seemed to want me to keep trying. I gave up.

"This is Jesse," Molly said. "He lives next door and he sort of shares Katy with me. He takes care of her when I'm at work."

"She shares Katy with me, is what she means," Jesse said. "I let her visit when she's not at work."

Molly laughed.

I liked her house. It was old fieldstone, smooth and clean, time-textured and welcoming in every way. The open porch had columns and a slate floor. Against one of the stone walls next to the front door was a woodpile, the logs kept organized by an old black metal open bin that had obviously been doing its job for a very long time. The house was a two-story A-frame with a high attic; the windows, colonial and framed in weathered but well-tended wood, took up a lot of wall. I knew those windows well because I'd once tried installing one in my small carriage house, and had a hell of a time getting the job done.

"I grew up here," she said. "We moved when I was eight, to Quakertown. My parents rented the house out but never sold it. I was at Jefferson med school last September, living in the dorm. But the tenants here left in December and I jumped at the chance to move in. I love it here. Always have."

"Big place to manage alone," I said.

"I had a roommate during med school. And also Katy—" the dog jumped up at the mention of its name. "Then just Katy." This time the dog barked.

We went in. There was a small rectangular anteroom before the living room proper, and in one corner of that small space was an old maplewood bootbench. The anteroom had a small porthole window at one end. I'd once built one like it in an old house in West Mount Airy. I thought I'd done a decent job, but this room put me to shame. It looked born, not made. As soon as I walked into the rest of the house, it was obvious someone had really sweated the details—and for a long time. Houses like this don't happen by accident.

Floor to ceiling, end to end, the place was wonderfully made. From the solid way the wood floors walked and were jointed, to the sanding and sealing on the moldings. The big stairway bannister was not just double-hung, but curved and polished with wax, layers deep. Just hand-rubbed wax. The furniture was every bit as carefully done. Every single item was solid wood and clearly hand-crafted, nothing trendy or cheap. There was nothing here I didn't lust after and that wouldn't have felt right and fit perfectly in any house I'd ever cared enough about to live in, build, or own.

The main thing in the living room was a huge stone fireplace, and the mantle was nicely done—one ten-foot long, two-foot thick slab of a single maple side from one tree, taken with one smooth cut, the way they don't do it anymore in these pressed-board, pretreated days. Up on the mantle was just one thing, a square wooden box of the same dark red wood that marked the character of the house like theme music. The lid of the box was open, and sticking up from a series of small open settings were old medicine bottles—I could see the labels—in a wide range of shapes and shades of old glass.

I walked over to look at it closer.

"Was your father a doctor, too?" I said.

"No," Molly said. "He got me that when I decided to be one. He's a cabinetmaker and owns a small shop that makes and sells old furniture."

"I'm impressed. But how come you became a doctor? Couldn't you get into furniture school?"

She laughed. "You're funny." She looked at me again. "You mean that, don't you?"

I shrugged, and waved my hand around at a few of the pieces in the room. "Taking care of people is fine, and all that, but good work doesn't get any better than this as far as I'm concerned. It's all his, isn't it?"

She nodded. Her father had put the inside of this house together, bit by precious bit. There was no mistaking that.

"He did have help on some of it," she said. "There are two other men who work in his shop, both good craftsmen. They built that, there." She pointed to a piece by a wall. I walked over.

It was a simple wooden desk. Simple, like a small wildflower in early spring—and every bit as pretty. It had a deep glow that said "warm" as if the word was spelled on its facing.

"It's beautiful," I said, and left it at that. "This place is a great gift."

"I know," she said. "My folks are up in Quakertown now, and don't get down here much. But my dad always asks me how the stuff's holding up. I think he feels like he ought to be taking care of it himself."

I ran a hand over the smooth desk top, then walked back to the big fireplace.

"I can't help wondering what you're doing at Clarke," I said. Somehow the question hadn't come up during the overnight. Maybe when she was actually taking care of a patient, it didn't matter much where it was. But in the light of day, I found it disturbing that she worked there. I was more and more convinced there wasn't any part of the place that wasn't in the business of hurting.

"I was a first-year family practice resident at Jefferson, but my mother got sick, and I took off to be with her. In residency, if you miss a few months, you have to skip the whole year, and start over in July. My mother was better by February, and I didn't want to not practice for seven months, and I needed the money. Clarke's a well-known place that runs on fillers, so I took the job."

"Fillers?"

"Yeah, medical school graduates who are just working and not in an educational—or residency—program. They're how a lot of hospitals get by. Clarke isn't a teaching hospital. Technically, it doesn't really have any residents, though they call us that. Just fill-ins, moonlighters. Mostly foreign med school grads. We're not in a training program, it's just a job. But it gives you experience, of course."

I smiled. "It seems as if it's more than just a job, at least for you. I like the way you went out of your way to help that kid the other night. I also like the way you're willing to help me find out what's going on at Clarke. You don't even seem to realize that most people routinely look the other way. On top of that, you're one of the few people I've met in a long time who doesn't have some gripe against their folks, or someone else, and isn't wearing it on their sleeve."

"Is that all?" she said. She laughed. "Feel free, of course, to continue."

"Maybe one more thing." I was standing right next to her, and I knew what I'd left out. "I like the way you look. Not just that you're pretty but that you don't make a big thing out of it. And that you're living in your dad's house, and haven't changed the furniture. I even like the dog. And the kid next door."

She took my arm in hers and held onto it, as if we were some old gentleman and lady about to go for a stroll. It was oddly restrained, but it seemed right. I'd been lucky that way lately. Every rough place I'd been had offered me, at some point, along with the threats and sorrows, one person who was a pearl. Nothing had yet worked out in a way that carried over long enough, and after a while, I always returned to my usual state, in my usual place, on my own, in the house a block away from the woods. But I meant to keep trying.

"Let's go out to Reading," she said. "We have a young man to visit."

It was just what I had in mind.

We parked in front of Peter's building. I'd found him home the last time, and even though I hadn't called, we went up the stairs of the rundown building, figuring to find him in. Depressed people stay home a lot, I thought. When we knocked, no one answered, so we went downstairs, then stood there for a minute, looking around. We decided to wait, at least until dinner time, and took a seat on the steps. All the neighbors who'd been there before were nowhere in sight, so we had plenty of room.

In half an hour, Peter pulled up on a motorcycle, one I'd seen parked near the building the last time. It was a big one, a Harley, high and with bulky weight. The metal all over was rough, and considering a new one costs ten or fifteen thousand these days, I assumed it was used, or that maybe he'd restored it himself. I admired the bike, whatever I thought of its rider right now.

Molly and I tried getting his attention, but he kept the cycle running and the engine drowned out all attempts at conversation. He made no move to shut it off. Finally I went over to him and yelled for him to silence the machine, and he did. I told Peter that Molly was a friend of mine, but left out the part about her being a doctor at Clarke. I asked him how he was doing, and he said fine, but it wasn't real. Actually, he seemed more distant than angry. It hadn't been quite this awkward the first time.

"We just came up for a ride, thought maybe we'd stop by the stadium," I said. "And I wanted to see if you'd changed your mind about the letter."

I figured I could wait until he let me know he was ready, and hold on to it for him until then. I was, in a way, calling him to stand before judgment, and maybe that's the way he felt. It probably wasn't an easy thing. In that letter were his father's final statements about him, last words straight from the vale of death, directed to a son. There was no more frightening a prospect. If the words were good, tremendous healing was possible. If they weren't, well, there were no limits to that kind of difficulty. I wasn't sure I'd run to read the thing too fast if I was him. It took more confidence and guts than most people had.

"I told you, I'm not interested," Peter said.

"I know it's none of my business," Molly spoke up, "but I think you ought to read it. I'm sure you're scared it'll say bad things but I doubt that that's the case." She was reading my mind. "People don't usually say bad things when they're dying. It's not a good time for that, and they know it. People who are dying usually want to make peace. It's all that really matters in the end, isn't it? I bet there are wonderful things in there for you."

"How do you know so much about what people write on their death-beds?" he asked her.

"I'm a doctor."

He glared at her and practically spit at me. Whatever gifts we had to offer, we still hadn't found the right way. He started the engine and put the big V-twin rumble between him and all our words, then roared off down the street.

We discussed following him, agreed that we couldn't possibly keep up, and concluded that even if we could we wouldn't know what else to say. I felt as though the whole trip had been a step backward, and Molly reminded me of the obvious, that the kid had to live his own life and make his own choices. That didn't make me feel much better, true as it was. I asked her if she'd mind a raincheck on the trip to the ballpark. She said she had no problem with that. We got in the car and drove back home.

CHAPTER 21

Abbott was alone Sunday afternoon when she heard the familiar rattle of Walker's keys outside the apartment door. This time she was irritated, unhappy that he would be intruding on her life. She had become involved with him personally because of what he could do for her at Clarke. She had always thought of Clarke as Walker's domain, the place he commanded. But now she felt very much in charge. She had power, money, new allies, and she no longer needed him. And if she could succeed without him at Clarke, did she need him at all? She had been considering asking for her keys back. Or she could simply ask him to leave. But she would do neither. She'd have to find another way, one he could accept or at least do nothing about.

As she waited for him to come in, she recalled that when they'd first met she'd relished the sound of him entering unannounced. She found it erotic, exciting. Sometimes, at night, asleep, having gone to bed alone, she'd feel his touch rousing her. He never said anything, his mouth on her nipples, his fingers teasing and probing, never hard or hurting, but insistent nonetheless. Often he simply lay next to her, curled up behind her, naked. What was always there, no matter what else occurred, was a sense of urgency, of need.

It wasn't only sex, she understood that. It was some intensity within her he sought to tap by exposing her to new, even extreme experiences with him. She saw what he did to other women, and sometimes thought that what he wanted to evoke in her as well was fear. But often, especially in their earlier days, she had enjoyed the extremes.

She remembered the first time she had seen him. They were in a conference with the medical staff. He sat in the first row, one of the senior people, not participating much, and frequently looking over at her. He came up to her afterward, introduced himself, and said he wanted to talk. They talked about the meeting, which had gone well from her point of view. Even then, after being at Clarke for only a few months, she was already aware of the opportunities, although unsure how she'd get her share. Walker was unusually direct.

"I think I know what you want," he'd said to her. "And I can definitely help out. Let's talk about it over dinner."

She accepted the invitation. It was late afternoon when they left the hospital, and they ended up staying out the night. They went to a first-rate restaurant and he told her stories about the practices at Clarke, and about the people there—all information that would help her to eventually move up. He headed all the important medical staff committees. He was clearly a strong factor in how things were done at Clarke. As dinner went on, she enjoyed the conversation and the food, the elegance of the place, and most of all, Walker's intense interest in her. Uncertain as she was, still new to the job, and lonely, she was attracted to him in every way. Aside from having influence at Clarke, he was also handsome and interesting. She was having fun with a man for the first time in ages and it felt good.

He talked very openly about sex. He pointed to a waitress across the room and asked whether Abbott found her attractive. She'd already had a lot of wine. She felt witty. She said she did think the woman was pretty, and she laughed about it. She wondered aloud how kinky he actually was. He went to make a call. When he returned, he said someone would be joining them.

"A friend?" she asked.

"In a sense," he replied.

A short while later, a woman showed up and sat down with them. She was beautiful, well built, a blonde. Walker asked Abbott if she liked the woman's looks. And Abbott said she did.

"Sometimes, I do anything I want to," Walker said.

He leaned over and whispered something to the woman, then turned to Abbott.

"Touch her," Walker said, and Abbott leaned over and patted the woman's arm. "Not there," he said, "between her thighs."

And although she laughed and hesitated, Abbott did what Walker said. When dinner was over, she felt exhilarated and excited, and not afraid. She and Walker and the prostitute went to Abbott's apartment, and the three of them had sex. After a while, the woman left and Walker and Abbott stayed up until morning, making love, but also talking. She told him everything, all of her longings, everything she wanted to do. And he encouraged her. He listened as no one before him ever had. And more than that, it was clear he understood. He guaranteed her that everything she wanted at Clarke could be hers. They made, in that moment, a pact between them, and so it began. By the time she returned to work the next day, she knew that everything in her life had changed, and for the better. In the years since, as she had inevitably taken over the hospital, Walker had simply continued on in his unpredictable way. Together they did the work she wanted done at Clarke, and in return she joined him to experience and witness his extremes in sex.

Walker came into the living room. Abbott could tell immediately he was drunk. She'd never seen him quite like that before. He carried an open bottle in his hand, which he put on the low living room table. He waved his hand over it as if making an incantation.

"Help yourself," he said.

She sat down on the big chair across from him. He always seemed to know what he wanted, or needed, to do. But now he looked uncertain, not only intoxicated, but something more; lost and worn. He took a glass from her cabinet and poured himself another drink. His hand brushed the pocket of his jacket. He reached in and pulled out a small rubber-topped bottle, and a capped syringe.

"What's that?" Abbott asked.

"Demerol—the physician's version of alcohol. What we have access to, we use. We're the true junkies, don't you know? Not that alcohol needs improving." He laughed.

He picked up the syringe and with quick practiced movements, uncapped the tip, turned the bottle upside down, and cradled it gently in his palm. He did everything with one hand, tapping the needle down through the rubber. The liquid in the bottle was water-clear, and a bit of it flowed up into the syringe.

He rolled the bottle through his fingers, moving the liquid back and forth in waves across the smooth round glass. The glass caught sun from the living room window like sparkling fine crystal.

"Look at that," he said. "Someone built this thing just to hold shit, and made a jewel out of it. What a glorious fucking accident everything is."

He went to the window. They were on the thirty-second floor, and there were no buildings between them and the river. The penthouse window was large, all one pane, and he stood there for a minute, squinting into the light.

"Bright," he said softly to himself.

He put the syringe and bottle down on the sill, and she worried for a minute, improbably, that someone might see the drug. He unbuttoned his shirt and took it off. As if he'd started a mechanical movement he no longer controlled until complete, he then took off his pants and shoes. He ran a hand down the hair of his chest, flattening it, then lightly felt his penis. It was half-erect. Abbott assumed he wanted her and she wasn't surprised when he turned to her and said, "Take your clothes off." It was what he said next that surprised her: "If you want to."

She looked at him. He stood up straight, his arms more thickly muscled than the rest of him, his stomach still flat, his chest tight, all of him in great shape for his age. She felt a touch of desire as she looked, but only faintly, then gone. He was troubled. She wondered why. Sex was always easy for him, but now he seemed indecisive. He leaned against the sill and picked up the bottle and syringe.

"Come on," he said. "I brought enough for two."

She drew back. He liked to see her extend herself, she knew, tread anxiously into areas she hadn't previously explored. But she'd never known him to use drugs before. She forced herself to stay calm. She wondered if he was trying to frighten her. But he didn't reach out for her, or even look at her. He didn't seem to care if she was there. The syringe was loaded with liquid. He stuck it effortlessly into his left arm.

"We're good at this," he said. "Don't even have to tie off. I can find the vein through two layers, no palpation. Just sight and slight feel. Look, here's another one."

He probed a short distance away on the underside of his arm, and thrust the needle in again, depressing the plunger, and discharged the rest of the liquid into his vein. She watched him for some sign of the effect of the drug. She didn't know what to expect. He slumped for a moment.

But then he looked up and his eyes were red and wide, his expression not dulled or peaceful at all.

In the past few weeks, she realized now, she'd noticed the beginning of this change in him. At the hospital, she had seen him come out of a room on the Pediatrics ward and lean against a wall for a minute. He seemed upset, as if whatever had gone on in there had bothered him. That was unusual. The next day, someone told her he had yelled at a resident. As good as Walker was known to be with patients, he was even better with the residents. He was their one role model at Clarke. Either the resident he'd yelled at was a particularly large challenge, or something about Walker had changed. She had also gotten calls about his ER coverage. The attending coverage was chronically thin and inept, but Walker had always helped fill the gaps. Lately, he hadn't been available when called. That had never happened before.

She looked at him naked, resting against the sill, reduced to playing with alcohol and injecting drugs. He was doing something extraordinarily dangerous, it seemed to her, in the ordinary setting of her own apartment. He was skydiving, letting himself fall freely, seeing what he could endure. But he was doing it with her, in front of her eyes. She wouldn't plummet with him, she vowed. He was an interruption to the process of living, she thought. That was the excitement he offered her. Four years ago, her life needed that. Today, it didn't. He could have the sanctuary of her apartment, for a while, if that's what he needed. But she made a firm decision he could no longer have her. She left the room. She left him alone with his changes. She didn't think he noticed her at all.

C H A P T E R

22

I suspected there was something wrong with the antibiotics and morphine at Clarke, but I needed to prove it. I had to have the drugs tested in a lab. I thought that with Molly's help we could do it at Clarke, but I was wrong. She said the job wasn't as simple as it sounded, that most hospitals weren't equipped to do that kind of lab work. She said we needed a chemist and she had one in mind, her undergraduate chemistry professor at the University of Pennsylvania. She called him and didn't have to describe much of what she wanted before he agreed to help.

The chemistry building at Penn was mostly labs. The corridors had shower nozzles set in the ceiling with big red signs overhead saying "In Case of Accident." There were "Hazardous Materials" signs on the doors. The man who let us in was tall and thin, but more noticeable than that was his enthusiasm. His manner made him seem much younger than he probably was.

"Dan Bailes," he said, shaking my hand.

Molly thanked him for seeing us on such short notice. He said, cheerily, "This sounds pretty interesting. What have you got?"

I handed him our collection of drugs. He walked us over to a long rectangular table with a slate top. He reached into the bag and pulled out the five vials of antibiotics and the plastic IV sack of morphine. He laid them out and looked at the labels.

"Five antibiotics and some morphine," he said. "But I guess if all you had to do was read the labels, you wouldn't be here, right?"

He pulled over a stool and sat down. "So tell me, what do you need?"

I told him my suspicion that the drugs had been tampered with in some way. "What we need to know is whether what's supposed to be in those containers is in there. And if not, what is? And we need to know it in as definite a way as possible and end up with a document, some written proof of the results. Can you do that?"

"No problem," he said. "For definite, we look right at the molecules. As for documentation, follow me. I'll show you a pair of very capable machines."

We followed him over to some tables set against a wall. The wall itself was dotted with more electrical outlets than I'd ever seen in one place. On the tables were big metal boxes the size of television sets side by side.

"This one," he said, pointing, "is what's called a chromatograph, on which we do a test called HPLC, or high performance liquid chromatography. It separates mixtures into their separate parts." He looked at Molly and winked. "Now I'm sure you remember all this, right?"

She grinned. "Absolutely," she said.

He turned back to me. "And this one," he pointed to another device next to the first one, "is a mass spectrometer, the tool that really tells us exactly what a substance is."

He slit the bags open with a small knife, poured the powders into flasks, and added distilled water. He placed each flask on a tripod and used the silent motion of magnets to stir the solution. In each bottle, the water formed a tiny rotating sea into which the grains of the drugs steadily disappeared.

One by one, he held each flask up to a bright overhead lamp. He nodded and frowned as he examined them. When he placed the last one on the table, he looked at us.

"Whatever these are, they're all dirty." He leaned one bottle on its side in the palm of his hand and motioned us over. "Look here," he said, pointing to something with a forefinger. There was a tiny smudge on the inside of the glass.

"Contaminated!" Molly said. Her tone was pure disgust. "These are all powdered IV solutions. The drug has to dissolve totally. If it doesn't, it'll either clot in the needle and the drip won't work or, worse, it'll clot in the patient. I can't believe it." She was outraged. "Damn, I've given patients that stuff!"

The fact that drugs were dirty at a place like Clarke didn't surprise me, even if it did her. But we still didn't know what was in the vials, aside from dirt. "You can run the tests despite the dirt, right?"

"Sure," Dan said. "That's the next step."

He took the bottles over to the machines. Syringes and needles lay in a holder. It seemed odd to me to see syringes there, with no patients in sight. Those were the swords doctors wielded and patients feared. Here in the lab they were just tools, like screwdrivers or wrenches. Dan used a syringe to draw fluid samples from the bottles and injected them through rubber ports in the machines. The instruments hummed to life. The noise they made was like static on a tiny radio, almost too faint to hear.

There was a clear glass tube on the left side of each machine. "If you look closely, you can see the drug sample make its way down the tube," Dan said. "Every substance known has its own rate of descent through the luminescence, makes its own trail in its own time. No two rates are equal. That's how substances are identified."

The three of us stood there, bent over, watching for several minutes as the liquids slowly flowed. To me, it was like watching slime race. But the professor saw things I didn't.

"Interesting," he said.

"What?" I asked.

"Well, you gave me five vials of antibiotics, each labeled with a different name. But I can tell you already that according to the chromatograph four of them are the same. They're identical. That means at least three of them can't be what they're labeled."

I looked over at Molly. If dirt had made her angry, I wondered how she'd feel about this. Major antibiotics given to patients at Clarke every day, and at least three of them were not what they were supposed to be.

There was some great and terrible scam going on at Clarke, and here was the physical proof. It hadn't taken much work in the lab to uncover it, either. The scheme was so thinly disguised that all you had to do was look. The perpetrators depended for their success on operating in a world in which no one was ever looking. Bailes was still studying the machine.

"The fifth drug contains a different substance," he said. "And the morphine shows two descent times, which means two substances. Assuming one of them is actually morphine, it's been mixed with something else. We'll know in a few minutes what they all are."

"So the morphine's been cut?" I asked.

"It's not pure. We don't know yet what's in there."

"Can we find out, for all of them?"

He nodded. "It's being done, as we speak." He pointed at the second and larger of the boxes in each pair. "The separated samples go automatically into the spectrometer. It's like a small radiation chamber, where electrons bombard the molecules and the pattern the electrons make as they pass through appears in the form of a graph. A graph for every known substance on the planet is stored in a computer data base at the National Institutes of Health in Bethesda. Once we have our graphs come up here, we can connect to the NIH computer by modem. The computer will make a match between one of our graphs and one of theirs. And bingo, that identifies all of your drugs."

Graphs started appearing on computer screens on the front of the lab's spectrometers. He typed on the keyboard and I heard the muted sound of a phone ringing and then the whistle of a modem connection being made.

"We're hooked up to NIH," he said. "It could take anywhere from a few minutes to half an hour." A minute later the terminal beeped.

"Wow," he said. "That was quick." He looked at the screen. "Of course. It started with the morphine. An easy match. They always check the narcotics first."

Even scientists were thinking like cops these days. The cursor was writing messages on the screen, strings of numbers as well as regular words.

"There is morphine in there. But not much. There is also milk sugar. I can't give you an exact breakdown."

He didn't have to. Milk sugar was the standard filler narcotics were cut with for street sale. Neither the junkies nor the patients at Clarke were getting full-strength relief. The computer beeped again.

"Another match," Dan said. He sat down. "Here's what four of your antibiotics are."

The word on the screen was a pretty familiar one: penicillin. Then the cursor wrote another word I recognized: ampicillin.

"Fast matches because they're all antibiotics," he said. "Pretty strange. Someone's substituting antibiotics for your antibiotics."

I didn't get it and I said so. "Why would anyone do that?"

"Money," Molly said, quietly. "What's supposed to be in those vials are some of the most expensive medications we have, first-line antibiotics, used only IV, for inpatients. Penicillin and ampicillin, on the other hand, are old-timers, no longer under patent, and very, very cheap. It's the difference between a few dollars a dose and a hundred dollars a dose. The old standbys are still used because they work in lots of cases. But they're no substitute for the newest ones."

"It makes sense," I said. Huge amounts of money at stake and all the victims poor. That always helps. "Extremely high volume, large price differences. But if the new drugs are better, wouldn't the switch be noticed?"

"I hate to say this, but not necessarily." Her voice was flat and hard. "I didn't notice." She paused, then went on. "If we put a patient on an expensive antibiotic, it's because the bacteria we've identified wouldn't respond as well to cheaper meds like penicillin or ampicillin. But once you put a patient on the expensive drugs, if the patient doesn't improve, you figure it's because the bacteria are especially resistant, perhaps because the patient's immune system is compromised or that the patient's still sick for other reasons. And sometimes the medications just don't work, and we never know why." She looked burdened by what she'd said. "God knows what's happening in that place. There are patients who probably died because they didn't get the right drug."

I asked Bailes for a written report. He said he'd send one to me right away, and in the meantime gave me the printouts from the tests. I wasn't sure what the next step would be, but I needed full access to Clarke's patient files. I told Molly, and she said she'd do whatever it took. There was no hesitancy now.

When we got back to the hospital, she went into one of the resident coatrooms and found me a white coat and an ID tag. We went together to medical records. She introduced me to the clerk there, saying I was working with her on a project. The woman didn't seem to care, and after a few minutes Molly left me alone, and I had all the access I needed.

I wanted to track the course of the patients given the mislabeled drugs, but that might be most of the patients at the hospital, so I limited it to a one-month period. In searching, I might come across another pattern, something else in the records, some treatment, some procedure, some indication of another scam. The antibiotics and morphine were being cut so openly, it was likely other things were being done, too.

The first twenty case files had nothing. As with Taft, as with most others, many patients had complaints about constant pain. Those on antibiotics were usually given one of the five drugs we'd identified. The twenty-first patient file was different. An old woman with kidney problems had been given an antibiotic called amikacin, which was not one of the five. Her pain medication was also different—Percocet, not morphine.

I couldn't tell whether her medical course differed from the others, but there were no nursing notes on her chart indicating she had complained of pain. That was unusual. Her attending physician was Dr. Walker. I recalled my first look at patient records a few weeks earlier; a very small number of them listed antibiotics other than the five. There were so few, I hadn't even bothered to notice which doctors wrote those prescriptions.

Attached to the old woman's chart was a "social work/discharge planning note," the type I'd seen previously on several other charts, including Taft's. The note said: "Pt. is a 77-year-old white female admitted for kidney problem. Will need continual nursing care. Patient is widowed, previously lived alone. Plan: screened and accepted for transfer to Brook Hall Convalescent Center."

Eight hours and two hundred cases later I'd found a pattern. Most of the patients had been put on one of the five antibiotics and given morphine for pain. But eighteen patients had been treated with different antibiotics. All eighteen were tended by Walker. None of them had been given morphine; the eleven who needed pain medication received Percocet. And those eleven had not complained of constant pain.

Molly was right. Walker was an exceptional doctor. He treated only a small percentage of the patients at Clarke but everyone under his care got better treatment—at least as far as medications went—and had less pain.

I needed to photocopy the records, but it was hopeless expecting a working copier at Clarke outside of administration. That meant I'd have to leave with the files. I didn't particularly want to steal records from a hospital, but I needed them. I took the page or two I needed to copy from each of the two hundred charts. I'd make copies and return the originals as soon as I could. I decided to sign the records out under the name of the resident whose coat and ID Molly had given me. I scrawled the signature badly enough to make it unreadable, and walked out. It was as easy getting out as it had been getting in. I took off the coat and tag as soon as I turned the corner, and left them on a chair outside a patient room. I took another minute to find a large file folder to put the papers in. I was on my way to the lobby when I ran into Carter, the security guard Abbott had called into her office. Bad timing, I thought, feeling the weight of the files under my arm.

"You haven't come to me for any help," he said. "I guess you've been getting around okay on your own."

I would have walked away but he kept himself in front of me. He was only standing and talking, but it felt as if he wanted to fight.

"I probably have the wrong attitude about reporters," he added. "I've always thought that you guys make up your facts as you go along." Then he took a long look at the file folder I was holding, as if he somehow knew what I had. He grinned. "But maybe you actually do some work. Maybe I should just follow you around, see exactly what you've been up to."

"Does this mean I'm under arrest? I didn't know security guards could do that." In fact, he didn't have the legal right to search me. Still, I was surprised when he didn't try. Instead, he laughed, then he stepped aside. "You'll see me around," he said, and walked off.

I took my package and drove to Temple University, where I found a photocopying machine I could use myself. I was well into the second hour of mindless copying, just finishing up, when it hit me. Maybe what was wrong was indeed in the records. I just hadn't seen it until now.

Walker was the chief of critical care at Clarke. He was always around the hospital, very involved, and spent time with patients—those were some of the reasons Molly thought he was so good. He was the only doctor I'd run across who didn't give patients the five mislabeled antibiotics. That was also good. Patients seen by Walker were getting the better drugs. But if none of those patients was getting the mislabeled drugs, then Walker must have known there was something wrong. And if he knew, then he must be involved in the scam, or, at the very least, he was allowing it to go on.

Yet I wondered why Walker would bother to protect a handful of patients if he was callous enough to let hundreds of others get hurt. Despite the scam, he managed to handle patients on whom he consulted in his own way. The thieves left those patients alone. And it wasn't as if he had a separate luxury floor where he treated his family and friends. The patients he saw were the same charity cases and neighborhood folks as everyone else. It didn't make sense.

One other large question also involved Walker. Twenty-seven patients treated by him had discharge planning notes in their files recommending transfers to Brook Hall Convalescent Center. They were all single with no family. Most of them were elderly. Twelve of those patients had been transferred to Brook Hall in the past three months, twelve signed out by Walker. He was the only doctor to sign transfer orders to Brook Hall, as far as I could tell. I wondered if the transfers were part of another scam. The explanations weren't in the records. I'd drive out to the nursing home tomorrow. Maybe the twelve patients could tell me what was going on.

CHAPTER 23

She ran most of the way to Walker's office. When she got to the door she stopped, and he waved her in. Molly caught her breath, then approached his desk slowly, sitting down in the big cushioned chair. She wasn't sure what to tell him. She looked around the room as she waited for the words to come. The office was a decent size, but seemed small because the shelves overflowed with books. Hanging from the bottom of one shelf and across the entire lower wall was a series of anatomy illustrations in red pencil and ink. She knew Walker had done them himself.

"There's something wrong, Molly." He leaned back and gave her his full attention.

"Yes," she said. "There's a problem."

She knew he was used to residents dropping in. Catching Walker for corridor consults was a resident's best hope around Clarke. He was one of the only senior doctors who was willing to listen, often at exactly the times when residents were most desperate, and felt most overwhelmed.

She told him what she and Gray had discovered in the lab.

He listened attentively as she gave him every detail. When she was finished, he stood up. "Come with me," he said.

Abbott was going over paperwork at her desk when she saw Walker and Molly Hale walk in. He had the same arrangement at the office as he had at her home: complete access. He hadn't specifically asked for it, but gradually, over the years, she had let others know that Walker was one of the people she would always see. In the past few months her feelings had changed, but her policy had not. She would have preferred that the administrative barriers that kept others away also barred Walker, but that was a difficult correction to make.

Abbott recognized Hale with annoyance. It wouldn't be a pleasant visit. She'd had two previous encounters with the woman, and both had been bad. Hospital policies Abbott had mandated—and finished with, from her point of view—had been questioned on both occasions, raising tensions among the staff. Hale was one of those people who believed that because she saw a problem and because she was sure she was right, she insisted things had to change, the problem be solved her way. She's obviously found another issue, Abbott thought, wondering why Walker was with her.

"Please have a seat," Abbott said.

Abbott expected Walker to take the lead, but he conveyed nothing. She looked the woman over, accustomed as she was to seeing Walker with prostitutes when he visited her. The resident looked tired, and clearly didn't pay much attention to her appearance. She was beautiful in a natural way, Abbott thought, and no doubt desirable to Walker.

Molly spoke first. "We have a serious problem at the hospital. It has to do with the drugs, antibiotics and morphine in particular. I think the supply's been tampered with—"

Abbott interrupted. "You mean someone's been stealing drugs?"

Molly shook her head impatiently. "I went to a lab and had some drugs tested. Five antibiotics, all new, first-line—Amigalycin, Cedrahyphinal, Deniphacylin, Koradraxate, Prinontocin." She counted them off on her fingers. "And morphine sulfate, one of our major pain meds. Every single antibiotic was wrong. The vials didn't contain what the labels said. And the morphine was so dilute it's like sugar. We tested unused samples, factory-capped, and morphine straight from an IV prep."

Abbott pulled a pad in front of her, and took notes. She asked Molly to spell out the names of all of the drugs, and after she was finished, she read what she had written, and asked if she'd gotten it right.

"We had this happen once before," Abbott said. "A year before I arrived, five years ago, there was a foul-up at the lab of one of our major suppliers, and we received a large batch of bad drugs. There was a recall, but for several days before the problem was detected patients actually took these things. I was absolutely shocked. I can't say for sure that's what happened this time, but we'll test our total supply immediately, and we'll have the suppliers in here stat."

"That'll take time, though," Molly said. "In the meantime, some of us could rewrite the orders, switch the pain meds to Percocet or something else." She turned to Walker to see what he thought, but he didn't say anything.

"That's not necessary," Abbott said. "I really mean I'll get on this instantly. We'll have our suppliers here in an hour, and all of the medications replaced, first the morphine, then the antibiotics. I guarantee you, I'll take care of this. Okay? I'm really glad you came to me right away. Thank you."

Molly looked at Walker but he still had no response.

"That makes sense," Molly said. "I'll be around if you need me."

Abbott asked Walker to stay, alone, so she could find out more about what Molly knew. Surprisingly, he said he was busy and left without talking to her.

When he was gone, Abbott picked up the phone. She got Gilbert right away.

"You know you warned me about the doctors here being a problem. Well, it's happened."

She'd already decided to lose these particular drug schemes. She had a dozen other ways to replace the income, and could come up with a hundred more if she had to. It was Walker that worried her. He was too unpredictable.

"Who?" Gilbert asked.

"His name is John Walker," she said. "And he's no idiot. He's the chief of critical care, the most respected doctor at Clarke, and he's been around a long time. He'll be hard to deal with." Having said that much, Abbott hesitated. If she told Gilbert that she and Walker were personally involved, Gilbert might decide she was also a risk.

"Look," Gilbert said, his voice weary. "I need to know everything you know about him and what he knows." He sounded as if he regretted the energy she'd made him expend in spelling it out.

She told him everything about Walker and Molly and what the two of them had said and done. She read the information from her notepad, leaving out none of the details.

"I don't see why we have to end the drug deal," Gilbert said. "If we handle those two, we have no other problems, do we?"

"It's not worth the risk, absolutely not," Abbott said. "If the two of them know, others might find out. Why take chances? We put this one to bed, and go on to the next."

"Okay, okay," Gilbert said. "I'll get you new supplies right away. And I'll also have a talk with Dr. Walker and his friend."

She had confidence in Gilbert. He was a professional, and she knew he had dealt with situations like this many times. He couldn't be handling the street end of the drug scheme without some ability to cope with intrusions. He was less likely to use violence than to use threats and payoff. But whatever he did, it might make for a clean break between her and Walker. She might lose a profitable drug scheme, but at the same time she might also conveniently lose Walker. Perhaps the day hadn't been so bad, after all.

CHAPTER 24

He liked the silence of the place at night. He always had. At night, the hospital, like most things in the world, slowed. It was quiet, but not where he needed quiet most. Within. He couldn't work and would have left hours ago but Walker wasn't sure where he wanted, or needed, to go. Nothing made him feel right these days. Not even drugs, not even sex.

He fingered the small glass bottle in his pocket, then took it out and placed it on the desk in front of him. He twisted off the rubber top and leaned over so he could smell the ether. For a second he felt dizzy, then pulled his head back, out of range of the odor. He stared again at the bottle. A few drops put you to sleep for a couple of hours. A mouthful puts you to sleep forever. The thought had crossed his mind before. He replaced the cap and put the bottle in his pocket. He sat back in his chair, feeling totally lost.

The door to his office was made of old wood, and it had three small, narrow, rectangular windows in the top half. From top to bottom the panes caught light differently, the dirt-distorted glare of hospital neons shining in from the still hallway. He absorbed himself in the colors and shadows, the abstractions of glass and wood. His sense of sadness grew. He grunted as if he'd been struck and the sound was so loud and clear he thought it came from somewhere else. He cupped his hands at the back of his head, his head turned up. His gaze met the high ceiling, and alone, of everything around him, it was clean and smooth and white. He filled himself with the sight of it. He felt isolated, bodiless, numb. He was suddenly, improbably convinced, against all logic, that he had already killed himself and that no one knew.

He had always thought his problem was fear. If he could make himself fearless, he could survive. The recent secret nighttime encounters with Molly in the resident rooms had taught him it wasn't fear that could destroy him, it was love. If her mere presence evoked such intensity and yearning, what would it feel like if she looked and touched and spoke with him of her own will? He hadn't realized it until now, but meeting her was the most important moment in his life. She made him feel complete. But now he also knew how incomplete he was. She's death for me, he thought. He wouldn't let her go. Because unless he found a way to quiet the pain within, he couldn't go on. He had told the residents many times that pain alone could kill. It was true.

Someone was at the door. The sight of another person startled him, as if he had been roused from a dream. He sat up straight and watched as a man pushed open the door and came in. He was taller than Walker, strongly built and young, perhaps in his early thirties. He looked confident and Walker marveled at the sight of such confidence, recalling what it felt like to be that way and wondering idly if it was something he could achieve again. The man wore a good suit and his appearance marked him, to Walker's eyes, as a businessman, perhaps a drug company rep. The only other possibility was that he was a relative of a patient, unlikely for Clarke, dressed as he was.

"Dr. Walker?" he asked.

When Walker did no more than nod, the man went on with enthusiasm just as if Walker had greeted him like a friend. His behavior settled the issue. Drug rep. Only people accustomed to being avoided were capable of unflagging enthusiasm in the face of disinterest.

"I'm Brandon Gilbert, from Rex. I've met you at several conferences but I don't know if you remember me. I wonder if you have a few minutes."

The man had already settled himself in as well as possible, both hands leaning for support on the back of the armchair. If Walker wanted to leave he would have to push past him. But Walker still didn't know what he wanted to do. Even deciding not to talk to the man seemed an effort. He wondered what came next and whether it would offer some measure of relief. Moments passed in silence. We are both uncertain, Walker realized, despite his confidence and the shattering of mine. Something is imminent, he thought. He felt it strongly. He only meant to take a breath but it turned into something else, a long sigh.

"Are you all right, Doctor?"

Walker stood up and the man stepped back.

"What is it you want?" Walker was surprised by the surge of anger he felt.

"I'm sorry if I've interrupted you . . ."

"Tell me what you want."

"I spoke with Nancy Abbott earlier today about the problem you came across with some of our drugs."

Walker nodded. He understood immediately that Abbott had sent Gilbert because she now perceived Walker as a threat. He wondered if it was because of the recent scene in her apartment, or if it was merely inevitable that she would come to distrust and fear him. He knew what she and Gilbert cared most about—the schemes, the money, the position she had at Clarke. Walker was indifferent to all of that. He had almost reached the point of ending his life, of removing himself from the world of routine problems and fears and plans. But he wouldn't let others decide that for him. First he would deal with Gilbert, and perhaps Abbott, too. Then he would deal with his personal problems. That decision made, he felt a bit more like his old self.

He opened his desk drawer and saw several bottles. Struck by a sudden thought, he picked up a bottle and tucked it in his pocket. But he couldn't use it here. The man was too strong. The lab was right down the hallway, he thought, and it was quiet and empty at night.

"I have some work to do in the lab," Walker said. "If you want to talk with me, we'll have to go there."

He pushed past Gilbert, who followed him to the lab.

"Haven't been in one of these places since college chem," Gilbert said. "Always feel like I ought to put on a fright wig and white coat. Did that once in college, actually. Fortunately, the professor had a sense of humor."

Walker nodded politely at the chatter. He looked around the lab, went over to the big two-door refrigerator in the corner. He needed to act, and the need inspired him, brought him energy and life. He carefully filled a big box with some chunks of dry ice. The box was deep and the light smoky haze didn't rise above the box's lid.

"So what will we do about the drug problem?" Walker asked, picking up a small knife and using it to shave the ice down into layers of sparkling slivers.

"That's what I want to discuss with you," Gilbert said. "We're very upset about it and we want to resolve the problem."

Walker kept at it with the knife. As he did, the haze rose, and Gilbert leaned over to see.

"What is that stuff?" he asked.

"Dry ice," Walker explained. "Keeps cell samples colder than regular ice. Even in the refrigerator, it keeps things colder."

Gilbert nodded. "I'll take care of the bad batch of drugs," the salesman said. "We appreciate your discovering the problem. We'd like to recognize your help in some way. There's a medical conference in the Caribbean coming up, something we sponsor. Would you be interested? There are also some research protocols we're funding at the moment."

The man was merely doing business, protecting what he had any way he could. The drug scheme must be working well for them, Walker thought. Abbott had never told him the dimensions of it, but he knew that money was the main way she soothed her fears. It worked like that for most people. You made as much as you could, you strengthened your family with it, you passed it on to your kids, or made or bought things to outlast your limited years. It was a good way to pretend you were never going to die. But it had never worked for Walker.

"I'm sure we can reach an arrangement," Gilbert said, encouragingly.

Walker smiled pleasantly and then threw the box of chipped ice in Gilbert's face. The drug rep's head was surrounded for a moment by a perfect circle of smoke, a thin airy sphere, and through it Gilbert's face could be glimpsed as if on a screen. He was jerkily opening and closing his mouth to get a breath, frantically rubbing his eyes. He yelled in protest. He tried to pull the pieces off and Walker realized Gilbert did not know that solidified carbon dioxide bonds to flesh. As he pulled the ice from his face and neck he took the skin off as well. The frozen numbing of sensation—another of the substance's properties—made him unaware of the damage.

Walker meanwhile grabbed a syringe and the bottle he'd taken from his desk. It was a new surgical anesthetic, a drug that removed all sensation and muscular control while leaving the patient conscious and alert. The drug was often used for scoping, when patients couldn't tolerate the discomfort of a tube going down. Walker grabbed Gilbert's right arm and held him above the elbow. His fingers folded up the skin, making an entry point for the needle. He pushed in the syringe.

In seconds, Gilbert lost control of his muscles. Like a tower of blocks built too tall, he came tumbling down. His knees slowly bent and his legs gave way, and Walker caught him just before he collapsed on the floor.

He gently lay the man down flat, cradling his head. Gilbert's eyes were active. Walker noted the pupils already wide with shock and fear. The drug's effects were primarily on large muscle and fine movements in the extremities, but it left autonomic functions intact. Gilbert could still breathe and his heart continued to beat; everything else was frozen. At this dosage, the condition would probably last five minutes. Another injection now could kill him. But Walker had already decided to kill him, so in a sense, it didn't matter. On the other hand, he wasn't ready for Gilbert to die. For one thing, he wondered, as confident as Gilbert had been before, how much he now felt fear.

He went out to the hallway to get a gurney, wheeled it into the lab, then locked the wheels in place. It took considerable effort to hoist Gilbert up onto the narrow bed. Walker paused for a moment to steady himself. His hands were trembling. He had a sense of crossing some boundary he'd established long ago. When he killed, the victims were always sick, or weak, or alone and out of place, like the resident Chaney. They were people without emotional connection to the world, or in some kind of pain. Death was close to them already. This was different.

The man's eyes, the only part of him capable of any expression, looked up at Walker. He's calming himself as best he can, Walker thought. He was beginning to move. Walker reached for the drug and filled the syringe again. He leaned over and picked another spot for injection, and stuck the needle in. Not too much, he reminded himself. The drug, like all things, required balance. It was the stillness, the helplessness of living he sought in the man, not the passivity of the dead.

His gaze fell on a box on a table. He opened it. Inside were shrink-wrapped pressure-treated bandages. He had used this sort of bandage before. They were instantly self-sealing, extremely adhesive on contact. He opened one of the packages and turned toward Gilbert. The very act of unveiling a new piece of medical equipment widened the man's eyes.

On impulse, Walker fit the bandage to Gilbert's mouth. The material expanded and adhered, becoming a new plastic layer of skin. Bent low to see, Walker noticed a new intensity and arousal, the struggle for life. Gilbert's nostrils flared to breathe. Because of the drug, there was no physical pain, no feeling at all, but there was full mental awareness. How much could a man experience and stay sane, imprisoned in his own body, unable to feel or to speak?

He grabbed another bandage and held it over Gilbert's face. He brought his own eyes as close to the man's as he could, looking within.

"It won't hurt," he said.

He pressed the artificial flesh over Gilbert's nose, the material locking itself, unremovable, closing off the last entry point for lifesaving air. Walker placed his hand on Gilbert's chest and felt the straining movements as he heaved and struggled to use the last air trapped within him. And then all motion stopped.

The eyes that stared up at him now were blood red. And even as Walker's senses returned, and he prepared to take the gurney to the morgue, he looked at the man's still face and saw instead a vision, clear and cold. He recalled with great clarity all the times he had killed. He saw the image of himself, and on his face at the moment of their deaths was a grin. It was the same grin he had seen on his mother's face, so many years before. He understood everything now. Since the earliest days he could remember he had lived with the fear that she could leave him, even that she could kill him. He had learned to feel better by emptying himself, and by being close to people when they died. But in killing them, he realized, he had become like her. He looked at the dead man on the gurney. The familiar death face stared him in the eye, and there was no escape.

He had killed. Yet he felt no relief at all. In all the weeks since things had been coming apart, his only intervals of true comfort were in the arms of his sleeping lover. Even seeing her earlier today had brought him respite. He wanted that feeling again. If nothing else could help him, she still could. He needed to be with her. When he found her, his agony would end.

CHAPTER 25

They called it a convalescent center. Brook Hall Convalescent Center. Even simple euphemisms like "nursing home" were obviously sometimes too plain. I'd driven the stone-walled roads of the Main Line to get here, passing the manicured gardens and set-back estates of towns whose names, at least in Philadelphia, had the sound of money: Bryn Mawr, St. Davids, Devon. The nursing home was a one-story ranch-style building, red brick, with lots of glass, not at all institutional. As I approached it from the parking lot, I could see green plants through the wide windows. A dozen people were sitting on the patio by the front door, and all of them were watching me. I figured they had little else to do. One of the patients caught my eye, and I nodded and said a casual hello. Then I went in.

There was a sweet-looking young woman sitting behind a desk at the reception area. She didn't question me, not even with her eyes, just smiled me on by. Obviously visitors were welcome. Behind her was an office, visible through glass doors and glass walls. There were file cabinets right behind the doors. It was a small place. The building was arranged like a wheel; at the hub was a nursing station, and along each spoke were patient rooms. I walked toward the station. It was four in the afternoon; not many visitors were around.

I stopped at the wooden outer ring of the station. It was low, but solid. I leaned against it, and waited. It didn't take long.

"Yes?" said a nurse, in a warm, helpful tone.

"I'm looking for a patient named Nancy Haupt." That was the first name on my list. The nurse didn't even bother to look it up. She seemed instantly familiar with who was there and who was not.

"We have no patient named Nancy Haupt."

"What about in another corridor?"

"No," she said, "there's no one by that name in the facility unless she's being admitted today."

"Maybe she was here, got sick again, and was transferred out," I said.

She shook her head no with certainty. "Never was here. I'd remember the name."

I looked at my list. "What about Frank Bagwell?"

"No, he's not here either."

"Sandra Stillwell?"

Same shaking of her head, same response.

"They're all on a Medicare list from Clarke Hospital," I explained, answering her unspoken question. "I'm with the state. We're doing a follow-up on nursing home placements from Clarke." I gave her nine more names. She stood there, listened patiently, never changed her answer: a definite no on every name. No one interrupted us while we talked, lost in the litany of names. I wondered how people who were almost real to me one minute could be lost so completely the next. I noticed that several old people were gathered in a small group behind me, a crowd of the persistently curious. The nurse acted as if our new audience made no difference to her. I guess it didn't.

I thanked her and turned to leave. A woman behind me blocked my path. She was slower than me, but knew how to use the angles. There was no avoiding her, which was fine. Officialdom hadn't been much help, maybe patients would be.

"You're looking for somebody?" she asked, her tone friendly and conspiratorial.

"That's right," I said.

She asked me to go through the list again. I did. She listened carefully, and said no, clearly and without hesitation, each time, just like the nurse. We got to the end quickly.

"Anyone else?" she asked.

"Tell me this," I said. "Is anyone here from Clarke Hospital?"

"Clarke?" Her voice rose at the end of the word. "That's in the city."

She thought about it for a minute, then stuck her face a little closer to mine. "No. No one here's from Clarke. Not that I can remember." It wasn't a ringing declaration, but considering what little I'd already seen, I thought it might be true. I thanked her and left, getting by her okay this time.

There was a short stretch of corridor between the nurses' station and the front-office reception area, where the spoke of the wheel curved a bit and the room entrances were slightly less visible to the nurses. When I was out of sight of the station, I stepped inside one of the rooms. I did it on impulse, just to take a look, see whatever was in there, searching for signs of someone from Clarke, whatever they might be.

There were two beds in the room. Some effort had been made to make the room homier than a hospital. Two matching dressers. Two mirrors on the wall. Bulletin boards across from each bed. One of the bulletin boards had several holiday-colored cards, held open in the middle with blue plastic tacks, the writing inside only a signature with no other message, the kind you send when you have to. The bed near that board was empty, although the sheets showed recent occupancy. The bulletin board across from the other bed was totally empty. The bed was not.

What looked to me like a very tall man was set just in the center of the mattress, on his back, the bedding tucked tight around his chest, his hands folded as if in prayer. His white bearded head lay straight back on the center of the pillow, the still precision of his placement masking any signs of life. At first glance, there were none. But the hands, clasped palm to palm fingers up, were moving, just slightly, up and down, like a rocket straining to rise, then settling back in disappointment. Up and down. It was the only sign he was alive.

I moved closer to the bedside, but he took no notice of me. His eyes were open but the stare was fixed. I heard now a shuddering sigh, moved by the same tidal rhythm that rocked his hands. I looked over the landscape of his body, the lines of him smoothed by the sheets like terrain displayed on a map. For some reason I turned around again to look at the room, the empty bed, the entrance out into the hallway. Then I turned back toward the window, the scenery outside a thick row of green bushes, and beyond that the landscaped beauty of a suburban mansion. I was in a still and separate world, outside the main herd, where the dying were stored, along with what remained of their lives, the size and depth and heft and weight of them no longer making any difference. I was looking for people I wanted to talk to, and yet if I'd found them, I'd be talking to them here, in this place, all of us together isolated from the world. But they weren't even here. They were gone, and I had no idea where they could be. I left the room and went to the office.

I gave the list of names to a secretary. She stepped into another office for a few minutes, came out, and told me none of those people were patients here. As I turned to leave, I noticed a big guy standing at the door of the office. He had a familiar look. Not a former cop, this time, but a former jock. Big, but young, without the skills and experience. The way I once had been.

I might have reached a dead end. But it was also possible I hadn't done enough research yet. So I went back to Clarke. I did the simplest thing first. I called patient information from a pay phone, to see if any of the people on my list were still registered as patients at Clarke. None of them were. I knew there had to be administrative hospital records in addition to the medical files. If patients were transferred from the hospital to another facility, there had to be some sort of documentation on paper, forms that recorded the date and time a patient was taken out in a van or ambulance. I went to three offices before I found the custodian of those files. No one at any of the offices asked to see my identification. No one asked who I was. They might have recognized me from my earlier visits or from the time I'd met with Abbott. Or they might have thought I was a doctor. Or maybe they didn't care.

I checked the twelve names on my list against the transfer files. They all came up blank. According to the hospital's own central records, none of those twelve people had been sent to a nursing home—or anywhere else.

So I double-checked my copies of the patient medical files. Nothing there had changed. All twelve charts still said the patients had been transferred to Brook Hall. In each case—and I hadn't taken note of this before—the transfer notes were written by the same social worker, Barbara Wilkens.

I went to the social-work office and asked to see Wilkens. The first person I spoke to said she never heard of her. The second person said the name was familiar, and he looked it up. He told me Wilkens was not on staff at Clarke, but worked there occasionally on a "per diem basis." He gave me her phone number. I called. It wasn't the social worker who answered the phone. It was the operator at Brook Hall Convalescent Center.

By the time I got back to Brook Hall, the friendly receptionist up front was gone for the day and the office was closed for the night. It hardly mattered that Barbara Wilkens wasn't there to talk to me because, the truth was, I didn't really need to talk to her. What I needed was to see the nursing home's patient and financial records. I used a screwdriver to pop the door to the empty office and pry the locks off the file cabinets. The security was bad; the locks were cheap. But these places didn't have to be Fort Knox.

Once I got in, it took less than ten minutes to find all twelve names. There they were, in alphabetical order, along with the other patients registered at Brook Hall. Each of the twelve Clarke patients was bringing in a hundred and fifty dollars a day in Medicare, for the "rent" on their rooms—over a thousand dollars a week per person; over ten thousand a week for the twelve. In addition, there were bills for procedures, for treatment, for all the attendant costs of caring for the very old and ill.

The charts were complete with doctor's signatures. On paper, it was as if the patients were actually out there somewhere walking around, or in their beds. They were getting very comprehensive care, too, I noticed. There were even records for consultations by a psychologist, and notes about behavior problems. The records were neat and clean and flawlessly filed away for inspection at any time. And there'd be nothing amiss to find in these files: no mistakes, no miscalculations, no phony dollar amounts. The only problem—and auditors would never even think to check for this—was that there were no patients by those twelve names in this facility. Somebody was making a lot of money on ghosts. And not just someone at the nursing home. The records showed also that weekly checks for exactly half the Medicare payments were sent to one of the medical companies owned by Nancy Abbott. She was the sole owner of the company. I had no doubt these payments were kickbacks to her, payments for transferring these ghost patients. If she was being very clever about it, then Brook Hall actually bought various products or services from her company. If she wasn't being clever, then it was all, in effect, a straight payment to her. Either way, it was a paper trail that could be nailed solid by a prosecutor making the case. If she made me take it that far.

There was a brand-new, first-rate copier right next to the file cabinets. It took only a few minutes to copy all the files. I was about to put the originals back when I heard a noise in the corridor. I managed only two steps when the office door came flying open. It was the big guy, the ex-jock.

"What in hell are you doing here?" His tone was loud rather than angry. Maybe he was happy to finally have something a big guy like him could do.

"Looking for missing patients," I said. "But it's okay, I found them."

"You broke in there?" He nodded at the open file cabinet.

"As a matter of fact, yes." I held my copies tight. "That's where the patients were. Amazing, isn't it?"

He pulled a blackjack from his side pants pocket, held it up and waved it at me.

"What I should do—" he began, and threatened me by lifting his arm. But he didn't attack. "Just stay there," he said. "I'm calling the police." He kept an eye on me, and walked over to one of the phones.

"Funny thing," I said, holding out the patient files to show him. "I could call the police myself. But I think I'll just leave instead."

I started toward the door. That surprised him. He dropped the phone and moved to cut me off. He first tried to block me, and maybe if he could have filled the whole doorway with his big legs, it would have worked. I think it upset him when I grabbed his shoulders and moved him aside. He let out a word that sounded like a curse, and swung at me with the blackjack at the same time. I was too big a target to get completely out of the way. I took the hit on an upraised arm, and it hurt. Then I grabbed his wrist and shook the jack loose. It fell to the floor. We were about to see who could punch harder when I heard a familiar voice call my name. Michael Carter, Clarke's security chief, was standing by the door.

The guard and I stopped what we'd started, and looked at Carter instead.

"You are such a bad guy," Carter said. He looked happy. I didn't know why. "And such a busy guy. I've been following you as much as I could, the past few days. You break in here, you break in there. You're a real credit to your profession, I'd say."

The other guy obviously knew Carter, but he didn't say anything. Neither did I.

"Let him go," Carter said to the guard. "I know him."

"Yeah," I told the guard, shaking myself free. "We're old friends."

The guard looked confused, but he shrugged and let me go. "He broke in here," the guard said.

"I know that," Carter replied. "And you and I are witnesses. But we're not going to do anything about it right now." He turned to me. "You can go," Carter said. I hesitated. "Go ahead, leave. Free as a bird." He bent over like a Victorian butler and waved his arm at the door. "Because I've got you. Even scummy rags like your newspaper don't allow their reporters to do stuff like this. Go ahead, finish whatever you've got to do. But you'll never get your story in the paper. When your bosses hear how you operate, that'll be the end of your career. I'm looking forward to meeting with them. And then I'll file the charges with police. So go ahead, leave."

He laughed, and I managed to look properly embarrassed and insulted. It wasn't until I got into my car, still clutching my copies of the Brook Hall records, that I finally laughed at the notion that Carter would go to "my editors." But by the time I got home I forgot about Carter completely. I couldn't get my mind off the twelve patients who weren't at Clarke. I had to find them.

CHAPTER 26

I thought about the twelve patients all night. There was documented fraud committed in their names. They would be ideal witnesses, or, at least, I could certainly say that to Abbott. But there was a better reason to track them down. I needed and wanted to find them. Something was wrong. They weren't in Clarke and they weren't at the nursing home. By sunrise, I realized there was another obvious place to check. Their homes.

I looked over the addresses to figure out where I should start and immediately saw there was nothing much to figure. All of the addresses were within a fifteen-block range in north Philadelphia, mostly in the Kensington and Fairhill sections. I knew the streets where I'd be knocking on doors, and I didn't look forward to it. These were among the poorest neighborhoods in the city, bad by anyone's standards, especially from the point of view of the people who lived there. In these blocks were white and Hispanic and black. Fairhill and Kensington offered equal-opportunity despair.

I drove up Broad and the streets kept getting worse the farther up I went. The skyscrapers eventually disappeared, as did the banks and the museums, and though the sky was more visible, which was good in its way, the buildings got older and more rundown. Ordinary things you took for granted about buildings disappeared. Like windows and doors. There were mostly boards where there should have been glass, and doorframes were either missing or replaced by thin sheets of unpainted pine, with locks thrown on.

The billboards changed, too. A typical display was a lawyer's ad with the words "criminal defense" in large letters. There were many ads for bug exterminators, and for cheap wine. There were pharmacies with Mom-and-Pop names, and check-cashing places on every corner. An occasional MAC machine for instant cash, but hardly anyone bold enough to use one. Incongruously, on a huge billboard, was the vision of a blonde woman in a white bathing suit, against a background of sun and sand and water and a big golden bottle of beer. I wondered what marketing whiz had made a deliberate decision to put it there.

I turned right on Lehigh. Everything I saw in the next few blocks made Broad Street, bad as it was, look good. What struck me first was how narrow the streets were, how close together it all was—the doors, the windows, the narrow sidewalks, the people bunched at stoops, the burnt-out cars, the garbage without the cans. It was a big city with small-town shanties, walls as thin as cardboard, that looked like they could be blown down by a stiff wind. And some apparently had been. What was there was dust-covered, dirt-filled, scarred and worn and punished. Philadelphia had some of the nicest houses in America. And some of its worst ghettos.

I found 2712 Cambria, written by hand in Magic Marker at the top of a wooden frame. The midsection of the door was missing, and all that separated the sidewalk from the inside was a three-foot-wide piece of plywood with one nail on each side. I leaned over the top and looked in. The only things I could see were a dark and empty room and some damaged wooden stairs rising up. I called out: "John Rutledge?" My voice was loud but no one answered. I tried again. "Hello? Anyone home?" No response. I waited. Sometimes you had to. A teenage girl whom I hadn't seen when I walked over came up behind me.

"Who you looking for, mister?"

"John Rutledge. I'm a reporter on the *Inquirer*."

The girl's eyes lit up. It was a low flame, the kind that burned on sparse fuel. I recognized the look. Newspapers mean something special in a poor neighborhood. They mean attention; in a world that spends all its time ignoring you, something with power is paying you attention.

"The *Inquirer?*" She spoke with perfect clarity, no jive, no street. "Can you do a story about me?"

I didn't answer, but she had no problem with that.

"You got a television camera?"

"No," I said, "just these." I pointed to my eyes.

She looked at me curiously, even at my eyes.

"Do you know John Rutledge?" I asked. "He's supposed to live here." I held onto the hope that I'd see him come down the stairs, walking firm and steady, healed and straight, poor, whole, and free, and full of explanations to soothe and satisfy my fears.

"You mean the old man?" the girl said.

I nodded. "You know him?"

"Yeah." Her voice was low. "He went to the hospital. Clarke . . ." I saw that she was skittish, reluctant to come to the end of whatever it was she had to say, and tense, like an animal about to flee. I looked at her a moment and tried to understand. And then it hit me. I had it all wrong. It was the other way around. I was the animal, ready to bolt. She was watching me, a human eye-to-eye with a deer. I'd suddenly come out of the woods and was caught in the frozen brightness. She was watching my movements, I realized, the slight tightness in my muscles, the way I stood, and the way I appeared to be preparing to leave. She watched me because I was someone different, someone new. And, for the moment, I was there. And she is right, I thought. I will go running off, because I really am from another place entirely. Not a deer out of the woods, but something stranger. A newspaper reporter, part of a people that goes everywhere they don't belong, just to see. I ignored all that, in my head, if not my heart, and I asked her, just the way reporters always do, another question.

"Do you know anyone else who knows him? Any neighbors?"

"Why you looking for him? He win something?"

"I'm doing a story about Clarke Hospital."

"Never been there," she said, with a wistful tone, as if it was a place worth going. "I been to Temple Hospital once, and my brother's been to Girard."

I had to go in. Just to be sure. I pushed out the plywood; it was easier than pushing open an ordinary door. The first floor was only a small room and an even smaller kitchen, both empty. The place smelled of urine. I went up the stairs. There were three small bedrooms and a bathroom. They were as empty as everything else in the house. The little furniture

I saw was worn and rotted. Whoever John Rutledge was, and however he'd lived, he and his world here were gone.

The girl waited for me at the bottom of the steps. When I came down she said, "Kids break in here a lot. That's why it's like that. They do drugs here." I stopped and looked at her one last time. "But I don't," she said. "Honest, I don't."

"I believe you," I said, and left.

Approaching the second address on my list, I saw a row of connected houses that were burned out. The place I was looking for was apparently one of them. I could still smell smoke, though the fire must have been long ago. I couldn't imagine anyone was in the buildings, but I stuck my head in doorways just to check. The first two were vacant. A group of people stood in the third. They were talking calmly, as if being in there was nothing out of the ordinary. Maybe it wasn't. I couldn't find anything to knock on, so I walked in.

"I'm a reporter from the *Inquirer*. Anyone here know James Parke?"

That started a debate.

"Doesn't ring a bell," one man said to the others, not to me.

"What are you talking about?" an older man responded, with a bit of anger in his voice. "You know him, he lived down the street a couple houses. The old man." He turned then, and looked at me. "He got burned in the fire and they took him to the hospital. An awful sight."

He had the ball rolling by himself. All I did was listen. "He used to work downtown for the city. Had the same job for years. Worked near City Hall."

A few of the others still shook their heads, no. The old man gave them a look, as if finishing an argument without having to use any words. "Why you looking for him?" he asked me.

"I'm doing a story about Clarke Hospital. I need to talk to him about his treatment. Is he around?"

"I told you," the man said. "He went to the hospital. He ain't never come back." His tone was final. I thanked him and left.

Mary Louise Marshall was listed at 2918 North Seventh Street. The address had a door, and a screen, and there was an immediate response to my knock. A young woman opened up.

"Mary Louise Marshall?" I asked, knowing it couldn't be someone that

young but willing to believe her if she said she was. She said she wasn't
Marshall, but she didn't say who she was.

"What's your name?" she asked me.

"Gray," I said, then added the part about being a reporter.

"I know her," the woman said. "She used to live here, but not anymore. She hasn't been here for three months." She paused. I waited for
her to continue. "Went somewhere and left this fine palace all for me."
Her hand was elegant in its motion as she gestured at the house. "Least
it's mine, for now." She was a model of small expectations and humble
assessments, but it had a bitter edge.

"She went to the hospital, to Clarke," I told her. "I thought she might
have come back here."

"I didn't know that," the woman said. She seemed apologetic about not
knowing. "So you're from the newspaper, huh?" She looked at me squinting, as if there was something more to see, and it took a sharper vision.
"Why don't you come in?"

The rich always turn you away. The poor invite you in. Every reporter
who's been around knows that. Reporters aren't looking for money.
They're looking for stories. The rich want to give you neither. The poor
invite you to take whatever you can, and to share something with them,
even if it's only time. I followed her in.

There wasn't much separating the inside of her house from the outside.
As soon as you went through the door you were in her living room. No
porch. No yard. No steps. The room was small and narrow. At the rear
of the room was a small bannister going up to the second floor. Under the
bannister, still part of the living room, was a little kitchen. The major
piece of furniture was a couch, which was just a box with a flat piece of
wood on top, and some cloth on top of that, and all of it looked home-
made. Next to it was a chair. It had a cushion on it, like the chairs street
people make for themselves from whatever's lying around. There was a
small black-and-white TV with rabbit ears pressed up against the front
wall. I started to sit on the couch. She stopped me.

"The chair's more comfortable," she said.

I sat on it.

"So what are you writing about?"

"I'm doing a story about Clarke."

"To make them look good or bad?" she asked, getting to the heart of
the matter.

"Whatever they are."

"If your story's any damn good, the place will look bad." She said it with certainty. And anger.

She was very thin, with dark hair a little more than shoulder length, tied in small tight ponytails. Her eyes were dark, her face small and well-formed. She was worn but pretty, and moved a lot even standing still, as if each part of her had occasional unrelated twitches. Her hands were small but muscled, and her petite size wouldn't have stopped her from forming them into fine fists. The word tough popped to mind.

She saw me looking at her and met my glance. "You notice I do drugs?"

"That's your business," I said.

She nodded, her lips tight, thin, set solid together, determined to do something. I wasn't sure what.

"I know Clarke," she said. "I've been there lots of times. A few months ago, to have a baby." There was no baby in the house, I could tell. No signs of a baby at all.

"They kept telling me to get off drugs." She was getting angrier. She didn't say who "they" were. "I told them I would. I meant it. But the baby came early, and I hadn't stopped the drugs yet." She stood right in front of me, her hands clenched at her sides. "So they wouldn't let me keep my baby." She saw me looking at her and turned away, then paced from wall to wall in the narrow room. "What kind of hospital is that? Said I couldn't have my own baby." She hit the wall with the heel of her hand, her palm open and flat, as if the point wasn't to let off steam or hurt something but to feel the impact herself. It was a hard, merciless blow.

"Treat you like you're nothing," she said. "Not a human being. Think I'm stupid because I'm poor." She bent over, both hands on her head, and rubbed it hard. "I'm not stupid. I know I did drugs, but I have a baby now." She straightened up. "I wouldn't—" She took her hands away.

I thought of telling her about Joe Taft and all the other patients I'd seen, and the dozen men and women I was trying to find. But I didn't. Maybe it would help her to hear about others' miseries. Maybe it wouldn't help at all. I got up to leave.

"I hope you find that woman," she said, "but I don't think you will. Don't trust that place, that's for sure. Something wrong there." I believed she was right about that. "Maybe if you write about it."

I went to the door.

"Write about it," she said again. "Maybe they listen to you." I opened the door, thanked her for her time, and went out.

"What you really ought to do," she yelled at my back as I walked away, and it was the same voice she told truths in, angry as she was, "is write about my baby."

The nine others on my list were also nowhere to be found. By the time I'd finished knocking on all the doors, I knew only one thing—that the world was too ugly, the sheer unending poverty too much to endure. There was a reason people tried hard to not end up in these neighborhoods, and struggled like crazy to get out when they did. It was a man-made hell. It is a given that in some places on this earth, people simply disappear. Philadelphia, whatever its lost virtues in recent times, was not supposed to be one of those places.

I was on the corner of Tenth and Cambria. Years ago I'd been here, as a reporter, and watched three cars full of policemen, lights on high and strobed, as they pulled up to the small, block-square cemetery right there in the middle of the neighborhood. It didn't even look like a cemetery. Looked more like another city street, but surrounded by low iron gates. It would be easy not to notice the small, round gravestones—as if the sacredness had been removed, as if there was nothing special about dying, not in that place.

The night I was there as a reporter, the three youngest cops, full of the obligations that came with low status and little time in, cleared away debris from a corpse, and wrote down details in their books. A dead body had somehow appeared there, unheralded and unburied, having, for its only marker, the usual street-corner brown metal can, full of its perennial fire, the druggie's shield against the cold. That time, years ago, I had sat in my car, running the heater against the chill, glad to be able to sit and observe, glad the cops were there to do their numbed and impossible job. I'd been eager to stay deeper into the night, to ask my questions, to learn a little more about how life ended on that corner, so close to its rightful place, and so far.

Now I was back, no longer a reporter, only pretending to be one, and what was tugging at me deep inside was the growing sense that the dead were all around me but I couldn't see the corpses.

I thought now, looking at the same corner, its small bands of young men still gathered around the garbage cans, that despite all the words and the money into this pocket and that, the mournful sympathies of the politicians and the well-meaning, and the intentions, good or ill, of everyone concerned, not a damn thing about Kensington or Fairhill had changed. However human and straining for dignity in their own way the people I'd just spoken to had been, the conditions of their lives had them anchored like concrete at the bottom of a pit of despair.

And yet, these people—these dozen names on my list—had surely lived here, sorrowfully perhaps, but they'd lived. So where were they? They were not in their rooms at Clarke Hospital. They were not at Brook Hall Convalescent Center. Patient records said they were at the nursing home, and Medicare monies were being collected in their names. But the paper trail said they never left Clarke. Maybe some of them never did.

CHAPTER 27

When I got back to Clarke I found Molly, told her where I'd been, what I'd done, what I still didn't know.

"I think these people are dead," I said. "And someone's using their names to collect insurance money. Hundreds of thousands of dollars. There may be no way to find the people because even if they're buried somewhere, they wouldn't be buried under their real names."

"If they're dead, maybe they're not buried yet," she said. "Maybe they're in the morgue."

"What are the chances of that?"

"Not very good, I would think." Then, hesitantly, she added: "But pretty often we do have bodies downstairs listed as unidentified. They die in the ER, or in ambulances on the way over here, and we keep them, pending some identification. For the homeless, we often get no ID's. We function as one of the city morgues here, so the city brings people in all the time. We could go down there and check, at least records or something."

"How long do they usually keep bodies in the morgue?" I asked.

"It's supposed to be one or two days," she said. "But the truth is, sometimes the unidentifieds stay here for weeks. They're supposed to get picked up by funeral parlors, private or city, and buried. But when there's no family, and no money, no one's in a hurry to do the job."

"Let's try it. Maybe you'll recognize one of them."

"People look very different when they're dead," she said.

I nodded. I showed her the list of names. It was the only memorial I had for them.

She looked it over. "I know most of these names."

I perked up. "Really?"

"It's not unusual. These are all old people, who were pretty sick. They tend to stay in the hospital for a long time. I'm pretty sure I'd have seen most of them for something or other."

"Let's go."

"In the basement, by the lab," she said, and immediately headed off. It was her world. I followed.

The morgue was locked. From the outside it looked like any other room off a hospital corridor. Molly went to locate someone with a key. She came back with a thin, young, balding man who introduced himself to me as Matt, said he was a lab assistant, and then opened the place.

It was a large square room, with lots of shelves and supply closets, doors wide open on all of them, and three large L-shaped metal tables. I stood by the doorway and looked around, while Matt and Molly went to a wall of large silver metal drawers, each with a huge hanging handle.

He noticed I hadn't joined them, and came back over to see what I was looking at. I thought he probably went through this with most of his visitors. It was hard not to stare at the shelf of liquid-filled glass jars, a human brain floating in each. I walked over to one of the long metal tables. It was actually a combination of table and sink. The end near me had a couple of drains built in. The only thing that wasn't metal was a squat thick block of wood, pale maple with a polished gleam, obviously very old, solid and worn.

"For their neck," Matt explained, following my gaze. I glanced down at the U-shaped indentation in the wood block and saw immediately how neatly it would support the neck of a body stretched out flat, the sink conveniently located to catch the excised brains and drain off the blood. His tone was casual, matter-of-fact, full of sure knowledge of exactly how it was in this place death was received and inspected. I liked his detachment, in a way. We usually got too excited about the dead, and not quite frenzied enough about the living. Molly called us over. She wanted to go through the drawers.

There were no visible signs on any of the drawers, and I wondered how you could identify a particular body. Altogether there were thirty-two drawers, eight across, four rows high. Matt seemed uncertain. I realized neither of us had told him just what we had in mind, and up until then he was automatically giving us the tour.

"Are they all full?" Molly asked.

"Eight," Matt replied.

"How do you know which ones have a body?" I wondered aloud.

"I keep track," he said. "But we also have this file." He pointed to a small dull green box of index cards on the bottom shelf on the left wall. I started to open the box, then stopped to get permission. This was his place. Matt saw me look at him; he shrugged. I opened the box. There was a thick sheaf of blanks and a thin pile of filled-in cards. The blanks were for the living. I didn't need to check my list anymore, to match it against the cards. They might have disappeared from this earth, but I carried their names in my head now.

Two of the cards said unidentified white male, one was similarly unknown and female. The other five had names, none of them familiar. We could just check the three unknowns, I thought, but it also made sense to look at the others. Being complete and compulsive had often paid off in my life. There was a small number on the upper left hand corner of each card, but there were no numbers on the drawers.

"Who do you want to see?" Matt asked. Not "which," but "who," I noticed. The dead were still people, at least to him.

"All of them," Molly said, saying the right thing without my having to.

Matt looked at her. He reached for a drawer and pulled it out. He had a calm expression and it didn't change at all when he drew back the sheet from the head. It was an old woman. Molly leaned over.

"I ran this woman's code yesterday," she said. "Joan Adams." She'd obviously been right when she said she'd recognize some patients. There was a good chance she knew all of the dead. Matt hadn't said so, but according to the cards I held, Joan was the woman in drawer one.

The woman had the expressionless face we all acquire when the spirit leaves. It was only when the refrigerated drawer opened that I became aware of the smell, not strong, and not the one of rot the live imagination braced for, but a slight flat staleness.

Molly, in her familiarity with this, and Matt, with his ease in the place, moved on. I hung behind them, looked over their shoulders, just watched, uncommonly passive, as they opened another drawer. I glanced at the card for drawer three. The name said Michael Jones. I added it automatically to the list in my head, not just the list of the missing, of the ones I wanted to find, but another, more general list, one I didn't particularly want to carry, but a toll paid to enter the room of the dead. Joan Adams. Michael Jones. The dead had simple names.

They were silent in front of me, and Molly started to close the drawer shut though I hadn't yet gotten a look. All I had to do was move forward a step to see. I was a lot taller than either of them. The bottom of the drawer was empty and at first I thought the whole drawer was. But a form filled the bag halfway up. This corpse was a child.

"Who is this?" Molly asked.

"I don't know," Matt said. "Just came down today."

"His name is listed as Michael Jones," I said, reading the card. "Six years old. He died of leukemia, it says."

I reached out between them and closed the drawer.

Matt opened the next one. It was a woman whose death mask was framed by a full circle of curly white hair. Her limbs were so thin I seemed to see through them, vision failing to spot the shift from the dull sheen of the plastic and cloth beneath her to the dry pallor of her skin. She seemed less resting upon the sheet than molded into it, the effect as if someone had shaped a human form from bedclothes. The card said: "unidentified white female."

Molly leaned a bit closer, as if she was going to rouse her from sleep, or brush the hair from her face.

"Martha Stenton," she said. "And I thought she'd made it home."

Not home, I knew. I'd been to her house earlier this very day, to the low squalid building where Martha had lived at least some of her eighty-two years. "No," I told Molly. "She never made it home."

There is sometimes a sudden realization, when doing stories, that you have moved from a long period of suspecting something is corrupt, to having a fairly detailed idea about the exact truth. And then, if you're lucky, you go one step further, and there is absolute certainty. Proof. Reporters and prosecutors have been known to jump up and down, and tremble and yell, when they find the smoking gun. Proof. Martha Stenton was dead. Not only were people at Clarke corrupt, I now knew—conducting a scheme in which government insurance monies were actively collected in the name of patients who were nowhere to be found—but the patients were, in fact, dead. Stashed in the morgue, right at the hospital, probably on their way, unidentified as they officially were, to an unmarked pauper's grave. They had little money when they were alive, but they were worth a great deal dead. One of them was right in front of me. I even had witnesses, though they might not yet realize what seeing her here meant.

"How did she die?" I asked.

"Sepsis, I think," Molly said, and then, before I could go on and ask: "Infection in the blood. All the organs just shut down."

"Looks more like she ran out of air," Matt said, and Molly and I both turned to him. He pointed to her head. He ran his finger across her lips, and Molly leaned over to look. Nodding now, she did the same thing, her finger too at the dead woman's mouth.

"Her skin's so thin," Matt said, "you can see the indentations through it."

"He's right," Molly said to me. "She must have suffocated. She sucked so hard to get air, her teeth made imprints on the inside of her lips."

We'd have to call in a pathologist, I knew. We'd need the expert examination and the tedious compilation of findings and facts. That was a given. But so was something else. Old women in hospitals don't suffocate by accident. Not while they're struggling to live. And that's the way I saw it. She'd been fighting, not just the infection in her body, but another person. She hadn't died of sepsis. She was murdered. And I thought I knew her killer.

CHAPTER

28

What a city medical examiner had found, after working overnight doing autopsies on all eight bodies, was that three of them had been killed. The three unknowns. The old woman had been suffocated. She also had two broken ribs, apparently crushed as the killer got the air out of her. Of the two others who were murdered, one had a broken neck and the other had been poisoned, it wasn't clear with what. The poisoned man had been on my list. The man with a broken neck had not. Molly had recognized all three as long-time patients at Clarke.

Molly assumed that when the medical examiner had finished his work in the morgue, he would call the police and report the murders. In fact, what he did—and this is what they always do, I knew—was fill out the necessary forms in triplicate, include a tape of his autopsy dictation in each file, and sign his name to the morgue ledger when he left. That was it. And if Molly and I hadn't been there, that may well have been as far as it went. In Philadelphia, medical examiners are political appointees. And inner-city hospitals like Clarke are major sources of patronage and payoffs for politicians, therefore protected. The last thing a medical examiner would think to do was file a report about a murder at a place like Clarke without being told to do so by someone higher up.

For a long time, the corpses had been almost invisible. And in this case, the killer was almost invisible, too. The initial impressions always had to be overcome, seeing them in their suits and their statuses, the offices, the degrees on the walls. Because we really are, all of us, chameleons. It is what we do best, in small ways and large—blend ourselves in with the surrounding social landscape, know how to do what pleases others and brings us rewards. It is a natural, human thing. And yet there is always the shock, when one of us turns out to be serpentine. Part of what shocks us is the effort they expend in the service of looking good.

People have been making masks for thousands of years. It is one of the oldest human activities. And when they put the mask on, they do what it foretells, and without it they are only ordinary. They work so hard to look good to the world. I sometimes wondered why. Maybe it's something they do on automatic pilot. They have no real idea how to behave, so they do what everyone else does. They follow the cues. They march in lockstep on some ordinary path. And no one ever sees the two sides. But the evidence was there. Now all I had to do was convince the police that the man under the mask had killed. Walker had done a good job of becoming the bedside hospital hero. And yet he killed.

I was certain Walker was the killer, but I didn't tell Molly or anyone else. I knew Molly had gone to Walker and Abbott when we'd learned of the problems with the drugs; I didn't want her doing that now. I didn't want her in that hospital while Walker was still free to roam, and I tried my best to convince her to leave Clarke for the day. But she insisted on staying and doing her rounds. The most I was able to extract from her was an absolute promise that she wouldn't tell anyone, no matter who, that there had been murders at the hospital. She'd even hesitated to make that promise, at first. She was used to fixing all the problems she encountered in life. But this was too big, and it wasn't in her realm. She finally left it to me.

In most murder cases, the best evidence homicide detectives manage to get is a statement from the accused. But even outright confessions are often confusing, and are not always believable. In Walker's case, we had something much better, thanks to all those patient charts and notes: a paper trail as solid as stone. Walker's signature transferred the patients to the nursing home. Documents at the nursing home confirmed receipt of the patients and collection of fraudulently obtained insurance monies. The bodies were right there in the morgue. Molly could identify the victims as former Clarke patients. The pathologist's report called it murder. Police and prosecutors rarely get a case this clean.

I went home to put together the case. I had to do it well. Walker was a senior doctor at a well-known city hospital and it would be difficult— even with the evidence I had—to get the police, let alone a jury, to see him as a serial killer. Political influence in Philadelphia had no limit. To make sure the police would move, I had to present them with an already investigated case. I wanted them to make an immediate arrest, or at least put some detectives on the case right away. I was assembling the file when I got a call from Ted Coleman, my editor friend in Reading.

"I thought you'd want to know," Ted said. "Joe Taft's son is in the hospital. They say he's lucky to be alive."

He explained that Reading police had found Peter, off the road, next to his motorcycle, out in the woods. It was an attempted suicide. Peter had asked police at the scene to let him die. He was now a patient at Reading Memorial Hospital. Ted didn't know the extent of his injuries.

I hated the thought of Peter being up there alone. Only days earlier I had been through a week of caring for his father in a hospital as he died. I wanted to go to see Peter but I had to finish my business with the police, which would take me at least a couple of hours. I called Molly, reaching her on her beeper. I explained the situation, and asked if she'd be willing to go up to see Peter right away.

"I can be out of here in an hour. I'll get someone to cover for me," Molly said.

"I really appreciate it," I told her. What I didn't say was that I was equally happy she was getting out of Clarke. By the time she got back, if things went well, Walker would be under watch by the police, if not already under arrest.

"I'll get up there later today and meet you," I told her. "I'll bring Joe's letter with me again. Maybe we can get him to read it this time."

"First things first," she said. "Let's see that he makes it through the day."

CHAPTER 29

He'd been at the hospital for two days. Walker's stubble and wrinkled street clothes under a still-white long coat made him quite a sight. He noticed the young residents glance with curiosity as he passed them in the halls. They must have wondered what project made his work days so long. His ritual years of putting in long hours were gone, of course, the rites of passage of medical training now passed. If he stayed around Clarke, as they did, it must be for some reason.

If only they knew. In truth, he had spent most of his time walking aimlessly, floor to floor, letting his goals be set by anyone who asked for a hand. He did everything listlessly—the nurses' requests, the residents asking advice, the mindless signing of charts and orders and notes held loosely for another day. In his mind, he was no longer in control of anything at the hospital. All he thought about was her.

He had a sense that he had been searching for something his entire life, and finally he knew what it was. He experienced satisfaction when he was with her—and that was the only time he felt that way. It seemed to him that all his life he had envisioned the possibility of another way. And now he saw what that could be. He could step away from death and fear and sorrow, and begin living anew.

It made sense to him. He could do it with her. She respected him and admired him already. Now he needed to take the next step. He'd been catching glimpses of her at the hospital all day. He waited for her at a nursing station, near where he'd seen her in a patient's room. But after ten minutes passed, he grew impatient and went to the room to see. She was no longer there. A resident walked past in the hall. Walker grabbed him by the sleeve, the resident halting in surprise. "Dr. Walker?" he said, seeming stunned.

"Have you seen Dr. Hale?" Walker asked, and though he was saying her name that way, he heard in the silence inside of him, just her first name, said alone, the way it would sound between lovers. Molly.

"By the ER," the resident said, and Walker immediately headed that way.

He broke through the double door too quickly. He took in the corridor in one fevered sweep of vision, not seeing her, feeling an oncoming burden of despair. But then when he arrived at the ER he was lifted and lightened by the sight of her. She was all the way at the other end, heading out the door. He followed.

She stepped outside and walked the distance to the hospital's parking garage. He saw her opening her car. Before he thought to do anything, she was inside and starting the engine. He looked down at his watch. Four in the afternoon. It was too late for shift turnover. Where could she be going? He scrambled into his car and pulled out behind her through the exit, keeping her in sight. The glare of the midday sun seemed unnatural; he'd been indoors for two days. She was driving an old blue Chevrolet that was easy to keep in sight. His own car was more distinctive, a two-year-old Saab—there weren't many on the road. She drove down Broad and took a right just before Hahnemann Hospital onto Vine. Up ahead was the Ben Franklin Parkway, then the two river drives—Kelly and West River. At the end of those routes were the various pretty little communities where many of the residents lived. Perhaps she was going home.

He found himself fantasizing about being in her house with her, mid-afternoon. There was a sweetness about the prospect that seized him with longing. She avoided the parkway and instead turned onto the Schuylkill Expressway. He swept quickly from the left lane to the right, to follow her. Cars honked in protest as he moved; it meant nothing to him and he settled in again behind her. She drove all the twenty miles to the expressway's end at Valley Forge, then got onto the Pennsylvania Turnpike, going west. She could be heading anywhere, he realized. Harrisburg,

Pittsburgh, Chicago. She was also heading toward Lancaster County, where Walker was born. The further she drove, the less Walker cared. He settled back into the seat, relaxed, as if some force beyond him was supplying the energy to move. Azaleas colored the rolling fields of Chester County. He felt as detached as he ever had. But he kept her license plate in mind—JXH808. Only one thing was important—keeping her in sight.

After a half hour, she took the exit for Reading. He felt himself drawn back to alert attention, and out of his languid daze. He was familiar with the area in general, but not with any of the street names. She entered a city avenue, passing some shops and a small mall. Then she slowed and turned into a parking lot. He saw with dismay a familiar sight: a medical building. A freestanding sign on the grass said Reading Memorial Hospital. A hospital was the last place he had hoped she would lead him. The long drive away from the workplace had essentially brought them back to work. His fantasies aside, whatever her reasons for departing so early in the day, it was only business. That's all a place like this meant, for both of them.

She left her car and headed for the entrance with a quick stride. He didn't even bother getting out of the car. The lethargy and emptiness flooded back. He wondered what kind of mission she was on. It was a long trip to see a patient, but sometimes residents were sent—and privately paid—to escort patients places and care for them on the way. Perhaps someone had hired her to take a patient from Reading to Philadelphia. More likely it was a favor for someone she knew. He'd never met her family or friends. Perhaps he could involve himself in a way that would somehow give him leverage with her. He got out of the car and went in. He still wore his white coat and doctor's ID. The lobby was entirely different from Clarke, larger, brighter, more open. The building, too, though smaller than Clarke, was clearly better kept. Nonetheless, he felt as familiar with it as if he was at Clarke. He'd lost sight of Molly, and rather than look for her on every floor, he stopped at the information desk.

"My associate, the young woman physician who just stopped here?" he said. "Which patient did she ask to see first?"

"Oh, that was Peter Miller," the woman said politely, immediately. "Room 405-1."

He went up to the room, still not sure of his intentions, but resenting the intrusion of this third party, a patient, into his relationship with Molly. He heard her voice as he approached the doorway, and stood outside it, listening. By his voice, the patient was a young man. His tone, more than the words, told Walker the man was depressed. Molly was trying to comfort him, her usual role with patients, he thought. It was the thing she probably did best. He wondered what connection there was between them.

"It was just an accident, that's all," Walker heard the young man say. "I'll be out of here soon."

"It was more than an accident," Molly said. "You told the police you wanted to die. I wouldn't have come up if it was only a matter of lacerations and bruises. Gray's worried about you."

There was a long silence.

"It was like I was alone," he finally said. "Like I always had been." Walker heard the soft sounds of a bed taking weight. He fought the impulse to go in. Her voice was strong, low, sweet. He felt lightheaded, his vision blurred.

"Maybe you've been alone," she said, "but you don't have to be."

Walker leaned against the wall, listening. Nurses occasionally walked by, but the scene must have looked familiar to them, mother and son talking something over inside the room, a doctor waiting. No one interrupted them. He felt a sense of isolation and connection at the same time. It was as if he now had a bridge, new to him, between himself and the world of other people who suffered: he was lonely, as other people were. He wanted her freed of all possible connections. He envied the shift in the sound of the patient's voice, the lifting of sadness, the burgeoning of hope. It was what Walker needed. Fear could be replaced by other things. His strength returned to him, along with the clarity he always had when he faced terrifying things and drove them away. The worst of these was loneliness. He could no longer deny it. The emptiness of the cornfield was not a victory but a reminder. What he needed now was love.

"Your father didn't have to die at Clarke," he heard her say. "Gray wanted you to know."

The twin mention of Clarke and even more so, of the reporter Gray, riveted Walker's attention.

"Your father would probably have lived if he'd gotten the right medication. Gray's discovered some problems in the way things are done at

Clarke, and your father was probably a victim, one of many. Someone's been stealing drugs, and making a lot of money."

"Money?" the man asked, not taking it in. Walker himself felt strange, hearing in this setting, from her, details of Abbott's schemes.

"It gets worse," Molly was saying. "Patients have actually been killed. Gray's gone to the police. It's why he's not yet here."

Now Walker was stunned. He thought about what to do. No one had ever even suspected a thing. He wanted to go into the room and talk to her. But Molly might already know him as a murderer. She was very headstrong. He wasn't sure he could control everything if she started to make a scene. The young man was another unknown. He wanted to get her out of there, but wasn't sure how. And then it seemed obvious. She was here for one reason: the patient, Peter. Move Peter, and she'd move with him. She seemed likely to stay in the room for a while. He went to find a pay phone. Getting patients transferred from one hospital to another is simple, if you're a physician.

After a series of appropriate questions of various personnel, he got what he needed. "This is Dr. Walker," he said, when he had Dr. Davidson, the resident covering Peter, on the line. "I'm an attending at . . ." he started to say Clarke, but Clarke was now tainted, and inhospitable for him, no longer home. ". . . At Lancaster Hospital," he went on, giving the name of the hometown hospital where he'd been born and where he got his start as a doctor. "You have one of my patients there at Reading— Peter Miller. The family would like him transferred to my care."

The resident had no problem with the request. Lancaster was familiar, less than an hour away. He gave Walker the number for the admissions office so Walker could make arrangements.

"I'll go write the orders," the resident said.

Walker thanked him sincerely, then called admissions and made arrangements to get an ambulance for the transfer. He specified that he needed just a driver, since a doctor would be in back with the patient. That was acceptable. At Clarke, the procedure would have taken hours. Out here, half an hour was the most it would take for the ambulance to arrive; the advantages of a small city. He just had to make sure the resident who was doing the transfer orders didn't talk to Molly and Peter until he was ready. He kept an eye on the door from a vantage point near the stairs. No one came or went from the room.

The patient was the bait for Molly, Walker was sure. She would follow wherever he went. In twenty minutes, he called the ambulance dispatcher from a pay phone; she said the ambulance would be there in five minutes. He told her to tell the driver simply to wait at the back of the ER, that he'd meet him out there with the patient and the transfer sheet. He went to a house phone and called the hospital operator. "This is security," he said. Years of acquaintance with the rhythms of daily hospital life served him well. "Please announce there's a car illegally parked in the doctor's lot. We need it moved immediately. It's a blue Chevrolet." He remembered Molly's license plate and gave the operator the number. He heard the call announced on the overhead page. After a minute, Molly came out of the room.

As soon as she was out of sight, Walker grabbed a gurney from the hallway, wheeled it to the doorway, and went in. Peter glanced up at him. Walker introduced himself, went over to the bed, and began examining Peter's bruises and cuts.

"Turn over, so I can check your lungs," he said.

Peter rolled over compliantly, facing away from him. Walker reached into his pocket for the familiar bottle, uncapped it with a practiced, rapid motion, and poured some drops of the ether onto a fold of the sheet. He put the metal circle of the stethoscope against Peter's back.

"Breathe deeply," he said, and Peter did. "Again," he said, and, just as Peter drew in a breath, Walker whipped the soaked sheet up against the young man's face, covering mouth and nose together.

For barely a second, Peter struggled hard against the suffocating restraint, but as he drew in the gas, he weakened. A few more seconds, and he was out. Walker brought the gurney into the room, and closed the door behind him. It only took a minute to wrangle Peter onto the gurney and strap him in. He covered him with a sheet, and there was nothing about the transport that looked odd in any way. He opened the door and wheeled him out. They were on the fourth floor and Molly's car had been far from the entrance. She'd be gone another few minutes, he figured, assuming she came right back. He had the time to get Peter off the floor. As he passed by the nursing station, the nurse called out, casually: "Hey, where's he going?"

"Transfer. Peter Miller," Walker said. "You already have the orders."

"Oh yeah," the nurse said. "Okay."

It was working. If Walker ran into Molly on the way, he'd deal with that somehow. He wanted to have both Peter and himself already settled into the ambulance when Molly arrived. He guided the gurney off the elevator and followed signs to the ER. He parked Peter's bed against a wall, and asked the nurse at the desk to get him the transfer papers. She didn't even ask him who he was.

"We're expecting a Dr. Hale to join us in the ambulance," Walker told the nurse. "We'll be outside, loaded up, waiting for her. It's Triple A Transport."

The nurse nodded, polite, busy, friendly.

"If I see her," she said.

Walker smiled. Molly would arrive at the ER in a surprised, maybe even frenzied state. The nurse would not miss her.

Molly walked off the elevator on the fourth floor scratching her head. She couldn't figure out why she'd been paged to move her car. There was no sign of a problem out there, and there were plenty of spaces around. She wondered when Gray would arrive. She was intensely curious about the full extent of the problems at Clarke. She recalled the scene in the morgue with a shudder. The notion that a doctor was actively killing patients was hard to comprehend. She'd assumed at first that Gray was talking about a physician helping patients commit suicide when they were intractably ill, something more and more common these days. But what he'd described was happening was murder. She walked to Peter's room. Before she entered, the nurse called to her.

"They already left," she said.

"What?" Molly went in a few steps, and saw the empty bed. She turned to the nurse. "Left for where?"

"Just a few minutes ago."

"I don't understand," Molly said. "Where did they go?"

"They'll still be in ER by admissions."

Molly turned and took the stairs. The ER was so different in appearance from Clarke's it took her a minute to locate the main nurse's desk. She didn't see Peter anywhere. The nurse surprised her by speaking first.

"Dr. Hale?"

"Yes?" Molly said.

"If you're looking for your patient, Miller, they're out in back in the transport. Said they'd wait for you. Triple A." She pointed to the door.

Molly stood still for a moment, looking behind her, then out the door.

She shook her head in confusion. She hurried out. There was only one medical van that said AAA, right outside the ER doors. The back of it was closed. Molly went to the driver's side window. A middle-aged man was holding up a CB mike, listening. Molly tapped on the window.

"Say, is this transport for Peter Miller?"

"Yep. In the back. We're ready to go."

She felt dizzy, taking steps, one at a time, going somewhere unknown. What was going on? She'd ask Peter. She didn't bother asking the driver. She walked to the back and opened the door. She saw Peter in the transport bed. He was strapped in, but more important, he was unconscious. She stepped up into the van. One of the ambulance staff was up front with the driver. He turned around. It was John Walker. Molly froze. Walker stepped into the back of the van and closed the ambulance doors. Molly couldn't imagine what he was doing there.

"What's wrong with him?" she said, pointing to Peter. "I was just with him and he was fine. And what are you doing here?"

She bent over Peter, not waiting for an answer. She realized immediately he was deeply asleep. His breathing was even, though slowed. His limbs were splayed and toneless, obviously from more than sleep alone. She raised his lids. His eyes were bright and clear, but he didn't rouse. She turned to Walker.

"Did you give him something? What's going on?"

"We're all going home," Walker said, his voice different somehow than any tone she'd ever heard him use.

She struggled to place it, to understand, make sense of what was happening. He was smiling at her in a relaxed, contented way, as if the two of them shared some secret source of calm and peace. It terrified her.

She heard herself demanding an answer, shrill and scared. "Where?"

He simply sat there, as still and as restful as Peter on the bed, eyes no less bright, and smiling all the while. "Home. I'm taking you home."

CHAPTER

31

Neither she nor Walker said much during the ride. She tried asking him several times for a simple, clear answer to what was happening, and nothing he said was reasonable. But one thing seemed obvious as the vehicle turned off a highway onto a country road, and Walker sat silent and smiling. Walker had done something to Peter. And she felt trapped.

Walker looked different. In one way, it was as if they were still in some familiar place—working at Clarke, the ambulance itself much like a patient's room, the patient on the bed between them, the two of them discussing a case. The more she focused on the quality of Peter's breathing and condition, the more familiar the situation seemed. She'd been with Walker on numerous occasions when she was trying to decide what to do with a patient. He was there to help, to guide. But the Walker here in the ambulance was not that same man. He had his white coat, wore his Clarke ID, even had the stethoscope tucked in the side pocket as always. But there was a quality she'd never seen in him before. His arms were folded in his lap, the hands clasped and hanging down, shoulders slumped, but his head erect as if held up by an entirely different set of muscles, eyes staring straight ahead.

She'd always had a talent for facing things. First things first. The fact that Walker was in Reading, that he had apparently done something to Peter—she suddenly knew what it meant. Gray had identified a physician at Clarke involved with the corruption, a killer. He hadn't told her who it was. It couldn't be any more obvious. It was Walker. That's why he was here. Perhaps the police were after him and he thought Molly could protect him in some way. Whatever it was Walker might want of her, she'd be best off if she knew what it was, and had time to prepare. She was worried about Peter. And she could use an ally. Combine the two things, she thought, go ahead. Try. You have no other choice.

"What do you think of his respiration?" she asked Walker, in a tone she hoped was eager enough to convey the proper respect for his expertise. "His breathing is regular. What—" she started to ask what Walker had given Peter, but thought better of it. "What did he take?"

"He's fine," Walker said, with an absent tone. The casual manner of his reply startled her. She had never heard him so detached from the very heart of his livelihood. He knew breathing, its rhythms, its sounds, its presence in the living, the silent absence of its muted piping in the dead. She had seen him cut holes through the flesh of throats, and force air into gasping supplicants through plastic tubes. She had seen him literally climb on top of patients in their beds, his strong arms beating their chests, seen him make them live, at least for a short while. Seeing his casual disregard for Peter's condition told her more than anything else he could have done.

"What are you doing here?" she asked, in a harsher tone than she wanted. "What's going on?"

"I followed you." His voice was the same dull monotone he'd used to describe Peter's condition.

"You followed me? What are you talking about?"

She didn't want to get him angry, but she couldn't control herself. Yet he sat there calmly, smiling at her in a familiar way. It was the way he looked when she did something he liked with a patient, a smile of approval, of support. Her anger ebbed for a second. It was as if he'd been somehow transformed, the known boundaries of him slipping away. He had been watching her as he spoke. He seemed attentive, shy, almost diffident in her presence. But he had kidnapped her and Peter. More than that, he was undoubtedly a killer.

It was only when she felt the metal wall of the car pressed cold against the skin of her back that she realized her shirt was soaked through. She was trying, impossibly, to back away from him, away from the realizations, piled one on the other, too many to organize, too much to make sense.

"Where are we going?"

"I told you, we're going to my home. I wanted to be with you. There's nowhere else for me to go." He sounded disjointed, lost in a reverie. "You have a beautiful body," he said. "Your neck, so bare, your ears, I cup them in my hands, feel the soft hair on your lobes in my palms. Your thighs don't meet. There's a thin, light line of hair, just at your spine, running down. I think about it all the time, the way you feel, when I'm pressed against you, my hands around you, your breasts—"

His words struck her like a blow. Could it be he had seen her naked? But when? He was talking as if he had actually been with her. It was impossible. She noticed the ambulance driver half turned their way, straining to catch his words as well. Walker was talking about her in this impossible, intimate way, and the softness of his voice, the longing she couldn't help but recognize, made it worse.

"Are you crazy?"

He stared at her. "It doesn't matter," he said, in that hushed voice. "I only know that when I'm with you, I feel good, and it's the only time I do."

"Does it matter to you that I'm not interested in that?" She was screaming at him now. "That I have a say in this? I won't let you. Whatever you've seen, whatever you've done, I won't let you go on with it. It's over." She reached over to the driver. He made no attempt to stop her. "You," she shouted. "You've been listening to this. He's crazy. Pull over. Stop." The driver slowed and she felt a surge of relief. Walker made no attempt to get in her way. She really could end this, she thought. She looked out through the front window. They were on a country road with no buildings or any other signs of life. She didn't have a plan, but stopping the ride itself was enough of a goal. The ambulance had a radio. That would come next.

"Pull over to the side," she ordered. The driver looked at Walker. "Just do it," Molly said. "Didn't you hear me?"

The driver slowed further, and the ambulance eased to a stop on a shoulder.

"Lady," the driver said, "we're only five minutes from Lancaster Hospital. We'll be there in no time."

"I don't care," she snapped. "I can't wait. Put your lights on, and use your radio to call the police."

"Okay, okay," the driver said. He reached for the radio. She glanced at Walker. He had a small brown bottle in his hand, the cap off, and he was soaking a small square of gauze with a colorless fluid. With a quick motion, his arm was suddenly around the driver's neck, pressing the cloth into his face. She smelled the distinctive odor of ether even as the driver slumped down in the seat. She looked around for something she could use if she had to defend herself. Before she could locate anything, Walker spoke.

"Don't," he said, his voice languid and weary. "You have to come with me. You have to. The driver's all right, but I couldn't let him call anyone. He'd only get in the way." He held out his hands to her, as if in supplication.

"In the way of what?" The question came out automatically.

"Please," Walker said, and she realized he was begging her, sweet, insistent, childlike. His act of violence to the driver was as unpleasant an interruption to his state of mind as the entire situation was for her. He was battered in some way, seeking shelter from some inner storm, dangerous in his desperation. His various aspects shifted before her like quicksilver. She hesitated.

"I won't come with you," she said firmly. She eyed the radio, and knew she had to get to it to call the police.

"We're only a few minutes from my home," he said, as if that fact alone would make it evident to her what she had to do. When she said nothing, he looked over at Peter. "You care about him," he said. "If you don't come with me, I'll kill him." The threat was made in the same low tone with which he had stated his need for her. It wasn't a threat as much as a burden he was willing to assume. He had the small brown bottle in his hand. They both knew that enough of a dose would kill. Maybe that's how he'd killed others at Clarke, she thought. She couldn't see a way to stop him. Peter was strapped in. Even if he was conscious, he'd be little help. She felt trapped and hopeless.

"All right," she said. "What do you want me to do?"

"Just sit there," Walker said.

He held the cloth over Peter's mouth for a moment, letting a few drops land on his face. It would probably keep him asleep for a few hours. She watched Walker carefully, not sure what she could do if he tried to hurt

Peter. But he didn't. He got up and moved into the driver's seat, pushing the driver over to make room. He drove the ambulance back onto the road and eased it ahead. In a short while, he pulled off to the side of a house. Across the road and nearby was nothing but fields and pasture. It was farm country. He pulled the ambulance up to a barn in back of the house and shut off the motor, taking the key with him when he got out. There was no way for her to flee and take Peter with her. She sat tight, determined not to leave Peter alone, but terrified for herself. The two feelings battled within her, and she had no way to resolve them. Walker swung wide the doors of the large barn. He got back into the ambulance, started it up, and pulled inside, then shut the motor again.

"Leave him here," he said, pointing to Peter. "Come with me."

She checked Peter's breathing. It was fine. Then she leaned forward to the front of the van to check on the unconscious driver. She put her hand on his throat. Nothing. She put her hand on his chest. It was still, rigid. She grabbed his wrist and arm, to straighten him out and try CPR. Perhaps she could revive him. Walker pulled her away.

"He's dead!" she said. "You killed him!"

"I didn't mean to," Walker said, and his voice held genuine remorse. "It shouldn't have killed him, the amount I used. He must have had a heart condition."

She was frozen in place. He put an arm around her to guide her out. She shook out of his grip, but followed him, forcing herself along. When they were out of the barn, Walker held her again with one hand while with the other he swung the wide door shut. She couldn't pull free. She consoled herself with one thought: At least for the moment, Peter was safe. So far, she thought, Walker hadn't hurt her, only frightened her with words. Except that he had killed the driver. They walked to the back door of the house. He opened it with a key. He pushed forward the door and held it for her.

There was no choice. She went in.

CHAPTER
31

I got to Reading Memorial at seven-thirty. It had taken me three hours at the homicide division in Philadelphia to complete the simple act of turning over Walker's file. Most of that time was spent waiting in a small room outside the captain's office. The fact that I knew two of the detectives in homicide didn't speed things along. It usually didn't. I happened to know them from newspaper days, but they didn't particularly like me, or like seeing me when I came to do business. Yet the strength of the case against Walker was too much for them to ignore. We went through all the facts together and, by the time I left, they were willing to guarantee they'd not only investigate, but send a man to Clarke immediately to keep tabs on Walker until they were ready to make an arrest. I figured Walker had, at best, one more day of life outside bars.

On the ride up to Reading I couldn't stop thinking about Peter and his father, Joe Taft. I had to talk to the boy. But I still wasn't sure what to say. As I drove, I thought more and more about the folded packet I'd been carrying with me since Joe died. There could be some guidance for me in there. There could be words I might say to reach the kid at least enough to get him to read the letter himself, because then it wouldn't be my words at all, but Joe's.

I put a hand on the envelope and fingered the edge of the letter inside. But I let it rest there, unopened. Taking the letter out meant ignoring what Peter had already told me, that he wasn't ready to hear it, that he didn't want to know. When he was ready, he'd let me know. All I had to be was available.

At Reading Memorial, I got Peter's room number from a white-haired lady at an information desk, the same woman who worked the information desk at every hospital in the world.

"Room 405-1," she said, and I went up.

I wondered if the place was anything like Clarke. It was certainly much cleaner. It looked friendlier, too, an easier, more relaxed place to heal. Still, it would have been no problem for an Abbott to run this place her way. When it came to hospitals, when it came to any business, looking better didn't usually mean being better. They were all in the same pit. The pit was human greed and the type and style of the endeavor rarely made any difference.

Room 405 was empty. The bedsheets were tossed aside, and the room looked used. Peter and Molly might have gone for a stroll. To check, I flicked open a few drawers. His wallet and keys and comb and some candy were all there. He could have been getting examined in another room. I went over to the nursing station and asked.

"Transferred," she said.

"That couldn't be," I said. "His clothes are still in the room." Why would Molly have taken him out of this place? I wondered. "You must be mistaken," I said. "I'm talking about Peter Miller, room 405."

"Right," she said. "He was taken out a couple of hours ago. Are you family?"

I didn't hesitate. "Yes."

"Check the ER. They'll have the transfer papers. I don't know where they took him."

The nurse in the ER picked up a sheaf of papers as soon as I asked about Peter. She plucked one of the forms out of the batch and handed it over. She waited a minute to see if I needed any help reading, and when it was clear I didn't, she turned to do something else.

The first place I always looked on any form was the bottom. That's where all the important information always is. Signatures, for one thing. The one on the bottom of this form was a name I knew, and it was a surprise. John Walker.

It made no sense. I was holding the original form, not something sent in or received by fax. A white piece of paper, with yellow and pink carbon copies. Signed only two hours earlier. Walker had been here. He had signed this paper. He had taken Peter out of here. In all likelihood, Molly was with them. I read the rest of the document. They were going to Lancaster Hospital. I asked the nurse how far that was. Forty-five minutes, maybe an hour. She gave me directions.

I pushed the car to extremes and got to the ER at Lancaster Hospital in thirty-five minutes. There were no patients in the waiting room. The man on duty was sitting on a fold-out chair and reading a newspaper. He told me no ambulance had arrived from Reading. Then he checked with one of the physicians. I again identified myself as a family member. The doctor checked with a nurse. She said they weren't expecting any transfers. Nothing listed under the name Peter Miller at all. The three of them looked sympathetic. I mentioned the name of the doctor who signed the transfer papers, Walker. Maybe they had another way to look up information based on the doctor's name. Instead, I got an immediate reaction from the nurse.

"We don't have any transfer pending, but I know a Dr. Walker. John, right?"

I nodded.

"He was an attending here, years ago," she said. "I know him. He's in Philadelphia now, been there for years."

"Yeah, that's the one. He's at Clarke Hospital in the city. He worked here?"

"Not only worked here. Born here, raised here. A Lancaster boy, from a farm just north of town. Made good and went off to the big city."

"When's the last time you saw him?" I asked her.

She thought about it. "Long, long time," she said. She laughed and poked the guy on the chair. "Can't believe it's been that long. But it has."

"I'm really confused," I said. "I was just at Reading Memorial, and they told me that Peter Miller was being transferred to Lancaster Hospital. Dr. Walker's name was on the papers. It might make some kind of sense for him to bring the boy here, since he used to work here. But no one seems to know about the transfer."

"You sure you have the right place?" she asked. "Maybe he's taking him to Clarke. That would make more sense, wouldn't it?" Of course she was right.

"Could you call up Reading for me, and check again?"

"Sure," she said. She picked up the phone and made the call. It took a few minutes, but when she turned back, she had the same look I did.

"You got it right," she said. "Definitely a transfer for here, but no one called us. A screwup for sure."

So we called Clarke, and there was no record there of an expected transfer and admission for Peter Miller. Nobody said anything for a minute.

"Where do his parents live?" I asked, because I couldn't think of anything else. When things get stuck, you do something simply to create movement. Walker had filled out the forms at Reading and said he was going to Lancaster. Maybe he was, but not to the hospital. I assumed he was crazy. That made almost anything a possibility and worth a try.

The nurse said she hadn't been out there since Walker left town, which was fifteen years ago, but that the place was easy to find. It was a small farm about two miles outside of town, no more than twenty minutes from here. I ran out to my car again and drove off.

I had to drive slow because somewhere along the way, all the light in the world started to fade. There were no street lamps and there weren't enough buildings in the countryside to offer light. Once in a while, a car headlight bloomed like the sun, but otherwise there weren't even shadows. It wasn't long before I got close to a straight stretch the nurse had told me about. The Walker house was supposed to be on the right hand side, with no other landmarks than surrounding fields and farm buildings.

The first thing I saw was a silo. It was empty. Thin strands of steel wound around air. As far as I could tell in the faded light, there were cornfields across the way, the land pale and brown, old dried stalks laying flat on the silent fields. I pulled up to a small clearing by the silo, a hundred feet from the house, and got out of the car. It was an old house, but without the virtues of aging, not solid or nourished by care. Molly's house was old and beautiful. This one was just worn. I didn't know why Walker had Molly and Peter, or why he had written on the hospital papers that he was bringing them to this town. I had a growing fear I might not find the answer. The house looked unoccupied, probably for years.

On impulse, I avoided the front door, and went around the side. I looked through the uncovered windows, but the rooms inside were dark and I couldn't see a thing. The house was turn-of-the-century, I guessed, patched planks of wood, not particularly well built. I knocked at the back door. No one answered. I knocked again. North Philadelphia or the middle of a cornfield. When things were devastated and down, no one was ever home. I was tired of chasing ghosts. I pushed on the door, prepared to break it in, if I had to. It was unlocked. I walked in.

CHAPTER

32

I was blind as soon as I got inside. It was pitch black. I felt my way along a wall, using my hand to guide me. Ten feet into the house the wall came to an end and there was a room. I reached around the wall and down, feeling first an empty space and then cold metal. My hand touched a grate and I recognized it was the top of a stove. I felt my way along a counter, old rubbed-smooth formica, and then I came upon the familiar outline of a small cardboard box. I picked it up and slipped out one of the sticks. I felt the rough strips on the sides of the box and struck a match.

The room brightened in an instant. I saw a sparse but neatly preserved scene from the 1950s. A square, white-topped table and four wooden chairs, one of them taller than the others and padded with black vinyl. On the formica counter top was a stack of coasters for small glasses, next to a portly old toaster. The windows were framed by frail cloth, old chintz. The ceilings glared in the matchlight, gleaming small square panels of tin. The inside of the home was neater and better preserved than the outside. I wondered where Walker's parents were. Their son had killed a good number of folks. I wondered how young he had begun. The house was silent. The match was burning my hand. I put it out.

In the next burst of flame, I found the light switch. I tried it. Nothing. No lights came on. I found the phone, an old rotary-dial black box on a wall by the entryway. I picked it up and listened, heard nothing. Next to the phone was a light switch. I tried that, too. No lights came on. The nurse thought Walker's parents might still be here, but she was surely wrong. Someone had cleaned up and made an effort to preserve things, but there were no signs of life. I went out through the archway and crossed a little distance in the renewed dark, moving slowly, thinking I'd come up against a couch or a chair. I lit another match. The room was empty. Against one wall, there was a small wooden desk attached to a chair. That was the only furniture in the room. At the back of the room, I could see a stairway. I reached the bannister before the match went out.

I decided to leave, but an old habit took hold of me, the same one that had led me to walk up the stairs of the shanty in North Philadelphia. It was a habit I'd never been able to break. It had worked for me too long, been a part of all the things I'd ever done—ballplayer, reporter, blackmailer. I always had to see everything; I could never stop partway. There was lots to be said for thought and skill and strength in this world, and I always tried to use a full measure of each. But sometimes what worked was simply to keep going, and hope you run into some luck.

I took the stairs. I felt a slight tendril of wind working its way into the house. The wind put the flickering match out and again there was only darkness. I hit the upstairs landing and felt along the wall to my right. I lit another match. Wary of the little wind, I cupped the flame with my hand, which made it harder to see. I looked around. Three doors for bedrooms, all closed. A bathroom door, opened. I tried the bedroom on the right. It was empty, a square blank box of space, nothing else. I crossed the small corridor to another door. I turned the handle and opened it slowly. As I stepped in, I lit a match, and turned my eyes away from the flare. This room was furnished. Lying still on a bed was a woman, her back to me. I knew right away it was Molly. She was curled up as if sleeping, her head tucked inside her arms. The little match light burned steady, but the shadows in the room still danced. As I took a step toward the bed, the match went out and darkness took over again. I reached for another match.

I sensed the movement behind me, but not in time. He grabbed me fast and rough around the neck and pulled me back. I kept my balance for a second, then smelled an acid odor, and my movements were quickened by fear. I pulled away, but he didn't let go. He pressed something wet against my cheek, a cloth with a stinging odor. I turned around and shoved him back, and heard a thud as he hit the wall. The smell lingered.

I started in his direction but it was like stepping into a hole, black all around me and a pit of it below. My legs gave out and I fell into the void. Everything was quiet. Either I passed out or I almost did.

Whatever he'd drugged me with made the floor tilt and move. But he hadn't finished the job. I wondered if he knew that. I was on my knees. I still had the box of matches. I took another one out. My hand felt disconnected. Lighting a match seemed impossibly difficult. I listened for the sound of him, staying as still as I could. The instant the flint spark took hold, I saw him coming at me again, and for the first time I could see his face. Walker. He was bare-chested, his chest and arms thickly muscled, and he was moving fast. He had a white cloth in his hand and I caught the bitter aroma before he reached me. He was aiming for my face. I put my hand up to block it, the match flaring bright. The white cloth met my hand and a huge square of fire blazed up. I jerked back and he cried out, his arm waving frantically, as if caught in the maw of a fire bird. He dropped the burning cloth to the floor.

A small tattered rug beneath him flared up. The fire spread and Walker was standing in a ring of flame. I had my legs back, and I scrambled up and aimed for him in one motion. I was thinking only one thing. If I got him, he couldn't get to her. I pinned and held him, my stance wide. He wasn't getting past me. I held him firm. He glared at me, and, as if his eyes controlled the flames, the fire on the floor got brighter. A cloth cover on a small table caught.

He lowered his head and butted me in the face. Blood ran from my nose, and my head hurt as if I'd been spiked above my eyes. I lost my grip. He was strong, but he was smaller than me. I shoved him away again. He hit the flaming table and it went over. The paper on the wall behind him flared up from the heat. He didn't seem to notice the flames. He dug into his pocket and came out with a thick brown bottle. Even if I backed away, I'd likely be splattered with whatever that was, and I'd already had a taste. That was enough. He opened the bottle with a quick easy motion. I stepped forward and punched him in the face. He tossed the liquid in my direction at the same time. I saw it coming and ducked. The liquid made a small arc in the air, a perfect half-circle, one end of it trailing from his hand, the other flung out to the wall. Whatever it was, it loved fire. A line of fire suddenly appeared in the air, and when the tip of the flame scythe hit the bottle, the glass exploded in his hand, spraying him with flame.

He came at me then and I couldn't avoid him. Fire licked faster at the old wood wall, and spread evenly across the dry oak plank floor as if someone had spilled a pot of flame. I could feel the heat intensely now, and yet he was barefoot and didn't seem to notice at all. His face was covered with blood and smoke, and he was still trying to get past me to Molly. His hands and arms were blistered and burned. He grabbed me by my sides as hard as I've ever been held, as if he wanted to root us in place, so we'd both catch fire and burn. My arms were free, and I threw punches at his head, again and again, as hard as I could, but he just stood there, his hair burning, his head shrouded in smoke. He ducked some of the punches and took the rest as if punishment was something he liked. And with whatever mad energy he could muster, he wouldn't let me go.

I heard a roaring sound, from far away. I knew the fire had broken through the back wall and was rolling to another room. He kept his arms tight to my side, his face in front of me, looking in me and through me. His skin radiated heat and he had a glow like an angel. I heard a crash from behind the wall. Something had collapsed. The room shook. I still couldn't shake free of him.

"Let go, Walker," I said. "Let go or we'll all die."

I braced my arm against his neck, and pushed full strength. His face flushed and his neck bent back, but didn't give. I was trying to kill him but he didn't let go. Then suddenly, he was no longer staring at me, but beyond me. I turned to see what he was looking at. Molly's bed and that side of the room started to go up in flames. Maybe he wants her, I thought, and doesn't want her dead. He let me go. I'd been keeping him up as much as he'd been holding me. The force of the blows he'd taken went through him like a wave, and he collapsed back. He staggered into the fiery corner of the room. It was like falling into an oven. I heard and smelled his flesh burn. His silence jolted me.

I went for Molly. The bed was about to go up. I swept her off of it with one motion. The thin drapes on the window were burning. I kicked right through them and the glass. The rush of air turned the room into a conflagration, wild with fire and smoke. Molly was still out, but stirring. I looked down. It was a ten-foot drop. It wouldn't be easy to take her weight, but I had no choice. I lowered myself by one hand from the sill, wrapping her arms around me. I let go of the sill. We hit the ground hard, but I took the brunt of it. I felt my ankle give, and I knew that at the least it was sprained, and maybe worse, but I could still move. I yelled when it happened, but the house was crackling and groaning with its bellyful of fire, and I couldn't even hear my own scream. I took a second to shake Molly. Her eyes were open.

I looked up at the window. Flames licked through, and the hot air blew the burning fabric out, a giant flag in a dark red wind. I looked for Walker but he didn't appear. Then, suddenly, I saw him at the window, a smoldering blackened silhouette of a human being. He wavered there for a minute, then he fell, tumbling head first and down, expelled by the fire, pieces of glass around him reflecting the light. He landed on the dirt a few feet from us. He was still burning, and somehow still alive. I didn't know if he could see, but he was face-up, looking our way. He moved, barely, in our direction, his hand out. Molly screamed. Walker's lips moved. I had no trouble hearing the words. "I'm scared." Then he wrapped his arms around himself, as if he was now aware of what was happening. His body shook for a minute. And then he died.

CHAPTER
33

It took a while to free ourselves from Lancaster. The police preferred us safely in bed at the hospital, while they gathered whatever independent information they could about a house fire, a dead ambulance driver, and a dead doctor. They had a point about keeping Molly, Peter, and me in the hospital overnight, we all knew that. But Molly extricated us from the place and their well-intended ministrations with more anger than I'd ever seen in her, using her status as a doctor with an edge and an arrogance that was unnatural for her. We'd agreed among the three of us, practically without speaking, that Molly's house was the place we wanted to be. It surprised us Peter didn't want to return to Reading, but he felt he had nothing there.

Peter, who was still out cold when Molly had taken me to him in the ambulance in the barn, was now in better shape than either Molly or I. She had bruises, minor burns, smoke inhalation, and a headful of fears that would take a while to ebb. I had burns and bruises as well, and an ankle that was swollen and stiff.

I drove and Molly filled me in slowly about what had happened while I'd chased them. There were long pauses while she talked, as if she was trying to sort it out. Walker had given her the ether a few minutes after they got to the bedroom, and she didn't know what he'd done to her after that. She could only guess—not just about last night, but about what Walker had been doing all along. Whatever it was, it left no physical scars. As we got onto the Schuylkill Expressway at Valley Forge, Molly asked me to pull over. I did, and waited a while for her to speak.

"I don't know how much of his crazy talk to believe," she said. "He talked as if he'd been with me, loved me, used me . . ." She hesitated, and I knew she was deciding as she went along, in every word she used, every shading of tone, whether to believe or disbelieve everything that happened.

"You weren't aware of what he said he was doing," I said. "Not at all. That must mean something."

"Does it?" I realized she was weighing the concept, plumbing the notion to see what relief it offered.

Peter was in the back seat. He leaned forward and put a hand on her shoulder. "You saved me," he said. "By going in the house with him. And he was crazy. I wouldn't believe anything he said."

He kept his hand on her shoulder. She nodded but said nothing, then he let go and sat back.

"He was one of the good ones at Clarke," she said, to no one in particular. "Good with kids." She shook her head and the sound she made came out like a laugh, but it wasn't. "And we all went to him with our problems."

She moved her shoulders the way someone does when trying to shrug something off, push it away. But she couldn't stop shaking. We sat there on the side of the road and cars whizzed by, their glass and metal tops gleaming in the night, all the drivers and passengers visible, one by one, separate worlds rolling down one path to different destinations. There was absolutely no way to know anything much about all our secret lives, however visible everyone was on the outside. Everything important was secret unless people decided otherwise. And people kept so much to themselves. It was the thing about the world I knew best.

"It would be easier if they all wore signs," I said, "the ones who come to us as friends and turn out not to be. It's shooting ground they want, some place close to our hearts to snipe from. We open up for them because that's the only way we can live, and then when they declare themselves, it's nothing but hardship. Every time it happens they catch us off-guard. And there's not a thing we can do to stop them."

She looked at me and nodded again, the way she had when Peter touched her. I wanted to touch her too, but I didn't. Instead, I drove her home.

I had planned to stay at Molly's house for as long as she and Peter needed the support. As it turned out, emotional needs took a second place to sheer exhaustion. Within a half hour of our arrival, the two of them had collapsed into sleep, and I was in the same healing state about fifteen minutes later, the time it took to drive home.

The next morning I went to police headquarters at Eighth and Race, the building known as the Roundhouse. From the sky the place looks like a pair of handcuffs. From the ground, it is a cement fortress, imposing, intimidating, and off-limits to you, whoever you are. It takes a certain courage just to walk in. And don't bother with the front door. Despite the welcoming sight of a bronze policeman holding a small child in his arms a few feet ahead of the front steps, the front entrance is always locked tight. The back door off the parking lot is the only way in. It is a perfect act of architecture—form and function mated.

The detectives had plenty of questions about Walker's death. It took four hours to go through everything, point by point by point. The thing I wanted most, I couldn't arrange, and hadn't expected to. The police would have to interrogate Peter and Molly, sometime soon. But at least the detectives didn't ask me anything about Clarke Hospital in general, and I had no interest in directing their attention that way. As far as they were concerned, this was a case of one individual crazy killer, who happened to be a doctor, and happened to work at Clarke. From their point of view, it was cut-and-dried. That was fine with me.

I knew when I'd first gone to them with the homicide case against Walker that I ran the risk of getting Abbott involved in criminal charges. That would have ruined any chance I had to make a deal with her. As it turned out, with Walker dead, Abbott's name didn't have to come up with the police. Her job at Clarke remained secure and intact, and that's exactly what I needed to do business with her.

Once I got out of the Roundhouse and into Clarke, I had to wait three hours to see her. One decision I made while I was waiting there was that I wouldn't even bother to discuss her security man, Carter. He had threatened to turn me in for stealing records, but in the light of day it was clear to me he was not in a position to do anything. Both Clarke and

Brook Hall were so consumed in their own corruption that no one from either place would dare go to police to complain about me. Having decided to do nothing about Carter, I still had three hours to kill.

Left to sit that long in a place I didn't like, and unable to do much about it, I did something I hadn't done in ages—read the newspaper. I went through all the stories in the sports section twice, and read all the stats in small type. But that only took forty-five minutes. So I read through the news pages, every one. It had been a year since I'd done that. I hadn't missed much. The world was still a rotten place, in all the usual ways.

When she finally let me in, in return for my patient waiting, Abbott agreed to give me five minutes. That was fine with me, because all I needed was to get in and say my piece. After that, she'd make more time.

"So what are you planning to write about us?" Abbott asked, when we settled in her office.

"I don't plan on writing anything."

She didn't seem to believe me. "Oh no?"

"I'm not writing anything because I'm not a reporter."

"Really?" she said, with a tight smile. "If you're not a reporter, what are you doing here? What do you want?"

"I want to make a deal."

I liked to say it straight out, a little because I enjoyed making it harsh for them, but more because I wanted to get it over with. Talking with them was unpleasant.

"Your end of the deal is you stop diluting the morphine; you stop giving your patients substitute antibiotics; you remove the incentives you put in place that lead your doctors to do unnecessary surgeries and amputations. In return—I leave you alone. That's the deal."

"Something might seem wrong to you," she said, "and still have a perfectly reasonable explanation. A lot of the things I do here are unorthodox, but the fact is this hospital was in much worse shape before I arrived. You may not like what you see at Clarke, and, much of the time, neither do I. But then, who likes poverty and sickness? What I've managed to do here is raise the level of care. And I've done it because I do things in an unusual way. I don't steal money from the government. I do whatever I can to get money out of the government so I can fund the things we need. You come along and you find things wrong. Well, welcome to the real world." Her voice rose, more with a sense of authority than anger. "Get out," she said. "I don't know what brought you here. Just get out." She got up, went to the door, and stood there with it open, motioning me out.

"I had your antibiotics tested," I said, quietly. "And the morphine as well. Your morphine is basically milk sugar and water. People in pain in this hospital are getting placebos, not painkillers. Your five most expensive antibiotics are mislabeled. None of them contain what they're supposed to. They're the cheapest possible drugs, instead, and even those are dirty."

"If you're trying to cash in on the problems we've had with our drug supplies, you're being ridiculous. We already know about those problems, and they're being corrected. Somehow you found out. What's your point?"

"The point is: you're a thief. This isn't some minor mistake we're talking about. It's a major felony. We're looking at a minimum of three point six million dollars in drug fraud in the past year. That is, for every dose of Amigalycin, you get a hundred and twelve dollars a day in insurance reimbursement, and you spend only seven dollars for the substitute. That's a profit of a hundred and five dollars a dose. And that's just for one patient one day. Multiply that by a hundred patients every day of the year. I have documentation for two hundred patients given the mislabeled drugs. The lab tests and the hospital's own medical records are not disputable. If you do everything I tell you to, the information I have doesn't go to the authorities and you don't lose your position, and risk going to jail."

There was a rhythm to it, like breathing, and it had become very natural to me over the years. I knew she was thinking of ways to get around my threats, and get me to leave. But if I kept on going, she'd fall into place. She didn't have much of a choice. Unless she was willing to risk losing it all—and they never were.

I took a small stack of papers out from the envelope I'd been holding. I dropped the pages on Abbott's desk. She closed the door.

"I have the originals stashed with lawyer friends, of course. At least forty patients were transferred from Clarke to Brook Hall Convalescent Center during the past two years. Those patients have brought in more than one and a half million in Medicare funds. All forty of them were dead on the day they were supposedly transferred out of here. And half of the insurance money, three quarters of a million dollars, has gone directly to one of your private companies. Not even to Clarke, but to your company. There are records that show that."

She walked slowly, reluctantly back to her desk and looked at the file on the table, then she looked at me. She shook her head. "This is incredible," she said. She sat down, and read through the pages.

I interrupted as she read. "I'm assuming you don't know that some of the patients you supposedly sent there were murdered."

She was stunned. "You're crazy," she said.

"Walker did it," I said.

"I don't believe it."

"It makes no difference what you believe. Walker was your partner in the nursing home scam. If I give the prosecutors the evidence against you—whether you knew about the murders or not—you'll be indicted for homicide, at least as an accomplice. And you'll probably be convicted, too. Because the paper trail of insurance money leads straight to you."

"You should be talking to Dr. Walker, then," she said.

"He's dead."

That last bit of information physically moved her back, just as if I'd shoved her with my hand.

"Even if you beat the homicide charge, you don't have a prayer of acquittal in the larceny and fraud cases. And those are federal, so your connections in Philadelphia politics won't help. Given the amount of money you've stolen that can be documented—and the number of scams you've run—I'd guess you're looking at a minimum of five years in prison. Before they consider parole. Think how it'll look in the eyes of a jury. You've given thousands of sick people contaminated medications and phony pain drugs, and those people suffered. It'll all be described in court. Some died. The jury won't like you much."

She edged the chair against the wall. She was afraid of me now, and that was good.

"Who are you?" she asked. "What do you really want? What?"

Usually they had trouble understanding what I wanted for their victims, or why anyone would care about that at all. Victims were invisible to them, and I was asking them to see. She had finally gotten around to asking me what I wanted, so I had to make it absolutely clear.

"I already told you what I want. You stop the antibiotic scam. Stop the morphine switch. Stop the unnecessary surgeries and amputations. Stop collecting money in the names of people of who have died. And one more thing. You stop taking money for yourself from Clarke's operating funds. That means that things like toilet paper, towels, sheets—and, most of all, medical supplies on all the floors—make a sudden reappearance at Clarke. And the heat goes up to normal temperatures in the winter. That's what I'm asking you to do."

It felt like we were doing business now. She was looking down at a page on her table. Maybe she was trying to calculate things out, see what kind of package she could get from me. I sweetened my end.

"You keep your car, your house, your boat, all the other expensive things you care about. You can keep all of that, and you even keep your job. If you agree to my deal."

She kept staring at the table, trying to figure it out, so she could give me what I wanted and still keep it all. Maybe it didn't make sense to her, even now, but she'd end up seeing it clearly enough. She could either lose her job, and lose in court, or make the deal with me. I got up and headed for the door.

"Add another figure to your calculations," I said. "My fee." I named a figure that seemed reasonable to me, considering what she had. It would pay for several months in the Caribbean, and some new construction projects on the house. I was long past the days I even hesitated about that.

She didn't look up as I left. That was unusual. In most cases, they made some kind of sarcastic remark when I mentioned my fee. But I think they actually like it, find it reassuring in some way that they are dealing with someone who is, after all, nothing more than a blackmailer. More or less just like them.

CHAPTER
34

I parked at the bottom of Molly's block, near the stone wall along the Schuylkill. A couple of old men were sitting on the wall, their long lines cast well out into the river as the early evening light spread over the calm water. I'm not sure anyone ever catches anything this close to the city. Maybe they don't want to and that's why they're here, to spend the better part of the day just sitting, looking at the water, or back at the green of the yards and the faded red of the old brick homes of East Falls.

So Walker was gone and Abbott was locked up neatly in the life of an ordinary administrator, someone who could still be corrupt in a limited way, but could no longer operate as a little god. It was a fate she would no doubt hate. Of course, she'd soon realize our deal was only that she had to stop the particular scams and protect the particular victims I'd identified. She'd soon find other ways to steal. I hated the inevitability of that, hated what it meant about the way the world really worked, and hated my own inability to change things enough. I hated it, but I absolutely refused to believe, even for a minute, that the world was a better place than I knew it was.

People like Abbott could be controlled, but only with a great deal of effort, every corrupt act countered, point by point. But they couldn't really be changed. There is never enough justice. Never. People like her and Walker hurt innocents. They wring an undue measure of suffering from too many. And whatever they are left with, life or power or freedom, by me or anyone else who gets in their way, always seems too much. And yet it doesn't solve the problem when you remove them—whether by jail or death—because someone else like them always comes along and takes their place, and functions for a while with no restraints at all. This is what I know, and knowing it is hard. On the other hand, even small hits that slow them down are victories, the temporary cessation of misery. For that I felt joy. It was the reason why, the motive for it all. In the end, it was all you could achieve.

I drove up the hill to Molly's house. I didn't see her black dog Katy, or the neighbor's kid, in her yard. I went in through the gate and up onto the porch. This was the second time in two years I had met someone special while working on a case. It was not something that ever had to happen, just something decent and unexpected. I was grateful for it. I enjoyed the feelings, and didn't doubt at all that these feelings—mine for her, and, I hoped, hers for me—were real. The only mystery I never solve is why there is love in the world that does not last, why things that feel good at the start do not keep feeling that way. I knocked on the door.

Molly let me in.

"How did it go?" she asked. I knew she meant with the police. She still didn't know what I really did for a living, and she had no idea I had been to Clarke.

"Fine," I answered her. "You'll have to talk to them sometime soon, but it will be routine questions, no big deal. Everything's settled and okay." That part was true, but I still felt uncomfortable with the part of me hidden from her, so I asked about Peter instead.

"He certainly seems a lot different from the first time we met him," she said. "Something's changed. All that anger, I mean. Whatever he was feeling then, it's more in the open now. He's lonely, I can see that. But he also happens to be a very nice guy. We've been talking." She smiled at me. Whatever it was she liked, I was getting part of the credit. I didn't mind at all.

We were at the entrance to the living room. He was sitting on the couch, but leaning over one of the arms to look at the underside of a small table. He caught a glimpse of me from his position upside down, grinned, and straightened up. He pointed at the furniture. "I cannot believe Molly's dad makes this stuff. It's so great."

He had to be exhausted, as much as any of us, but he sounded rejuvenated. Perhaps, I thought, the experience with Walker, and especially having been part in some way of some evil having left the world, had been good for him. The point of suicide, I thought, was to obtain some final relief, but it was also an attempt to put some action and meaning into a life that's been emptied out. However he had meant to do that, he had found another way and ended up here at Molly's place, reconnected to the world.

He got up off the couch and walked over. "I'm ready for that letter now," he said, and I knew he was.

I had it with me. I'd been carrying it everywhere I went for the past month. I wasn't sure at times I'd ever get to give it to Peter. But I hadn't given up on the idea. As soon as I handed him the letter, he handed it right back. I only had a second to look puzzled before he spoke. "You read it," he said. "Read it out loud."

I knew right away what he wanted. It made sense. I had known his dad, and he had not. There are privileges we have that we do not notice at all. A series of moments years ago had been special to me. Tossing a ball back and forth with Joe Taft, sitting next to him on the bench as he taught me how to think about the game, watching his intensity when he waited on the ball. I had had all of those things with Joe, and this boy, his son, had had none. I pulled the letter out of the manila pouch. It was just a few sheets of notepad paper. I remembered too well what Taft looked like in the hospital those last days. Given his condition, the writing was in a remarkably steady hand. I walked over to a big red couch, its deep color reflected off the surfaces of the roomful of polished wood. Molly and Peter found spots for themselves in a set of facing armchairs across from me. I spread out the pages and started to read.

Dear son,

The night you were born, your mother, Carolyn, died. I did something that night I've never stopped thinking about since. And even now, after eighteen years, it is hard sometimes for me to understand. I made a vow to find new parents for you, and to give you away. And then I did.

I don't know where you are, Peter. But I know now that I'm never going to see you again.

When I decided to give you up for adoption I was certain that I couldn't be a father, not a good enough one, anyway. Playing baseball is the only thing I've ever been good at, all my life. There isn't much that's ever felt right to me aside from that. I met Carolyn, and that seemed right. And then, because I had her, and she wanted you, that seemed okay, too.

But I needed her to raise you. I was absolutely sure about that. If I'd done it without her, I'd have caused you nothing but problems. I didn't know how to be a father, because my own father was a very angry man, and the only thing I remember about him sometimes is the cold expression on his face. Especially when he looked at me.

He was a ballplayer too. Basketball, in the earliest days. Before all the money and the leagues. He was not tall, or powerful, just quick. But people who saw him play tell me he moved the ball like he owned the floor. And I know what made him good was his anger. Because he had more of that than anything else.

On the court, he had his enemies. And at home, he had me. He always treated me like an enemy, or at least that's how it felt. I said something nice to him once, when I was watching him shave. And he got mad. That's all it took for him to lose his temper. He had his things to do, and all I was to him was someone who interfered. Whatever it was with him, he passed it on. When I wasn't playing baseball, I was always in a rage.

I've thought about these things over the years. I understand them now, and maybe it even makes sense. When your mother died, they let me stay with her for a while, just holding her. I finally spoke to her out loud. I told her that without her, I had nothing, I was nothing. Then I cried. It was the only time in my life that I've cried. That's when I made the vow, and I truly believed it was right. It wasn't fair to bring you into the world with me as a father, without her love. A nurse at the hospital found parents for you. I decided I'd never see you again.

But I couldn't live with that. For years after, I looked for you around Reading, not even knowing what you looked like, who you were. It was hard not knowing you. It was hard giving you up. It was hard to keep that secret all my life. I lied to everyone I knew, told them you were dead. And it never got any easier.

One day, five years after I gave you away, I found you. I used to watch the kids line up outside the stadium before the games. That Sunday, I saw you on the line. I knew it was you. I don't know how. Because the last time I'd seen you was the day you were born, but I knew it was you, Peter, I knew. Because you looked just like her . . .

My God, I thought, all those games. Taft with his quirks, the guys nodding to each other, wisely, we thought, all of us: He lost his kid and he goes out to the stadium gate before every game, dressed in his pin-stripes. The old man, the catcher, the tough guy, cracking open the back door just a little, watching all the kids, the long line of them. He's heartsick because his son had died. He just wants to see the kids, and wishes one of them was his. Little did we know that he was waiting all those years to see the one most important kid in the world, the one he gave away. He really had a son, and he knew he'd see him some day.

It's okay, Joe, I thought. We found him. I almost said it aloud. And then I read the letter once again.

> . . . *After that I stayed in Reading, even when the season was over. I volunteered to be a coach in the fall training camps because I thought I'd have a chance of seeing you again. But you never came. And I never saw you again.*
>
> *I've thought about it a lot, why it all turned out the way it did. Why I couldn't make it work for us. When I gave you up I was doing what was best: for you, maybe even what your mother would have wanted, and for me.*
>
> *But I was wrong. I was afraid, and all I did was what felt good to me. I don't expect you to forgive me. I don't ask for that. I know the world is mostly a rotten place. But maybe it doesn't have to be that way.*
>
> *The mistake I made when I gave you up was I didn't see the possibility that things could change. Maybe I could have been a father to you after all, or even made the world a better place. I didn't even try, but you still can.*
>
> *I try to imagine who you are now, and the biggest fear I have is that you might become like I was at your age. Angry and bitter and absolutely certain that life has to be that way. I don't know anything about love anymore. But I think it means trying to make things right for somebody. I wish I could do that for you.*
>
> *I don't know what else I can tell you. Baseball is the life I had without you. I was never a big success. I worked at it hard as I could, every single day. I don't have money or anything more to give you. I wish I had more to say. I wish we had the time. I don't. But you do. You have time to make a life for yourself. I truly hope you do.*
>
> *I love you,*
> *Your father.*

A month passed. It had been Molly's idea to bring Peter up to Quaker-town, to meet her parents and see the place where her father did his work.

Peter had kept telling her how much he loved the craftsmanship, and finally she asked him if he'd like to meet the craftsmen. He was thrilled at the idea. He'd ended up apprentice carpenter, at least for now. He fit in well, according to Molly's parents' detailed progress reports. I had trouble picturing him as I'd first seen him, only two months before—a lonely, angry, troubled young guy standing in the doorway of his desolate apartment.

I didn't know about the long term, but he had some strong things going for him now. Molly's parents and their particular ability to nurture, mainly, and the beauty of the objects with which he was now surrounded. A lot of warmth in that little shop. There was at least a good chance he could heal from everything he'd been through.

In that same month, Molly got to hear about the other parts of my life. Truths took shape between us, changing the way we were. At first, it was hard for her to understand what I did. But she'd also seen the good that it could do. And she understood why I'd waited so long to tell her. We'd been together, in her house and mine, as much as we could when she wasn't working. I made my usual plans, to take off for the Caribbean, assuming she'd come along. She wanted to be with me, she made that clear. But she also wanted very much to finish her time at Clarke. I thought her desire to stay there and to take care of her patients had something to do with Walker, and what he'd done; wiping the memories away. So instead of going to the islands, we spent our time together in my house in Chestnut Hill. This time it felt like home.

I awoke one night with the odd sensation of having become a child again, in my boyhood home. And it wasn't Molly who was with me, but other people I'd loved, and then lost. I lay quiet and still, and heard the country house noises in the night, and then willed myself back to sleep. I dreamt I was a child, and naked in the daylight in front of my old school. I ran home, only four blocks away, seeking the shelter of parents and home. But the house I knew was gone, and my parents were gone, and no one knew me at all.

It was the kind of dream that often frightened me when I was young, but this time I woke without fear. I had a sure knowledge of what my dream conveyed. We lose the loves of our lives one by one, and for each one gone we go less and less protected in the world. And there is that last moment when everyone close to us is gone, and there is nothing that holds us to the world and steers our way.

It was four in the morning and not yet light, but I got up and went out and wandered to the edge of the land at the back of the house. I looked up at the trees, and then, through them, the sky. I didn't have Molly's father's skill, but I measured the heights and crannies of the wood with my own practiced eye. I didn't think, as Molly's father undoubtedly would, of the small comforts I could evoke from the wood. Instead, under this canopy, I saw the things it took to build a place solid enough to live. An early morning light in the sky came up, and opened a circle of vision around the stand of trees. The natural land stood in soft contrast to the solid roofs and peaks of the houses in the distance. This is what we do, I thought. We take what is offered, and we build.

Before the sun was fully up, and while I stood there in the quiet of the cool dew, I saw Molly come out from the house. She asked me why I was up, and when I told her, she said she'd had a bad dream of her own. She'd been thinking about Abbott and Clarke.

"As much as I hate what she did to Clarke," Molly said, "I think about what you said, that a lot of what she did is what goes on, more or less, at all hospitals, all the time. It really is an ugly picture."

"I know," I said. "That's what always gets to me. How little you can change things in the end. People like Abbott see the world the way it really is. And then they use that knowledge to exploit people and hide their trails, and to steal as much as they can."

"So how do I go on?" she said. "It bothers me there's so much corruption. But I'm a doctor and I want to work in hospitals."

"Thank God it bothers you," I said. "You keep on doing what you want to do. In your case, that means you help people. You can do it even at a place like Clarke. On the large scale, maybe it balances out some of what the Nancy Abbotts do. I settle for that. Maybe you can, too." The sky was turning various shades of pink.

"What the hell," she said, taking a step away and motioning me to follow. "Let's go for a walk in the woods."

It was just what I had in mind.